ALSO BY JUDITH A. BARRETT

Maggie Sloan Thriller Series

Grid Down Survival Series

Riley Malloy Thriller Series

Donut Lady Cozy Mystery Series

Deadly Equity

Riley Malloy Thriller

Book 5

Judith A. Barrett

DEADLY EQUITY

RILEY MALLOY THRILLER SERIES BOOK 5

Published in the United States of America by Wobbly Creek, LLC

2023 Georgia

wobblycreek.com

Cover by Wobbly Creek, LLC

ISBN 978-1-953-870-35-3

DEDICATION

Deadly Escrow is dedicated to farm utility vehicles and to horses, miniature ponies, and farm dogs.

PREVIOUSLY. . .

RILEY

My name is Riley Malloy. I'm a vet tech, and I understand what animals tell me, which must be why people call me a "dog whisperer." When the clinic where I was working in my hometown abruptly closed, Toby, my five-year-old black and brown German Shepherd-Labrador Retriever mix, and I moved to Barton to live in my Grandma's old cabin. I found a new job at a fantastic animal hospital with wonderful people, but best of all, I met Ben Carter, a cute, tall deputy sheriff with brown hair, greenish hazel eyes, and a smile that melted my heart.

Not that we're competitive or anything, but I enjoy reminding Ben that I love him more. Did I mention we are married?

Ben's in training with the Georgia Bureau of Investigation; our original plan was that while he was in training, Toby and I would stay with his parents, Jake and Melissa Carter; I looked forward to working with his uncle, Doc Seth, a veterinarian who specializes in farm visits, but it didn't work out as well in real life as it did on paper. Ben was miserable being away from me five and sometimes six days a week, and I wasn't all that crazy about it either.

My mother-in-law's friend, Mugsy, who owns the Big Mug Coffee Shop in Carson, found a house for us to rent only twenty minutes from Ben's classes, and we moved two weeks ago. Ben said the house was creepy outside because of the peeling paint and overgrown yard; he wasn't wrong, but it feels like home inside.

BEN

Riley is brilliant, has a remarkable talent for communicating with animals, has fiery red hair, and is the prettiest girl I've ever seen. Her talent is a little more than dog whisperer; she talks to animals and understands what they are telling her when they respond. I know it's a stretch to believe, but I've seen her in action, and it's true. I thought she should become a veterinarian, but she is burned out by classes, loves being a vet tech, and sees no reason to change. I respect her wishes, but I do wish she'd stop being the target of murderers.

Mom said some people hinted to her that we rushed into marriage too quickly, but they abruptly changed the subject when Mom dared them to tell Riley. In case it comes up, I loved her first.

CHAPTER ONE

Ben kissed Riley as she handed him his lunch for the day. "Keep dancing, babe; I wish I'd known your grandmother."

Riley leaned against his chest while he hugged her. "She would have loved you. Grandma said the best advice she could ever give me was to keep dancing, so I'd remember to study my enemies, watch for trouble, and protect myself."

Ben hugged her. "Still goes."

After he left, Riley said, "Let's go outside, Toby, and check the yard for any downed branches after last night's windstorm."

Toby trotted alongside her as she strolled around the back part of the property until he dashed into the woods after a squirrel.

Riley dragged small branches to a central location then took a break as she put her hands on her hips and examined her growing pile of branches. "I'm not sure if this is useful or not, but I'm outside and getting some exercise, so I guess it is."

As she struggled to pull a large, downed limb away from a stand of trees, Toby yipped then barked. She rushed to see what he'd found.

Her eyes widened at the dirt that clung to his paws and face. "Did you find an armadillo hole? I'll bet the armadillo escaped by its back door and is long gone."

Riley examined the spot where Toby had been digging. "That's flat in the middle. Did you hit a rock?"

She knelt in the dirt and tried to clear away enough soil to see how deep the hole was, but the rock was larger than she thought. "I need a shovel to dig around this rock, but I don't think this is an armadillo hole; maybe you found a rodent like a woodland vole that Grandma called a field mouse."

Riley hurried to the barn to see if she could find a shovel, but it was empty.

"I need gardening tools," she grumbled. "I might want to plant geraniums or jalapeno peppers."

She returned to her struggle with the heavy limb but was interrupted when her phone rang.

"Are you in the middle of anything?" Seth asked.

"Just dragging branches; it's my excuse to be outside."

"Good. I heard from an old friend, Ned Halsey, who provides veterinary services for farmers and ranchers Tuesdays through Thursdays and has office hours the other two days. He's approaching eighty but is as strong and sharp as he ever was. When he called me, he told me his partner heard that you had moved close to their office, so he checked around then asked me if you would be interested in farm visits."

"You know I love farm visits, and three days a week would be ideal; I wouldn't mind talking with him to see what we could work out."

"I thought you'd say that. I gave him your number, so he could call you, but he might call you from the end of your driveway to ask if he can drop by." Seth chuckled. "Let me know how it goes."

When Riley headed toward the house, Toby trotted to join her.

"If I'm going to be working three days a week, I'll have to think about meals that don't take a lot of time. I'll talk to Mom."

Riley heated a pot of water for tea, but before her tea finished steeping, her phone rang. *Mugsy.*

"How are you doing, Short-stuff? You aren't having any trouble with creepy house vibes or anything are you?"

"Not at all; the house is homey inside; I think the rough exterior is to scare away any bad guys."

"Whatever works." Mugsy snorted. "Melissa and I thought we might come see you for lunch. Melissa's already preparing a basket to bring, so don't think you have to scramble to fix anything. An ambulance is transporting Ryan from the trauma center in Atlanta to the hospital in Carson this afternoon, and I'm too antsy to be nice to customers more than another hour."

"I'd love to see you two," Riley said.

Toby yipped.

"Toby wants to know if Duffy, Finn, and Cookie are coming too."

"Cookie wants to come, but she gets carsick. As far as Duffy and Finn are concerned, it depends on whether Melissa can sneak out without them noticing."

After Mugsy hung up, Riley removed her tea bag from her cup and sipped her tea. "A little bitter, but it's still warmish tea."

Toby flopped down on the floor, and a few tufts of dog hair rolled away from him. She frowned at the kitchen floor then left her tea on the table while she hurried to the living room; Toby followed her.

"It looks fine, except I need to sweep, dust, and maybe rearrange the furniture a bit."

Toby growled.

"I'm not anxious; I'd just like for the house to look nice, but if I do too much, Mom will notice and her feelings will be hurt because I'd be treating her like company, not family."

Toby snorted then returned to the kitchen and lay down next to the back door.

Riley pulled out her dust mop and ran it across the wood floors in the living room then took the mop outside and shook it out. Toby stayed in the yard when she went back in the house.

"The kitchen floor looks bad now." Riley swept the floor and chased dust bunnies to a corner with the broom then picked them up with her hands and slowly walked to the trash can. When she opened the lid and dropped the dust balls, half of them floated to the floor instead of into the can. She exhaled, picked up the can, and kicked the fluff before she set the can on top of the errant, flyaway dog hair.

She put away her broom and poured out her tea. *I'm driving myself crazy. I'll just peek at the bathroom then go outside and plan where I'll plant geraniums.*

She replaced the hand towel with a fresh one and reached for Ben's towel he had hung on his towel rack then pulled back her hand. "Geraniums."

Riley tossed the hand towel into the washer and rushed to the back door. When she went outside, she breathed in the fresh air. "I was making myself crazy."

Toby grinned, beelined to his hole to sniff for any new clues of the invader in his territory then wandered around the yard while Riley furrowed her brow. *Maybe I'd rather have the geraniums in large pots.*

When she heard her phone ring, Riley raced into the house and was out of breath when she answered.

"This is Ralph Wagner; did I call at a bad time?"

"Not at all; I was out back picking up some limbs from the storm," Riley said.

"I was contacted by a guy who was interested in buying the barn then dismantling it for building material, but then one of my customers introduced me to an investor who is interested in helping me with the house. I haven't signed a contract yet, but I talked to the investor, and he agreed the old barn might be fine with just a little work. I talked to an old friend who offered to work on it with me on the weekends, if that won't be too disruptive. I'd like to come by on Saturday to see how much we'd have to do, and my potential investor said he'd like to see the house too."

"I agree with you, but that might be because I love barns."

"As far as the barn's concerned, you wouldn't have to be home on Saturday if you have something planned because I wouldn't have any reason to go in the house. If Saturday isn't convenient, let me know, and we'll make it another time. I'd like to bring my tractor on Saturday too, so I can mow around the house; I'll bet the weeds are worse than I remember from the rain we've had the past few days."

"I like the natural look of the yard, but the tall weeds don't add much," Riley said.

Ralph chuckled. "That's what I was thinking too. Another fella called me and said he heard I was fixing up this old house; he told me he had a way for me to take advantage of the equity I have in the house from the updates I've done, so I wouldn't have to wait until I could afford to upgrade the exterior. He made it sound like it was free money, so I'm a little skeptical. He said it was like an equity conversion loan except it was a grant with the money held in escrow, so I could withdraw funds when I needed them. Have you ever heard of a reverse mortgage? That's what it sounded like to me," Ralph said.

"I always thought a reverse mortgage was a loan for retired people to access the equity they had in their home without having to move out; when they die, I think the heirs can pay off the loan balance, but they don't have to, and the lender then sells the property. I probably have some of the details wrong because I'm not an expert at all."

"The more he talked, the more complicated it sounded to me, so I told him I wasn't interested, but he was in a selling frame of mind and told me he'd check back with me later. I better let you go before you start thinking I'm a persistent sales guy too."

"I did have a question for you. Toby was digging in the yard and came across something flat and hard, like a rock."

"Really? I'd heard the property had a koi pond on it somewhere, but no one seemed to know where it was, and I couldn't find it, so I decided it must have just been another story to add to the mystique of an old house. Are you interested in raising koi? I could dig it out for you and have it tested to see if it still holds water."

"Oh, no. I can just see Toby jumping into the pond with his koi friends then coming into the house."

Ralph chuckled. "You have a point there. Let me know if you change your mind."

After he disconnected, Riley called Claire, her closest friend and confidante and the office manager at Doc Julie Rae's clinic.

Claire answered on the first ring. "Are you okay? Did you shoot somebody? I'll be your alibi and swear you were with me the entire time."

Riley smiled. "I needed a breath of fresh air, and you never fail me. What's going on there?"

"Zach still hasn't proposed. We're thinking about disinheriting him and finding Kayla a new boyfriend. How's the new house? Do you have a job yet? I knew you wouldn't last a month without finding the perfect vet tech position for you. What is it? Farm visits?"

"You're good. How did you know?"

"Doc Julie Rae keeps her veterinarian radar on at all times. She knows the vet who works with Doc Halsey, and he told her Doc Halsey was going to talk to you. Doc Julie Rae said Doc Halsey is highly respected in the veterinary field and loves to teach, so tell me about the house."

"The exterior paint is peeling, and the yard is overgrown with weeds…"

Claire interrupted. "And you love it, don't you?"

"I do; it's homey inside and the outside is like an old-time southern belle who pines for the long-lost love from her youth."

"I'm fanning my face with a folder and pretending to clutch my pearls in sympathy with your house. How does Ben like it?"

"We could be living in a tent on the property, and Ben would be perfectly happy because he has only a twenty-minute drive home at the end of the day."

"Thad and I had a bet that Ben wouldn't last the entire sixteen weeks being so far away from you, but we had to declare a tie because we forgot who said what, just like we always do. Now, tell me why you called me."

"Ben's mother is coming here for lunch, and this is the first time she's been here. What if she hates the house?"

"You collapse into soul-searing sobs, clutch your bosom since you don't have any pearls, and come back to Barton until Ben finds a new mother. You can live with Zach and Kayla."

"Clutch my bosom?" Riley snorted. "Your plan makes as much sense as my panic over Ben's mother coming here."

"Thank you," Claire said. "Happy to help."

After they hung up, Riley smiled. *I can always count on Claire to set me straight.*

Riley's phone buzzed a text.

Mugsy: "We're five minutes away."

Riley hurried to the front porch and listened. When a car turned from the road to the driveway, she grinned. *Almost here.*

Melissa parked, and Riley ran out to greet them.

"Oh my gosh, I love your house, Riley." Melissa hugged her while Mugsy groaned as she lifted out a large box from the back seat.

"I'll carry that," Melissa said.

"I've got it," Mugsy said. "Open the door, Short-stuff, and I'll set what Melissa called a little nosh on your kitchen table."

After Mugsy set the heavy box on the table, Melissa pulled out plastic containers and handed them to Riley. "All the meals are four portions, so you can have leftovers for your next meal; these two containers of chicken noodle casserole go into the freezer. This is Greek chicken pasta; put it in the refrigerator and warm up half of it tonight and the rest tomorrow night."

When Riley put the last container in the freezer, she said, "I hope this is it because the freezer is full."

"Here's a list of what you have in the freezer, and I'll send you the recipes for everything later this week." Melissa pulled out a folded sheet of paper from her purse then smoothed it out on the table.

Mugsy snorted. "You're lucky I was driving because she wanted to stop and pick up a gallon of ice cream."

"I have sandwiches for lunch." Melissa sniffed at Mugsy then handed a large lunch bag to Riley. "We made sure we'd have time for a house tour and lunch before we have to leave, but we need to talk first. Let's sit."

After they sat at the kitchen table, Mugsy said, "We stopped for gas in town and heard very disturbing news."

"A farmer near a town south of here has been struggling with his debt, and evidently was approved for a loan or grant, the details weren't clear, but something must have gone wrong because he sent his wife and children to visit her parents who live in Alabama. A week later, in the middle of the night, he took a neighbor's boat and rowed out to the deepest part of the lake." Melissa bit her lip.

"They found him at the bottom of the lake with an anchor tied to his legs," Mugsy said. "I guess a lot of farms in this area are having financial difficulty, and everyone at the gas station was shaken by the news."

"That is terrible. I feel so sorry for his wife and children," Riley said.

Melissa nodded then cleared her throat. "We wanted to tell you before you overheard people talking in town."

As they strolled through the house, Melissa said, "The wooden floors are beautiful; the owner has put a lot of work into the house, hasn't he?"

"It's not all cosmetic, though," Mugsy said. "My friend told me Ralph updated the electrical and plumbing systems to bring them up to code."

When they went upstairs, Melissa peered into two bedrooms. "I'd be tempted to tell him to leave the upstairs alone because there is so much old charm in these bedrooms."

"I told him I loved them the way they are, so he's not going to touch them while we're here."

"Good because I want the bedroom next to the upstairs bathroom as our guest room when we come to visit. We'll bring a bed," Melissa said.

"Jake and Ben will have a fit if you try to furnish all the bedrooms because they'll have to lug the furniture upstairs then back down four months later," Mugsy said.

"You're right; I'll have to rein in my decorator side." Melissa's eyes crinkled as she smiled. "Does this mean I should cancel my trip tomorrow to the antique store?"

Riley giggled as Mugsy groaned. "You're incorrigible."

When they went to the backyard, Toby rose from his sunbeam spot in the kitchen to follow them.

"You have a decent pile of branches and limbs for a bonfire," Melissa said.

"I started with clearing the backyard then decided it was a great excuse to be outside and moved to clearing the woods," Riley said.

"I'm starving," Mugsy said.

While they ate lunch, Riley told them what she knew about Doc Halsey. "I haven't talked to him yet, but I talked to Claire earlier, and she told me that Doc Julie Rae said Doc Halsey is highly regarded by other veterinarians, and he loves to teach."

"That's good; I'll check with Seth to see what he thinks," Melissa said.

After they ate, the three of them strolled around the house to the front porch while Toby trailed along.

"It's so peaceful here, Short-stuff; I'm sorry we can't stay longer. We'll wear out our welcome next time."

Melissa smiled. "Absolutely."

Riley and Toby stayed on the porch and waved until Mugsy's car disappeared down the lane.

"The visit was too short, wasn't it?" Riley scratched Toby's ears, and he moaned.

"I'll remind Mom to bring Duffy and Finn next time. I talked to Ralph, and that rock you found buried in the backyard is actually part of a fish pond."

Toby whined.

"No, we're not going to have a pond in the back yard."

Toby hung his head and returned to the porch then flopped down with his back to Riley.

While she pulled more branches to her burn pile, her phone rang.

"This is Ned Halsey; is this Riley Carter?" a man asked.

"Sure is, Doc Halsey; Doc Seth told me you'd be calling."

"Good; then you know I'm looking for a vet tech like you to help me with farm visits on Tuesday through Thursday every week. My last appointment in the office is at three today; I'll pick up my wife, and we'll come see you around five. Will that work for you?"

"That's perfect. My husband may be home about that time, and I know he'd be interested in meeting you too."

"I met Seth's nephew one time, but that was ten or fifteen years ago. I look forward to seeing both of you."

After Doc Halsey hung up, Riley sent Ben a text. "Quick question but not urgent. What's your schedule this evening?"

Ben replied. "Home by five thirty."

Riley smiled. *Perfect.* "See you then."

"Ben will be home early today, Toby."

Toby wagged his tail and waited for Riley on the porch.

When they went into the house, Riley said, "I'll make a big pitcher of sweet tea. Should I make something for a snack? Grandma and I made crackers one time, and it wasn't that hard. I could make crackers real quick and see if I have some cream cheese I could spread on the crackers; maybe Mom snuck some smoked summer sausage into the refrigerator when I wasn't looking. I could…"

Toby interrupted her with a howl.

"Fine; just sweet tea," Riley grumbled. "After I put it in the refrigerator, I'll read a book."

Riley woke when Toby nudged her elbow.

She stretched then spotted her book that had dropped to the floor. "I guess I needed a nap."

As she picked up the book, Toby quietly woofed. "Somebody's here?"

She and Toby hurried to the front porch as an old white pickup rolled to a stop then parked near the barn. Doc Halsey, a spry man with thinning, gray hair, hopped out and assisted a woman out of the passenger's side of the truck.

Riley returned their waves as they strolled together to join her and Toby on the porch. Toby sat patiently next to Riley; she smiled at his furiously wagging tail that sent the dust on the porch flying. *Both of us are excited about meeting new people.*

When they reached the porch, Doc Halsey said, "Riley, this is my wife, Lizzie."

"It's so nice to meet another shorty." Lizzie, who had silver streaks in her brown hair and was curvy just like Riley, beamed as she held Riley's outstretched hand with two hands.

"Come inside," Riley said.

Lizzie glanced around the living room. "Ralph has done a great job on this old house, hasn't he?"

"I love it; I'm kind of hoping he leaves the exterior alone, though."

"I agree completely; it definitely gives the house a sense of character, doesn't it?"

"Would you like some sweet tea?" Riley asked.

"I'm fine," Lizzie said. "I heard this old house has a back porch."

Riley led the way through the kitchen to the back.

"That was Lizzie's sneaky way to see the kitchen too." Doc Halsey chuckled.

When they sat on the back porch, Lizzie said, "This is nice. You two can talk business now; I've finished my home inspection, and it's lovely."

"I heard you have a way with animals," Doc Halsey said. "Tell me a little bit about yourself."

Riley told him about her first job as a vet tech then moving to Barton with Toby. She talked about different cases and going to Lindsey's horse farm with Doc Julie Rae.

"That Julie Rae is a crackerjack vet, isn't she? Some of her classmates thought she was crazy to open her business in a small town in south Georgia because she could have opened one of those boutique practices in Atlanta and raked in a lot more money with minimal effort, but all us old country vets understood why she did: her boys will grow up surrounded by nature not concrete."

Lizzie stroked Toby's face while Doc Halsey talked about his practice.

"You carry, right?" Doc Halsey asked. "I keep my deer rifle and my concealed with me at all times, and I know Seth does the same."

Riley nodded then smiled when Lizzie said, "Of course she carries; she's a country girl."

Toby yipped then jumped off the porch and headed to the front of the house.

"Ben's home," Riley said. "I'll bring him out here."

Riley hurried through the house and met Ben at the front door.

He hugged her. "Who's our company?"

"Doc Ned and Lizzie Halsey; they're out back on the porch. He's looking for a vet tech to help him with his farm visits three days a week."

Ben chuckled as they headed through the house toward the back. "Word gets around fast, doesn't it? I think I met Doc Halsey a long time ago."

"Ben Carter," Doc Halsey said when Riley and Ben came outside, "you look just the same as the last time I saw you, except just a little taller."

As the two men shook hands, Ben said, "You haven't changed a bit, Doc. Nice to meet you, Mrs. Halsey."

"Please call me Lizzie, Ben. Your wife is delightful; I'm so happy for both of you."

"Riley and I were just finishing up our chat," Doc Halsey said. "Riley, can you start tomorrow, or do you need a little time to think about it?"

Riley smiled when Ben chuckled. "Ben knows I'm ready to work; tomorrow is great."

"I can pick you up or meet you at the office; we'll use my old truck to visit the farms. I heard Toby went to work with you at Julie Rae's; do you suppose he'd like to hang out with the office staff?"

"What do you think, Toby?" Riley asked.

Toby grinned, and Lizzie laughed. "I've never been accused of being a dog whisperer like they say you are, Riley, but I feel comfortable saying that Toby loves the idea."

"Is eight too early for us to meet at the office?" Doc Halsey asked.

"Not at all," Riley said.

"Pack a lunch because we're not always close to anywhere to pick up a bite to eat." Doc Halsey rose from his chair and helped Lizzie to her feet.

"Do you think Riley and Ben would be interested in the meeting this evening?" Lizzie asked as the four of them walked around the house, and Toby stayed behind.

"I didn't think of that," Doc said. "Riley, I realize it's short notice, but Lizzie and I are going to a meeting this evening at seven thirty at the Baptist church in town. There's a presentation for farmers that's sponsored by several of the farm organizations. It would be a good opportunity for you to meet some of our clients."

Riley glanced at Ben, and he gave a slight nod.

"We could do that," Riley said.

"We'll save you seats next to us," Lizzie said. "I like to sit near the back."

Doc helped her into the truck. "We arrive early whenever we attend any functions because Lizzie likes having her escape route in case she gets bored, which is fairly often."

After the Halseys left, and they strolled to the house, Ben asked, "How was your day?"

"Mom and Mugsy dropped by for lunch. Ryan was supposed to be transferred to the hospital in Carson, so Mom rode with Mugsy to Atlanta. He'll travel by ambulance, and I think they'll follow the ambulance. I didn't understand why Mugsy wanted to go to Atlanta instead of waiting in Carson for him, but our bonus was that Mom filled our refrigerator and freezer."

"I'm not a bit surprised; I've been wondering how Mom was going to find a way to bring us meals," Ben said.

Riley furrowed her brow. "Do you suppose going to Atlanta was their cover story, and they returned to Carson from here?"

Ben snorted. "I wouldn't put it past Mom at all."

Riley chuckled. "Mugsy would be happy to have a way to do something for the day besides stew about Ryan, and she'd love a good conspiracy."

"Neither one of them will ever admit to it, will they?"

Riley shook her head. "We're having Greek chicken pasta for dinner tonight and tomorrow night. Mom packed four portions of a meal in each container, so we can have leftovers the second day. Mom promised to send the recipes later this week." Riley opened the refrigerator and pulled out the container with the Greek chicken pasta.

"Do I have time for a quick shower?" Ben asked.

"Go right ahead."

While the pasta dish warmed, Riley fed Toby, set the table, and poured sweet tea.

"Supper smells great," Ben called out while he dressed.

CHAPTER TWO

When Ben came into the kitchen, he picked up his glass of sweet tea and downed half of it. "I was dry because I didn't slow down long enough to refill my water bottle. I need to remember to hydrate better than I did today."

He refilled his glass then talked about the class and the upcoming field work while Riley dished up their servings.

After they ate, Ben said, "I'll do the dishes if you'll put away the leftovers."

When the dishwasher was loaded, Riley said, "Come see my burn pile."

As they stood with their arms around each other and admired the huge mound of branches, Ben asked, "You did all this today?"

"It was a good excuse to be outside, and I enjoyed the exercise," Riley said.

Ben rolled his eyes. "I'm glad you'll be working with Doc Halsey, so I don't have to worry about you taking a chain saw to the woods. Uncle Seth and I used to visit Doc Halsey when Uncle Seth had a particularly complex problem he wanted to discuss. Mom didn't understand why Uncle Seth didn't just pick up the phone and call Doc Halsey, but Dad told me she always gave Uncle Seth two or three jars of her jam for the Halseys. Mrs. Halsey was a nurse and didn't have time to can in those days. I remember how happy Doc Halsey was to get his favorite jam. I always thought Uncle Seth was paying for Doc Halsey's time with jam."

After they went inside, Riley asked, "Don't you have homework?"

"I worked on it during lunch; I could finish it after we return home from the meeting, but maybe it would be better if I finish it up before we leave."

"Good; otherwise, I'd worry the entire time and keep asking you if we needed to use Miz Lizzie's escape route."

Ben opened his laptop and focused on his homework while Riley made their lunches for the next day then hurried to their bedroom and packed a backpack with what she'd need in the field.

As she carried her work backpack into the living room, Ben grinned then snapped his laptop closed.

"I'm done; what have you been doing?" he asked.

"Our lunches are in the refrigerator, and I packed a farm visit backpack with your old butcher's apron, my rain gear, and a change of clothes."

"What about a warm coat and extra ammo?"

"I included extra ammo; be right back." Riley returned with her heavy coat and dropped it on top of the backpack. "Done."

Ben stared at his laptop. "I might want to take notes."

"Why don't I take a notepad and take notes?"

"That's a much better idea; I got stuck in my student lane, but people might get the impression that I'm surfing the internet if I'm on my laptop. Do we have a second notepad for me?"

"I'm sure we do; we can write notes during the meeting." Riley checked their closet and returned with a notepad in a black portfolio.

"This is nice; why don't you take it?"

"It goes with your student-self. According to Miz Lizzie, I'm a country girl; I wouldn't have any use for a fancy folder."

As they headed toward the door, Riley said, "We won't be gone long."

Toby padded to the kitchen, flopped down near the stove, and closed his eyes.

On their way into town, Riley asked, "Do you know where the Baptist church is?"

"No, but I know how to find it; we'll follow the pickups."

After Ben parked his truck next to another truck, they strolled into the church and were greeted by a low rumble of voices at the end of a hall to their right.

"I know where the meeting is," Riley whispered.

"Now you're catching on, babe." Ben winked.

When they went into the large meeting room, Lizzie motioned to them from the back row near the exit door.

"I'm glad to see you," Lizzie said when they joined her. "Ned's up front talking to a couple of farmers. He'd like to introduce you two around. Put your notebooks on your seats, and I'll put my purse on Ned's seat."

As they headed toward the front, Doc Halsey met them halfway. "I have some people for you to meet, but no one expects you to remember names."

After Ned introduced them to the farmers in the small group, the men's wives joined them to meet Riley and Ben.

"We didn't want to mob you right away…" one of the women said.

Another woman continued, "…which is why we're mobbing you now."

Her husband stared at her then chuckled when another woman elbowed her and snickered.

A woman introduced herself and invited Riley to visit her anytime then carefully explained how to get to her farm, complete with the instructions to turn left at the white house with the red barn. Riley blinked then covered her face with her forearm as she faked a cough to keep from laughing.

Ben put his arm around her. "We might want to take our seats and get settled, babe," Ben said.

Riley nodded. As they headed toward Lizzie, he whispered, "What was so funny?"

"When I moved to Barton, Aunt Millie told me that the driveway to Grandma's cabin was right after a white house with a red barn, and I spent almost the entire afternoon driving all over two counties trying to find the right white house with a red barn."

Ben chuckled. "I'd forgotten all about that, and I'm glad I did because I'm not certain I could have been as restrained as you were."

Before they reached Lizzie and their seats, Ben peered at the entrance. "The sheriff just came in, and I'd like to talk to him. I won't be long."

After Riley sat next to her, Lizzie said, "It seems to me the whole town is here, not just the farmers. I had heard the farm organizations were sponsoring it, but one of my friends who is on the board of directors of one of them told me that the farm organizations weren't invited to attend and aren't sponsoring it at all, so it's not quite as well-supported as we all originally thought."

As more people poured into the room, everyone spoke louder to be heard over others. A woman carried in a large tray of cookies and placed them on a table that stood against the back wall; another woman behind her rolled a utility cart with a large coffee pot, cups, and packets of sweetener on it and placed it next to the table.

The excitement in the conversations and the noise level grew as people lined up for coffee and cookies.

Lizzie leaned closer to Riley. "I wondered if there were going to be refreshments. Do you care for any coffee?"

"No, thank you."

"I'm in awe of those people who can drink coffee in the evening; I'd be awake all night if I tried that."

When a man in a dark gray suit and two men in jeans and long-sleeved plaid Western shirts came into the room, Riley said, "I think the presenters are here."

Lizzie glanced at the men. "That one definitely has the banker look, doesn't he? They're obviously not from around here because I don't think there are many local men who own suits, including our local banker, and those that do probably can't fit into them anymore, and those Western shirts are straight off the rack because they've never been washed."

"You can tell their clothes haven't been washed just by looking at them?" Riley squinted at the men.

"Well, I cheated. That one guy still has one of those clear, long stickers with XLs running down the front right side of his shirt. See it?"

Riley raised her eyebrows. "I do now that you've pointed it out."

A woman in her early thirties with pale skin, hazel eyes, tattoos on her neck and arms, and dark-brown, purple and green-streaked hair sat in front of them then turned sideways in her seat. "Hi, Riley, I'm Hope, but you can call me Toby's best friend. I'm Doc Ned's office manager, and Doc told me Toby will spend the day with me. I'm excited because I'll finally have someone to walk with me at lunchtime. Does he walk with a leash or without?"

"Without; if you want him to carry his leash for appearances, he'd love to show off."

"Ooo, he sounds like my kind of guy. My friend's sitting close to the front, but I wanted to say hello before the program starts; see you tomorrow."

After Hope left, Lizzie chuckled. "Hope loves animals; she told me once that she can't believe she spends her days bossing people around and doting on dogs and cats and is paid money to do what she loves."

The three men strode to the front of the room and sat at the table, facing the crowd. As people noticed them, more people drifted to seats and the level of noise slightly decreased.

Riley shifted to have a better view of the men at the table, and Ben sat next to her. One of the men in jeans made his way to the podium and clutched it with both hands before he leaned close to the microphone and spoke, but the microphone screeched from the feedback. He backed away from the microphone and swallowed hard as he stared at the man in the suit.

"Can you fix it?" The man in the suit spoke in a loud voice to the young audio tech who sat at a table behind Riley's row.

"Working on it, bud," the audio tech mumbled.

"Try it now, sir, but not so close," she called out.

The man near the podium exhaled, then he approached the microphone. "Let's try this again."

Everyone applauded, and the man's face reddened.

"Good evening," he said.

"Good evening." Almost everyone in the room automatically responded, and the man's face paled.

"Definitely not a public speaker," Lizzie said.

He pulled out a sheet of paper from his back pocket and unfolded it then stared at it so long that chairs creaked as people shifted in their seats.

He cleared his throat then quickly read aloud in a monotone. "We'll start the evening off with a prayer. Lord, lead your people to do what is right. Amen."

"Amen," a few in the audience responded.

Lizzie whispered, "Very odd and two big mistakes: he didn't give the men in the room enough time to remove their ball caps before the prayer, and he should have asked the Baptist minister to pray for the meeting."

Riley nodded and glanced at Ben who frowned at the speaker.

When the man at the microphone exhaled, the microphone amplified his breath to mimic the whoosh of a gust of wind. Riley glanced back at the audio tech who rolled her eyes.

"I'm not a public speaker..."

Lizzie elbowed Riley, and a few men and women chuckled.

When he glanced up at the audience, the man forced a smile.

Painful to watch this.

"I'm John, and I've been a farmer my entire life." He followed the words with his finger as he read. "I always knew I'd die happy working in my cotton field." He cleared his throat. "Until last year when the bank threatened to foreclose on my farm and take away all my machinery. My farm has been in the family for generations. Mr. Clausen, here..." John turned toward the front table and motioned; the man in the suit nodded.

John furrowed his brow then ran his finger down the sheet until he found the place where he had paused. "Mr. Clausen came to our church and told us he could help us pay off our loans, so we weren't obli...um..." He bit his lip then improvised. "bound to the bank no more."

Beads of sweat broke out on his forehead as he stared at the paper, then he abruptly said, "Mr. Clausen."

He hurried to his seat at the front table.

The room was quiet until Mr. Clausen began applauding, and the people near the front joined in. Riley glanced at Ben, and he shrugged.

Mr. Clausen continued applauding as he approached the podium. He smiled and nodded at the audience before he turned to the table. "Thank you, John. We all appreciated hearing your first-hand experience; I'm certain it's still painful for you to discuss."

John stared at his hands on the table.

Mr. Clausen gazed at the first row. "Pastor, we appreciate the use of your fine building for our meeting, and we particularly enjoyed the surprise of delicious refreshments provided by the best cooks in the state. Thank you so much for your kind hospitality."

Pastor rose from his seat in the first row. "It's our honor to serve the people of our county."

Ben leaned close to Riley. "Quite the contrast, isn't it?"

She nodded. *Seems overly contrived to me.*

After Pastor resumed his seat, Mr. Clausen's smile disappeared, and his face became solemn as he slowly scanned the room before he spoke.

"Two years ago, my brother was in the same situation that John just described for you, but my brother was fragile and didn't survive the stress of losing his farm. I vowed at his funeral in front of his young, grieving widow and my three young, fatherless nephews that I would make it my life's calling to never see another man suffer from that desperate situation of fear for his family's future like my brother did."

Mr. Clausen paused then wiped near the outer corner of one eye with two fingers before he cleared his throat. "Sorry; it's still painful."

He shook his head then continued, "I gathered my closest friends, and we talked to the smartest people we knew who cared about keeping farmers in business. With their help, we created a foundation and developed a simplified process that didn't rely on the government."

He paused and smiled as a few men murmured their assent and nodded.

His voice rose in emphasis. "Our goal is to help farmers tap into their equity that has been lying fallow for so many years to pay off the large, institutional banks and to remove that crushing stress that no man should bear. We're calling the program Step Up because you are stepping up to reclaim what is rightfully yours."

Riley raised her eyebrows as the sound of the affirmative murmurs and the number of nodding heads increased.

"My good friend and associate, Jim; stand up, Jim."

The third man at the table rose, smiled, and waved then remained standing.

"Give Jim your name, address, and phone number if you would like to hear more about Step Up and the possibilities the program has for you. We'll stay here this evening as late as Pastor allows to answer questions and to chat with you."

"Take all the time you need," Pastor said.

"Thank you, Pastor. John has my business cards; please take one and call me anytime you have a question. Thank you for coming tonight, and thank you for your kind attention. God bless."

Mr. Clausen beamed and turned off the microphone, and the applause was deafening. As men and women filed to the front of the room, a few men and women gathered separately in small groups.

"I want to pick up a business card," Ned said.

"I'll go with you." Ben rose from his seat and strolled with Ned to the front.

After John gave Ned a card, Ben shook John's hand and asked John a question; John set the stack of business cards on the table, and his face relaxed as the two of them moved away from the table for a conversation.

"Your husband must be a most talented interrogator. Did you see how quickly he put John at ease? He'll be a great GBI agent," Lizzie said.

When Riley side-glanced Lizzie in surprise, Lizzie smiled. "Noticing details was a valuable skill in my career as a nurse, and since I've retired, I've found watching people is actually very entertaining sometimes. Ned told me you're a dog whisperer; I think your Ben is a people whisperer. Try looking at the individuals up front instead of seeing the group."

Riley exhaled then concentrated on examining each person in the group that surrounded Mr. Clausen. "I didn't notice the sheriff until now. He's standing partially removed from the group and is closely observing Mr. Clausen and listening carefully to the conversations."

"Fascinating, isn't it? Do you think Ben and our sheriff are conspiring to work together?" Lizzie asked.

"Just like you and me?" Riley giggled.

A woman strolled to their aisle of chairs and stood next to Lizzie. "Excuse me for butting in, Riley, I'm Madge. Everybody knows your name, and we're all excited that you'll be working with Ned. What did you think, Lizzie? My husband is seriously considering the offer. He signed up for more information; after all, like Jim said, it doesn't cost us anything to learn more about the program, and our farm has been in my family for over fifty years."

"What would you do with the money?" Lizzie asked. "You don't owe anything on the farm, do you?"

"No, but we'd like to have the equipment to plant then harvest the cotton. We've been contracting that out for years, and it would be nice to have some equipment of our own to do it ourselves."

"Is that your husband talking to Mr. Clausen?" Riley asked.

The woman glanced at the front. "Sure is; he's usually not that forward, but he told me he had a couple of questions."

"Shouldn't he be sitting down? It looks like his knees are bothering him," Riley said.

Lizzie peered at the group in the front. "Riley's right, Madge; how much longer would he be able to do the work by himself if he bought all that equipment? I thought the arthritis in his knees was hitting him pretty hard lately. Isn't he limping even with his cane most days?"

Madge exhaled then sat next to Lizzie. "We were so excited about the idea of being less dependent on others that we didn't think about the details: the extra work he'd be doing in the field, how hard it would be for him to climb up and down from the big machinery, and the stress on his knees. I'm glad we talked because you're so practical, Lizzie. I need to talk to a couple of the other wives because we all got caught up in the idea of flashy new farm equipment for the men and extra money for updated appliances in the house. We don't need the fancy, new things, but I can see the value of the program because there are some people that are in a bad place and need to bail themselves out of foreclosure, just like John."

Riley said, "I'm not sure I understand how they could help people avoid foreclosure; do you have any ideas?"

Madge narrowed her eyes then glanced at the front of the room. "I'm sure he said, but I don't always understand things like that. I wish some of our local lenders were here; we'd all heard they'd been invited. Did you see anybody, Lizzie?"

"No, but I'd heard they hadn't been invited; there seems to be some confusion," Lizzie said.

"I'll talk to Pastor right now." Madge rose from her seat. "Can you make some calls, so we can have a meeting tomorrow night with the lenders here? Pastor can invite Mr. Clausen back, but we need more information before anyone signs on the dotted line."

"Maybe it makes more sense to talk to one or two of our local lenders first to see if they are interested," Lizzie said.

"I guess. My sister and her husband are desperate; I'll offer to drive her to the bank south of us to talk to their lender. She went to school with our local banker's mother, and she said she's too embarrassed to talk to him."

"Let me know what the lender says. I can talk to a friend in Atlanta to see if she's heard anything about Step Up. She's an officer at a big bank and would have better information than I could find on the internet. We can compare notes," Lizzie said.

"Thank you." Madge scanned the room then hurried to a woman who was with three other women who stood near the coffee and pulled her aside.

"I'd like to hear what Mr. Clausen's saying to the group up front," Riley said.

"You're the newcomer and would stand out too much if you tried to join the group around him. The line to sign up is fairly long, so if you stand with me, you'll be close enough to hear Mr. Clausen's conversations."

"You gave me an idea. If you go stand in line, I'll join you if my idea is a dud; otherwise, see what you can hear." Riley strode to the table behind them as the audio tech packed away the equipment while Lizzie headed toward the front.

"Hi, Riley. What can I do for you?" The audio tech shrugged when Riley's eyes widened. "You walked back here like you were on a mission. I'm Shelby, by the way."

Riley smiled. "I'll have to work on that. Shelby, how well do you know this room? Is there a good place to stand where I can clearly hear the conversations up front?"

"Nobody's ever asked me that before, but I know the answer. Pick up the smaller case and the rolled-up cable and come with me."

The tech picked up the large case, and Riley followed her to the front; the tech continued to a door and led Riley inside before she closed the door.

Riley glanced around the room that was crowded with folded tables against one wall and a stack of chairs against the wall that faced the door. The tech unlocked the storage closet door that was opposite the folded tables and turned on the light. "This is where I keep the audio equipment because it's expensive. Listen."

"The contract is all legalese, but that's how lawyers are, isn't it?" Mr. Clausen chuckled. "The bottom line is that after you sign the contract, your debt is assumed by the foundation, then you receive a check to give your farm operation an extra boost."

Shelby pointed to a chair at a small desk. "Enjoy; I won't stay because I have a few more adjustments to make in the main church. Close the door when you leave if I'm not back; it automatically locks."

Sounds like Step Up provides grant money, not loans, but won't the foundation eventually run out of funds?

Riley sat at the desk and listened as Mr. Clausen repeatedly assured each farmer that the debt would be transferred to the foundation, and the farmer would receive a check.

A man asked, "What if my debt is greater than my equity?"

"Good question; I should have brought this up earlier. The foundation assumes the debt, but you may have to supplement your operating costs for the first year; after that, you pay your operating costs from your previous year's profits."

"That sounds reasonable," the man said.

"Did you sign up on Jim's list?" Mr. Clausen asked.

"I'll do it now." The man chuckled.

Riley's phone buzzed a text from Ben.

"Where are you?"

"Be right there. Helped with audio equip."

Riley turned off the light and closed the storage closet door then double-checked to be sure it was locked before she went into the large meeting room.

Ben and the sheriff stood near the empty audio table in the back.

"I'm Alex Baker; everyone here knows you're Riley," Sheriff said as they shook hands.

"Babe, Sheriff Baker and I have a few things to talk over. Do you mind going to the diner for coffee?"

"That's fine, but why don't we go to the house? I'll put on a pot of coffee, and we have Mom's peach pie; your conversation will be more private at our kitchen table than at a diner."

Ben nodded. "Sheriff?"

"She got me at Mom's peach pie." His eyes crinkled as he smiled.

On their way home, Ben said, "I'm having trouble with one of my classes, and I asked the sheriff to look over my last two assignments with me. It was brilliant to invite him to our house because all my study material is there. Sheriff told me there's always a difference between classwork and field experience, but at my level there shouldn't be a conflict, which is why I think I'm misinterpreting something."

Riley sighed. *I thought I'd have a front row seat while they discussed Mr. Clausen and the Step Up program; I'll read a book.*

"You and John seemed to hit it off," Riley said.

"He was a last minute fill-in. The farmer who usually speaks with the Step Up group canceled at the last minute. I thought I recognized John, and I was right. He delivers and stocks potato chips for grocery stores in Macon; Mr. Clausen approached him in the grocery store this afternoon and begged him to read the real John's talk." Ben chuckled. "He told me Mr. Clausen paid him well and gave him that Western shirt to wear to the meeting, but he'd never do anything like that again."

"He actually did fairly well, considering his short notice," Riley said.

"That's what I told him. He told me it felt slimy to pretend to be John, but Mr. Clausen was a very persuasive man and assured him it was not a legal or ethical problem at all."

After they went into the house, Riley started the pot of coffee while Ben and Toby went out back.

Ben pulled out his study documents to review, then after Sheriff Baker arrived, the two men sat at the kitchen table with their coffee and pie. Riley took her pie into the living room and opened the last book she had been reading; Toby hopped up on the sofa with her and lay next to her.

She was immersed in her book when Ben said, "Babe, Sheriff's leaving."

Riley put her bookmark in her book and glanced at the clock on the fireplace mantle. *I've been reading for two hours.*

After the sheriff left, Ben said, "Sheriff Baker agreed that I found a significant error in the facts of the case in our textbook. We checked the original case, and my findings agree with it. He'll make a call in the morning to my instructor for a heads-up, then he'll call the head of the department to make an immediate correction. I'm glad he's doing it because I'd rather not tackle the entire department until after I get my certificate."

Riley hugged him. "I'm so proud of you."

"It was a relief to find out I'm not totally incompetent. I would have thought I'd be too wound up to go to sleep, but I'm exhausted. Ready to go outside then go to bed, Toby?"

* * *

While Ben took his shower, Riley started the pot of coffee and fed Toby. After she showered and dressed, she hurried to the kitchen to eat breakfast with Ben.

"I grilled the biscuits Mom made, so we have sausage biscuits for breakfast," Ben said. "Since we'll be leaving at the same time three days a week, we'll need to get up earlier. I appreciate that you made our lunches yesterday. Gotta run."

Ben grabbed his sausage biscuit, coffee, laptop bag, and backpack then rushed out the front door. Riley gaped at the door.

One minute later, he raced back in, kissed her then headed to the door.

Riley shouted, "Coat."

"Coat," Ben grumbled as he grabbed his warm field coat then left.

"He's right, Toby. We need an earlier start; he would have frozen without a coat today if they have a field exercise."

Riley put on her heavy coat, dropped her breakfast into her lunch bag, and picked up her computer bag, backpack, and work backpack, then she and Toby headed to her car.

CHAPTER THREE

After she parked at the office, Doc Ned parked next to her. "Good timing, Riley. Let's take Toby inside; you can tell me when he's comfortable enough for us to leave."

When they went into the building, Hope said, "Toby, you are so handsome. Come see our reception area where I work, then I'll show you our kennel that we call sick bay."

Toby investigated Hope's chair and desk then inspected the waiting area before he yipped.

"I think both of us will have an exciting day, Toby," Riley said. "Are you okay if I leave now?"

Toby grinned, and Riley hugged him.

When he whined, Riley said, "He's ready to check out sick bay. One of the things he did at Doc Julie Rae's office was to keep the injured and sick dogs and cats company."

"I'm not a bit surprised," Hope said as she and Toby walked down the hall. "You have very kind eyes, Toby."

After Doc Ned and Riley were in the truck, he said, "You have your carry piece, right? One of the farmers called me with disturbing news last night. A farmer in the next county disappeared yesterday during the day. He left early in the morning to plant soybeans; when he didn't return home for lunch, his wife called his cell phone, but he didn't answer. She didn't think anything about it because their cell coverage isn't that great, so she packed his lunch then went to their fields to find him. She found his tractor but not him. She called around to the neighbors then finally called their county sheriff. Word is that the farmer had some money problems and was severely depressed, but his wife told the sheriff that her husband had a complete reversal in his attitude a week ago because he'd found a way to save their farm. She's afraid that he became ill and confused then wandered into the woods trying to get home. The other farmers are concerned that someone harmed him. His neighbors plan to conduct a coordinated search led by a retired search and rescue expert later this morning."

"I suppose it could be nothing, but I can understand why everyone is concerned. His wife must be frantic," Riley said.

"All we can do is watch for a lone man, particularly one not dressed for today's weather since yesterday was so nice, and today has turned colder."

"You think he could have wandered this far by foot?" she asked.

"No telling." Doc furrowed his brow then exhaled. "Let's discuss our first appointment: it's more of a get-acquainted visit. We have a new farmer who has goats, and he wants them checked. He didn't say if he was worried about anything in particular. What do you know about goats?"

"Nothing, really."

Doc Ned chuckled. "I stalk the Ag Extension Service regularly for brochures. This is my goat folder, so you can be just as much of an expert as I am by the time we get to the goat farm. After we get there, if we have any questions, I'll give the extension agent a quick call."

Riley opened the folder and began reading the first document. After she finished reading the last brochure, she said, "This is a lot to digest in one reading; I understood maybe half of it."

Doc Ned snorted. "That means you're ahead of me. I told the farmer we'd be happy to check his herd, but we'd need to return if we find any problems."

"That's good. I have a notepad. I can take notes while we're there then type them into my laptop to document the visit after we're on the road."

"Taking notes as we go is a huge advantage of having the two of us working together, but there's no need to type them into your computer. I've got a voice to text transcriber, similar to what medical doctors used to use, except mine is automated. You can record our findings on our way to the next visit. Hope will review the text then mark anything that seems off to her for us to review and correct; it's a fairly simple process, but it has worked fine so far, which is no surprise because it was Hope's idea."

When Doc Ned parked at the goat farm, he said, "The farmer told me he has two does with kids and three juvenile does. He doesn't have any bucks, which is good because all new farmers don't think about starting off as simple as possible while they're learning. He intends for the goats to be meat goats, and his cross-bred New Zealand Boer goats were a good choice. We'll assess their shelter, examine the food and water, and take measurements."

"I saw the recommendations for a shed in one of the brochures, so I have a pretty good idea of what all to measure. Will we use those as a guideline?"

"The recommendations give us a reference, and I like that brochure in particular because it also explains the basis for their recommendations: why a shed might need an elevated slatted floor, for example."

Riley nodded. *I am going to learn so much.*

"There's a tape measure in the glove compartment. After I get the niceties out of the way, one of my first questions will be how much each animal weighs. If the farmer hasn't weighed them, we might be in trouble because all of the dosages are weight dependent, and I don't carry a scale. I want to hear what the farmer knows and has done, then we'll assess each goat and measure their shed and troughs. I suspect we'll have a follow up visit, but we won't know the purpose of it until we finish our examination."

As Riley and Doc Ned strolled toward the goat shed, Riley said, "You know my head's going to explode, don't you?"

Doc Ned chuckled. "I understand completely."

A man and a woman hurried out of the house to join Doc Ned and Riley.

Doc Ned shook hands with the couple. "I'm Doctor Halsey, they call me Doc in the office, and this is my veterinary technician, Riley."

Riley shook hands with them as the man introduced himself and his wife. "We bought the farm a year ago with the idea of having chickens for the eggs for our own use and raising goats; we plan to eat some of the meat and sell the rest."

The woman handed Doc Ned a folder. "These are our records; we have attended several classes so far at the Ag Extension Service, and we followed the template they recommended we use."

Doc Ned and Riley looked over the records together. "You're being thorough," Doc Ned said. "Where's your scale?"

"We'll show you. It's in the barn," the farmer said.

Doc Ned and Riley followed them to the barn.

Doc Ned said, "These are smaller stalls than I typically see in a barn. Did you modify them for your goats?"

"We did," the man said. "We wanted to have a maternity ward and a nursery then realized we'd also want to be able to quarantine any new goats that we brought onto our property."

"I'd like to have a copy of your records for our files," Doc Ned said as they all returned to the goat shed. At the end of two hours of questions and assessment, Doc Ned said, "I'd like to come back in a month to see how everyone is doing. Do you plan any changes before then?"

"Not really," the man said. "We'd like to be comfortable with our operation before we try to expand, and we're not planning on selling the does as long as they are nursing."

"My staff at the office will review your records; if they have any questions, they'll call you, but I think that's unlikely because from what I've seen so far, you're doing everything right. Do you have any questions, Riley?"

"How often are you changing the bedding?" she asked.

"About every week or so," the man said.

"Even though your shed is well-ventilated, I'm catching a light ammonia smell from the bedding. You might want to change it twice a week for the kids because their faces are closer to the bedding, which makes them more susceptible to respiratory problems. With our weather turning cold, the kids need all their extra reserves to stay healthy."

"Thank you, Riley, we'll do that," the woman said.

"Call the office for an appointment in a month, and feel free to call any time if you run into any problems or have any questions," Doc Ned said.

After they left the farm with their copy of the records, Doc Ned said, "I didn't smell any ammonia, and I'm not going to make a short joke because I'm married to a height-challenged woman and too smart for that."

"I didn't smell any either at first, but the older doe was worried about her kids; I bent over to check the eyes of the smaller one, so I could take a whiff of the bedding."

"A doe told you she was worried?" Doc Ned asked. "You're as unusual and talented as everyone says, Riley."

"What's our next appointment?" Riley asked.

"Check your phone. You should have received a text early this morning."

Riley pulled out her phone from the inside pocket of her coat. "I don't see a text of the appointments."

"Computers are great except when they aren't. Call Hope and tell her you didn't get today's appointment text. She'll shoot it right out to you and troubleshoot where the glitch is."

After Riley called Hope, her phone buzzed a text, and she reviewed their appointments for the day. "The schedule allowed all morning for the goat farmers; I wouldn't have thought we'd have been there that long, but we were."

Doc Ned nodded. "We had new farmers, a new goat herd, and it was our first appointment as a team. Perfect trifecta of needing extra time. What did you pack for lunch? A sandwich?"

"Sandwich and a bottle of water."

"There's a small diner nearby. What do you think about a small bowl of chili to go with your sandwich and coffee or hot tea? They don't care if we bring in our sandwiches, and we can eat inside where it's warm instead of in my drafty truck. I wouldn't have thought of it, but those dark clouds are headed our way, and the wind has picked up, hasn't it?"

"I can feel the cold from my window; I'd love hot chili in a warm diner."

"We can talk about our visits for the day without our teeth chattering." Doc smiled.

When they hurried into the diner, a tall woman with gray hair and eyes and skin as dark as coal called out, "Chili or chicken soup?"

"Two chilis," Doc said.

The woman chortled. "Doc, I know it's too cold to be outside; find you and Riley a seat and figure out what you want to drink, but we're plumb out of mimosas."

Doc snorted. "Miz Abigail is a terrible tease."

Riley glanced at the menu board near the cash register. "They have hot chocolate, and I'll bet it's not a packet of powder shaken into a cup of hot water."

Abigail approached their table. "I know you want coffee, Doc, what about you, Riley?"

"Hot chocolate."

"Hot chocolate with a dollop of whipped cream." Abigail set napkins and spoons on their table as a middle-aged couple came into the diner and stared at the menu board.

"Welcome, y'all; it's nice to see you. Come on in, warm up, and find yourself a table."

After the new people sat three tables away from the front door, Abigail asked, "Did you see anything that sounded good to you?"

"I'd like a bowl of chicken soup," the woman said.

"Chili for me," the man said.

"Coffee, hot chocolate, or hot tea?"

"Coffee for both of us," the woman said.

"Got it; while you wait for your soup and chili, you might want to study that dessert board. Our pies are made fresh every morning."

When Abigail returned to Doc and Riley's table with their hot drinks, Riley's eyes widened at the tall mound of whipped cream.

Abigail chuckled. "This is Cook's interpretation of a dollop."

Riley tasted her whipped cream. "Mmm. I think Cook nailed it."

"Honey, I'm not going to tell her that because next she'll want tablecloths and fresh flowers on the tables."

The three men sitting at the counter nodded and chuckled.

"Can't you just see that?" one man asked. "This place would have to change its name to the La-de-dah Café, and we'd all have to wear ties with our overalls."

All the customers in the diner laughed, including the newcomers.

When Abigail brought the bowls of chili to their table, Doc and Riley unwrapped their sandwiches.

"I brought you a knife, Riley, so you can cut your sandwich in half and have the second half for a snack later this afternoon. You won't want to skip the sour cherry pie with a dab of ice cream."

While Riley and Doc ate their lunches, Riley asked, "Is a dab like a dollop?"

"You catch on quick, Riley," Abigail said as she gave a man his change at the cash register.

After Doc finished his dessert, a man at the counter asked, "Doc, do you have a minute? We've got a couple of fishing questions for you."

Doc took his cup with him to the counter, and Abigail refilled it then poured a cup for herself and sat with Riley.

"It's my break, and I hate to see anyone sitting alone," Abigail glanced around then lowered her voice to a near-whisper. "I heard you were at the meeting at the Baptist church last night. My sister and her husband have got themselves into a bind. They had planned to talk to their banker, but now they are considering Step Up, and my brother-in-law signed up for more information last night. I'd rather they worked with folks they know, but they're worried they're going to have to file for bankruptcy, and they're too proud for that. What did you think about the whole presentation?"

"If it was my sister, I'd encourage her to talk to her banker. Mr. Clausen was a good speaker and a great salesman, but he didn't share any details at all last night. I would have thought his sales pitch would have been backed up by a brochure explaining the program or a list of frequently asked questions with the answers. Mr. Clausen's card had his cell phone number and an email address with one of the common email service providers; I would have expected his email to be clausen at stepup dot com or something similar, and I didn't see a website listed for the Step Up foundation either."

Abigail nodded. "I heard you were a talented vet tech, but you've answered all those nagging questions I didn't know I had in the back of my mind. You have a rare knack for digging through the layers of bull to get to the truth. If you ever need any help, give me a shout: here's my cell phone number." Abigail tore a blank ticket from her order pad then printed the number neatly on the paper and gave it to Riley.

"Thanks, I'll put your number in my phone right now."

Abigail nodded then rushed to the cash register to take a customer's money.

Riley entered Abigail into her contacts with her phone number then ate her last bite of pie before she wrote her cell number below Abigail's then headed toward the counter.

"Here you go," Riley said as she handed the paper to Abigail.

Abigail glanced at it. "Ah, thanks for the idea."

"It's time for Riley and me to hit the road," Doc Ned said. "I could talk fishing all day, but some of my favorite farmers would not be happy if I played hooky."

"Your fishing buddies picked up your lunch tab, Doc," Abigail said.

"Thanks, guys, you didn't have to do that," Doc said.

"We treated Riley on her first day on the job; you should thank her for your lunch being on her ticket," the man who had called Doc to the counter said. Doc and the other men laughed.

As Doc Ned pulled away from the diner, light rain splashed on the windshield, and he turned the wipers on low. "Our next appointment is with a rancher who raised horses for rodeo riders for years. Two of his favorite horses that he had raised and trained retired from the rodeo circuit a few years ago. Their owner offered them to the rancher because the two quarter horses had always been together, and the rancher was happy to have his old friends back. He told Hope they appear to be fine, but he has always scheduled regular checkups for them."

"What a kind-hearted man," Riley said.

"He has the reputation of being an irascible old cuss; nobody except his wife, Sharon, and a few of us oldtimers know about his soft side," Doc said.

When they reached the ranch, Doc turned at the driveway that had a rustic ranch gateway sign at the entrance.

"The running horses in the metal sign remind me of wild mustangs running free, and I love the name, 'Tossin' Broncos Ranch' because if somebody thinks they're going to tame a wild horse, they need to think again."

"Exactly, so can you guess what our rancher's name is?" Doc asked.

"Tell me," Riley said.

"Buck."

"Of course." Riley giggled.

Doc smiled. "Not everyone gets it; Sharon gave him the nickname after his mother warned her when they were engaged that he never followed any rules that didn't make sense to him. He'll be in the barn with the horses."

As Doc parked next to the barn, the wind and rain intensified.

"You want to wait in the truck?" Doc asked.

"No, I'll go in with you; give me a second to throw on my poncho over my coat."

Riley zipped up her warm coat and tossed on her rain poncho then snatched up her backpack as she jumped out of the truck. Doc hurried behind her with his umbrella and bag. They dashed for the barn through the blinding rain.

"Glad you made it here before the storm got any worse," Buck said as he and Doc shook hands.

A black Labrador Retriever nudged Riley's hand, and she knelt to rub his face.

"This is Outlaw, Riley; it's a pleasure for both of us to meet you."

"Any weight loss or concerns?" Doc Ned asked as he approached the horses.

"This past week both of them were extra skittish in the morning and stomped their feet when I came into the barn, which is unusual for them. By early afternoon, they seemed tired and sluggish; I had to coax them to go out to the pasture to graze and get a little exercise. I've wondered whether they're getting a good night's sleep." Buck stroked the neck of one of the horses.

Doc Ned examined one horse thoroughly and paid particular attention to her mouth then carefully inspected the other one with the same thoroughness. "Everything looks fine except they seemed a little nervous when I checked their lower legs. Have you noticed any signs of arthritis flareups? Are either one of them limping?"

The larger horse snorted and raised an eyebrow which indicated fear or stress by showing the white of her eye then noisily blew out through her nostrils.

Buck stroked her neck and cooed, "Easy, girl, easy."

When the horse shuddered, Outlaw whined.

Riley asked, "Have you noticed any signs of coyotes around the ranch?"

"I thought I saw one running from the pasture toward the woods at dusk last week, but there wasn't much of a moon, and my eyesight's not as good as it once was. I haven't seen anything since then. Should I think about getting some coyote bait and putting out some traps?"

"Yes, sir; I think that would be a good idea," Riley said.

The older horse nodded and stamped her foot. Buck stared at her then glanced at Riley. "I already have traps; I'll get the bait after the storm passes us. Old Outlaw loves to sleep in the barn; maybe Outlaw, Sharon, and I will hang out with the horses the next couple of nights."

Doc Ned chuckled. "Smartest thing you ever did was marry a woman who thought sleeping in a barn was an adventure."

When a lightning flash was immediately followed by a loud crash of thunder, the horses jumped and crashed into the bars on their stall doors in an attempt to bolt. Riley slid close to them and hummed, and both of them settled down as she stroked their necks and continued to hum.

Buck relaxed on a square hay bale. "She's something, isn't she, Doc? Did you go to that meeting last night? I've heard mixed reviews from those that did: some think the speaker was a shyster, and others swear this new program will save their farm."

"I think your second group heard what they wanted to hear; I was there and listened to the same speech, but I didn't come away with any hint on how the program could save a failing farm operation."

"I was afraid of that," Buck said. "I got a call from a friend to go with him to a meeting at the Methodist church tonight with that Clausen fellow. I think it's a waste of time, but I'd like to help him out because he's skeptical but desperately wants the program to be real, not a scam. What do you think, Riley?"

"I was there too, and Mr. Clausen is highly skilled at delivering a polished sales pitch, but there was no one at the meeting who explained the details of the program or even presented a summary of the contract that a farmer would sign."

"My friend said he wanted me there to keep him from doing anything he would regret if he didn't understand the program, so I guess I'm going."

"While we're waiting for the storm to slow down, tell us about the horses' careers on the rodeo circuit. Were they always together?" Doc sat on a hay bale, and Riley stayed near the horses.

"They sure were; Sharon and I went to as many of their rodeos as we could." Buck told the story of the horses' first rodeo and how irate Sharon was when someone made a comment about first-time rodeo horses.

Doc chuckled. "Even though it was their first rodeo."

"That's right. I was smart enough to never question her about it, though."

Buck continued with another story about Outlaw's first rodeo when he was just a pup and met a cute collie that they still visited every time they had a chance.

When the rain slowed, Doc said, "I'm sorry to say the weather is clearing up; I suppose we'll have to leave. I do recommend more frequent checks of these two."

Buck's eyes twinkled. "For the stories?"

"Absolutely." Doc rose from his hay bale. "Let me know how that meeting tonight goes."

Doc stopped at the end of the driveway and called their next appointment. "We got caught in that bad storm. We can be there in thirty minutes, but it's getting late, so if it isn't convenient for you, we can reschedule."

Doc Ned smiled. "You've got yourself a deal." He chuckled after he hung up. "We have been challenged: we can have hot chocolate and cookies if we're there in twenty-seven minutes; we're actually about twenty minutes away, but I always like to give myself a little cushion."

On the way, Riley's phone buzzed a text from Ben. "Call?"

"Do you mind if I call Ben?" she asked.

Doc Ned shook his head.

"Are you okay?" she asked when Ben answered.

"I'm fine. There's a study group tonight that one of the instructors is leading; we may order takeout if the session goes long. It isn't mandatory, but I'd like to attend. What do you think?"

"Go ahead. Doc Ned and I waited out a bad storm in a barn, so we're running a little behind schedule anyway. I'll see you later, but don't leave your class early because Toby and I will be fine."

"That worked out," Doc Ned said after she disconnected.

"It wouldn't have been a problem for me, but he seemed relieved that I would be home later than usual too. Where are we going next?"

"Our next visit is a cattle finishing pasture, a small operation. The owner is seriously considering a feedlot, which is grain finishing, because he can accommodate more cows."

"I'm not sure I understand," Riley said.

Doc pointed to a folder. "There's new research that shows the latest energy efficiencies of grain-fed finishing in a feedlot generates more beef per animal in a shorter amount of time than pasture finishing."

After Riley read all the information, she said, "This is interesting; the study reports that grain-fed is not only more efficient but also takes fewer people to manage, which is critical according to the article, because staffing has been an ongoing problem for the past five years. What about the increase in concentrated nitrogen-rich manure and methane if he expands his operation?"

"Ahh. The cow manure environmental runoff and the methane air quality controversies. New technology can manage both of them in ways that we never imagined even five years ago."

Riley continued reading. "Popular opinion has been that grass-fed beef is better for the cow, the consumer, and the environment; probably because of marketing, but this article that was published in a journal and jointly written by two authors, a veterinarian and a nutritionist, says the claim about grass-fed versus grain-fed is a marketing myth because research shows that there is no difference. I never realized what a great resource the Ag Extension Service could be for us."

"Fascinating, isn't it? Question everything is my motto."

"I can't believe all I'm learning, and this is just my first day." Riley smiled. "On top of all this, we get a bonus of hot chocolate and cookies. This is the life."

"We're here," Doc Ned said as he slowed to turn into a driveway past an open pasture with grazing cattle.

"They've got their backs to the wind," Riley said.

"If the wind gets any stiffer, they'll head to their shelter."

When they neared the shelter, a man, who was working on a tractor, set down his tools and waved then strolled to the back of his pickup and opened the passenger's door.

Doc Ned parked next to him as the man pulled out a thermos and a tote bag.

After Doc Ned and Riley climbed out of the truck, the man said, "Let's go into the shelter to get out of this wind. My wife brought me a hot lunch because the weather turned so cold and decided we needed hot chocolate and some of her snickerdoodle cookies that she made this morning."

While they sipped on their hot chocolate that the farmer had poured into three large mugs and snacked on cookies, Doc Ned asked, "What are your plans for going to a grain-fed operation?"

"My son's a senior at the University of Georgia College of Agriculture in Athens, and he is researching the best practices for transitioning from a pasture-fed to a grain-fed operation and writing a paper on it for a class; he's using our farm as a case study. Our soil survey was completed last month, and we're in good shape; we need your opinion on our planned feedlot population." The farmer handed Doc Ned a folder. After Doc Ned and Riley read the documents, he asked, "How do these compare to the extension service recommendations we have, Riley?"

"The specifications for space per animal are more generous than what the extension service listed as the ideal, but it makes sense to me to start off slow."

Riley looked through the documents again. "Do you have a plan and schedule for expansion?"

CHAPTER FOUR

"That's a good catch," the farmer said. "I'll relay your question to my son because even though his current course may not require it, he could go above and beyond or use the information as a basis for his next paper; either way, it certainly will help with our plans."

After the three of them walked around the area for the planned feedlot, the farmer said, "Thanks for coming today; I didn't want to slow down my son's paper."

"My office will send you our report and recommendations first thing in the morning. Let me know if there's anything else we can do to help," Doc Ned said.

"That was very exciting to be a part of planning a feedlot; will we be involved in anything else?"

"We'll drop by from time to time while they're in the middle of construction because I'm nosy," Doc Ned said.

"So am I." Riley smiled. "I love learning."

Doc Ned chuckled. "I heard you had a scholarship for school, but you declined. You're having too much fun to fall into the trap of veterinary college, aren't you?"

"Absolutely; I am over academia, I don't have any desire to run a business, and I love spending my days with animals and having the freedom to pick up and go with Ben wherever that may be on a moment's notice."

"You're very rare, Riley; there aren't many people who can clearly articulate what they want out of life."

On their way back to the office, Riley's phone rang, and she raised her eyebrows. "Lizzie's calling me."

After she answered, Lizzie asked, "Did Ned forget to tell you that I'd call you if I had something to tell him?"

"It seems to have slipped his mind," Riley giggled.

"I knew it. Can you turn on your speakerphone?"

"Speakerphone is on," Riley said.

"Ned, I've received four calls about the meeting at the Methodist church tonight; did you hear about it?"

"Sure did; a friend of Buck's asked him to go," Ned said.

"From what I can tell, just about everyone who was at the meeting last night has asked at least one other person to go with them to the meeting tonight; hence my four calls. Are you game?"

"I suppose. What about you, Riley? Would you like to go with us since Ben's going to have a late study session?" Doc asked.

"Come have dinner with us," Lizzie said, "and bring Toby; we always have dog food, and he can go to the meeting too."

"I don't know. Are you sure?" Riley asked.

"I'm positive," Lizzie said.

Riley glanced at Doc Ned, and he nodded.

"Okay, but we sit where you want, so we can bolt if it gets too boring or goes too long."

"You got it; see you two when you show up. Ned, take Riley's car home then the three of you come here; there's no sense in her and Toby being alone on the road late at night."

After Lizzie disconnected, Doc Ned said, "Thanks for agreeing to go, Riley. I wonder if this will be informative or more razzle-dazzle."

"I suspect we'll know within the first five minutes."

When they went into the office for Toby, Hope smiled. "We had a great day, Riley, and we're looking forward to tomorrow, aren't we, Toby?"

Toby yipped.

"See? Unanimous," Hope said.

"You're just guessing," A woman called out from the back.

"You don't know that, Elsie." Hope wrinkled her nose, Riley giggled.

Hope knelt next to Toby and hugged him as he leaned against her. "I'll see you in the morning about eight. Maybe the rain won't chase us back to the building when we're halfway around the block."

"Halfway?" Riley asked. "That must have been brutal to run back the rest of the way to the building."

"Believe me, it was." Hope kissed Toby's nose then rose. "What do you have for me, Doc?"

"I'll call in our report for the feedlot operation as soon as I get home; I'd appreciate it if you'd make it a priority in the morning to review it then send it to our client."

"Will do, and I've set up Riley's phone to get each day's schedule in the mornings."

When they reached the house, Riley opened the back door of her car, and Toby jumped out. *My raingear might still be damp.*

After Doc Ned parked, he opened his back door for Toby.

"I'll be back in a second; I'm pulling out my raingear, so it can dry." Riley dashed into the house and spread her raingear over her dining chair then dumped the rest of her things on the kitchen table in case they were damp; she hurried back and hopped into Doc Ned's truck.

"I hope I didn't slow us down too much," Riley said.

"We've got plenty of time," Doc Ned said.

When Doc Ned headed down a long driveway that became a narrow path through the woods, Riley said, "You're definitely not too close to the road."

Doc chuckled. "Lizzie and I bought this property right after we graduated. It was our belated wedding present to each other because we were married when we were in college. I was a first-year veterinary student, and she was a graduate student. You'll have to ask her for her version of our short courtship because it's my favorite. Both of us were broke and didn't have anywhere to live. I hadn't applied for student housing because a friend of mine with questionable judgement swore that living off campus was cheaper; it wasn't. Lizzie's books cost her far more than she expected. We met in the cafeteria after I watched her make tomato soup with the free hot water, ketchup, and hot sauce, and I copied her. When I sat at the table with her to find out what other miraculous ideas she had for free food, we decided to join forces. We lived in her car for a semester then realized we could get into married student housing which was very cheap, and so we were married."

"That's why you got married?" Riley asked.

"That's my version; you might want to hear Lizzie's."

Riley gaped at the cabin at the end of the path.

"We didn't want a fancy house, so we found an architect who understood our vision of a secluded cabin in the woods. The only concession we made was the firebreak of a fifty foot clearing around the house."

After Doc Ned opened the back seat door, Toby jumped out and investigated the yard until Lizzie opened the front door.

"Come inside and warm up. I've dished up a treat for you, Toby."

Toby dashed to the door; Riley and Doc Ned followed him.

"Come into the kitchen; our supper will be ready shortly."

After Toby ate, Riley zipped up her coat, then she and Toby went out back for a quick break. Riley listened to the din of the katydids and crickets and the screech of a barn owl. The sky was dark, with no light pollution from any nearby towns.

Doc Ned opened the back door. "Time for our supper."

"Come on, Toby," Riley said.

After they ate a dinner of fried chicken, mashed potatoes, gravy, and English peas that Lizzie had canned earlier that summer, Riley helped Lizzie clear the table while Doc Ned loaded the dishwasher.

"Ready for dessert?" Lizzie asked.

"Not really," Riley said.

"Good. I'll send you home with dessert, and you can share it with Ben tonight or tomorrow night."

When Doc Ned pulled into the Methodist church parking lot, he crept around the lot for a vacant spot; on his second pass by the church entrance, he said, "The entire county must be here; why don't I drop you all off? I know where to find you, honey."

Lizzie and Riley hurried to the front door, and Toby trotted along with them.

After they were inside with the warmth and bright lights, a man with a scar that ran from the top of his cheek to his jawline greeted them. "Good evening, ma'am. The meeting is in the church proper because there are too many people here for our meeting room."

As Lizzie and Riley continued toward the double doors to find seats, a large man with sparse brown hair that began at one temple then circled his head to the other temple and only a few wisps on his crown cleared his throat. "I've been looking for you; you're supposed to be helping Mr. Clausen."

The greeter's cheeks reddened, and his jaw twitched as he ground his teeth. "Right."

Riley furrowed her brow. *I don't think I've ever seen shoes with perforated toe caps before.* She exhaled. *Now my curiosity is piqued; I'll have to do a little research.*

"The minister must be weeping in his office over tonight's attendance; these pews are almost completely filled," Lizzie whispered as they went into the church.

Lizzie paused as she scanned the room then led Riley to a pew in the back that was occupied by a large pile of coats. When Lizzie loudly cleared her throat and held up one coat after another in disgust with her thumb and one finger, the sheepish owners claimed them.

When Doc Ned joined Lizzie, Riley, and Toby, he slipped past them and sat next to Riley and Toby.

Doc Ned whispered, "She always finds spots in the back."

"I can't see," Riley whispered.

"I can't either," Lizzie said. "There is plenty of room between our pew and the one in front of us to stand up. When a meeting begins, I stand if I think there's anything to see because I can't see over all the tall people in front of me, if it drags on, or the speaker is boring, I move to the back and lean against the wall or walk out."

"She usually leaves, but I'm happy to be right behind her," Doc Ned said then glanced at his watch. "Five more minutes."

As the time for the meeting to start drew near, people hurried into the church and searched for seats; the conversations turned to murmurs at seven thirty then the room quieted.

"Do we stand now?" Riley asked.

"Nobody's talking; we'll wait," Lizzie said.

"Did you know the man who greeted us at the door?"

Lizzie furrowed her brow. "No, I didn't, now that you mention it. Why?"

Riley shrugged. "No special reason: he called you ma'am, and it seemed odd."

"He's not a church member here because I know all of them; he did act like he was an official greeter, didn't he?" Lizzie asked.

"Did you notice his shoes?"

"Those wingtips? I haven't seen shoes like that in ages," Lizzie said.

"Is that what they are? I'd never seen shoes like them before."

"They were a little old-fashioned and a trifle fancy for his khaki pants and collared polo shirt, but that might be the new thing."

After five minutes, the murmurs began again then by seven forty-five, the conversations became a little louder and had tones of impatience.

At five minutes to eight, shushing sounds came from the front of the church, then a man stepped out from a door on the side of the main area at the front of the church; a middle-aged woman with light brown and blond streaks in her hair and dressed in a custom-fit, dark blue suit followed him.

"That's the Methodist minister and probably our replacement speaker," Lizzie whispered to Riley. "Their best microphone would be set up in the pulpit because that's where he delivers his Sunday sermon."

The people in the church hushed, then the minister said, "Our scheduled speaker has been detained, but Mrs. Fleet assures me she will provide the information you need. Let us take a moment of silence to calm our spirits, then I'll begin our meeting with a prayer."

Riley closed her eyes then peeked at Toby, who had laid his chin on her knee. A tear slipped down her cheek. *What a sweetie: his eyes are closed.*

At the end of the prayer, the minister motioned to the pulpit as he sat on one of the nearby chairs.

Mrs. Fleet stepped to the pulpit, adjusted the height of the microphone, and spoke in a clear, cheerful voice. "Good evening, everyone."

She paused while her audience responded.

"I must apologize for the meeting beginning later than was scheduled; Mr. Clausen was called away on a family emergency and asked me to speak to you. I am not the speaker that Mr. Clausen was, but no one is, don't you agree?"

Riley raised her eyebrows as heads nodded.

"She pulled them in quickly, didn't she?" Lizzie whispered.

"My name is Ava Fleet, and I'm one of the original directors of the foundation, so I can help you understand what the foundation can do for you. We aren't a one-size-fits-all organization, so I won't spend the evening explaining all the possible programs because what you are interested in hearing about is a program that fits you: your farm, your circumstances, and your family." She paused at the murmurs of assent and nodding heads.

"I understand being tied to the land. My husband was a fourth generation farmer: a godly man with a drive to provide for our family of five children. Sadly, he died in his sleep at the young age of forty-one. The doctor said it was a heart attack, but I saw the stress from the burden of escalating costs of farm expenses and unstable crop yield and prices dragging down his spirit and his life energy, and I'm convinced that's what killed him."

Ava paused and gazed at the women in the audience. "You've seen that too, haven't you?"

"Whoa, she's good," Lizzie whispered, and Riley nodded.

Ava continued, "So that we can better understand your circumstances and find the right program for you, I've reserved the beautiful bed and breakfast on the edge of town for the weekend beginning on Friday evening. We'll have exclusive use of their large common room for your privacy and comfort, and my son, Orson, and his lovely wife, Pam, and I will be staying there, so we'll be able to accommodate your schedule."

Buck sat two rows in front of them at the end of a pew next to the wall. After Buck raised his eyebrows then motioned his head toward the exit, he and the man who sat next to him slipped out of the church.

"We're allowing an hour and a half for each appointment, so no one will feel rushed, and we will begin at five thirty in the evening on Friday, then for anyone who is an early bird, we'll begin on Saturday and Sunday at six in the morning then continue until midnight on all three nights, so you don't have to take any time away from your farming operation or your place of employment. Because we're at the bed and breakfast, Orson, who is a master at coordinating events, made arrangements for a caterer to work with our wonderful host, so our morning appointments at six and seven thirty include a continental breakfast, our eleven thirty and one o'clock appointments include a light lunch, and our evening appointments at five thirty and seven include a simple buffet dinner; all our other appointments include a light snack for you, not me because three delicious meals a day for three days would make me even rounder, as they say." Ava rolled her eyes.

She paused while her growing number of supporters in the church chuckled, then she smiled. "At the back of the room, your church has set up a large table for you to sign up for an appointment."

While people turned to look at the back of the room, Ava continued, "Orson will be at the table to help you find a day and time that works best for you, and I'm certain you understand that means both of you if you are married. Pam will have a sheet for you with a list of what are commonly called frequently asked questions or FAQs. I think they should be called AFAQs for answers to frequently asked questions, don't you?"

Ava gazed at her audience and smiled approvingly at the nodding heads before she turned to the pastor. "Would you please close us with a prayer for wisdom and safe travels for all?"

Ava stepped away from the pulpit then bowed her head as she surreptitiously surveyed the audience then smirked while the minister prayed.

Riley narrowed her eyes. *Why is Ava so pleased with her performance?*

The amens at the end of the prayer were enthusiastic; Ava shook the minister's hand then quietly left the church through the back door as people filed to sign up at the table.

When Orson's wife came into the church with a stack of paper, Toby softly growled, and Riley gaped. "Pamela Suzanne?"

"You know Ava's daughter-in-law?" Lizzie asked.

"It's a long story," Riley said. "Here's the short version: Pamela Suzanne was good friends with one of Ben's cousins and was convinced when she and Ben were in high school that she was semi-engaged to Ben. It became an ongoing family joke at the Carter family events that Pamela Suzanne always attended, but as far as Ben was concerned, it was all in good fun, so he went along but didn't take it seriously."

"Ooh, boy, but she did," Lizzie said.

"Very. She was irate when he didn't give her the engagement ring she expected and even more irate when I showed up."

"How long were you and Ben engaged before you were married?"

"Not all that long." Riley snickered. "That's a different story."

"In a nutshell: Ben was engaged to Pamela Suzanne for years, then he met and married you, and that canceled the engagement; do I have it right?" Lizzie asked.

Riley stared at Lizzie.

Doc Ned coughed. "Seems a little extreme on Ben's part, doesn't it? Why didn't he just tell Pam?"

"Because he didn't need to; Riley took care of that," Lizzie said, and Riley giggled.

"Is that true, Riley?" Doc Ned asked.

"It's partially true, and I love Lizzie's version," Riley said.

"Another story?" Doc asked, and she nodded.

"Are you going to sneak out or say hello to Ben's old pal, Pam?" Lizzie asked.

Riley snorted. "No question: I'm a hundred percent sneaking out."

"Let's use the side door near the pulpit; it will be convenient because we'll be near where I'm parked," Doc said.

Toby softly growled again as he faced the back of the church then trotted alongside Riley when she and Lizzie headed to the side door. After they were outside, Lizzie said, "Ned gave me the keys to the truck, so we could wait for him out of the cold wind. He wanted to pick up one of Ava Fleet's FAQ sheets."

After Doc Ned joined them and they were on their way to Riley's house, Lizzie said, "Ava Fleet was much smoother than Mr. Clausen."

"She was, but the program is murkier than it was last night. I scanned their FAQ sheet, and I still don't know how this equity thing of theirs works. There has to be a contract with fees, a repayment schedule, but all I saw tonight were sparkly phony smiles and a list of questions and answers that could have come from any lending agency for anything from a standard consumer loan to a variable rate for a housing loan," Doc said.

As they neared Riley's driveway, Lizzie said, "You're being awfully quiet, Riley. What are you thinking?"

"I'm surprised I didn't hear anything about Pamela Suzanne's wedding because it would have been an extravaganza."

"That you would have been grateful to miss, I'm sure," Lizzie said.

Riley nodded. *I'll call Mom.*

"We'll sit here until you go inside," Doc Ned said. "See you in the morning."

"Thanks for going with us," Lizzie said as Riley and Toby hopped out of the truck.

Toby raced to the house and nosed the door. Riley unlocked the door, and they went inside.

"I need a cup of hot tea, a book, and my boots off," Riley turned on the burner under the tea kettle then opened the back door for Toby before she pulled the dessert from Lizzie out of her backpack and took a peek before she put it into the refrigerator. "Yum, peach cobbler."

While she waited for the water to heat, she called Melissa.

"Everybody okay?"

"We're fine. Do you have a little time to talk?"

"Sure do; what's wrong?"

"Everything's fine. I heard that Pamela Suzanne was married. Did I miss that juicy bit?"

"If you did, so did I; you know, I haven't talked to Pamela Suzanne's mother in ages. Actually, I can't stand to talk to her. I think I'll give Mugsy a call; she'll find out what's going on. Anything else?"

"That's all."

"We'll chat more another time." Melissa hung up.

Riley brewed her tea then opened the back door for Toby.

After she and Toby sat on the sofa, Riley pulled off her boots, put up her feet, and found her place in her book.

An hour later, her phone buzzed a text. "Be home in twenty minutes."

She hurried to turn on the oven and put the peach cobbler in an ovenproof dish to warm before she checked the container of ice cream. "We're set."

When Ben came into the house, he lifted Riley off her feet with a hug. "You are more gorgeous than I remembered."

She giggled, and he kissed her.

After he set her down, he said, "Something smells good."

"I had dinner with Doc Ned and Lizzie, and she sent me home with enough peach cobbler for both of us, and we have ice cream."

While they ate their dessert, Ben told Riley the details the study session covered. "The entire class was ready to quit the program earlier today, me included. The extra time on the material made a difference for all of us."

Riley yawned but moved too slowly to cover her mouth. "I guess I didn't realize how tired I was."

"I didn't mean to keep you up, but thanks for listening; I was wound up from the stress of that class."

Toby yawned, and Ben chuckled. "I'll go outside with you, then we'll all get a good night's sleep."

* * *

After a quick breakfast, Ben said, "Your lunch is in the refrigerator; I made it while you were in the shower." He kissed her. "Didn't want to forget that again, babe. I don't expect to be late tonight, but if that changes, I'll let you know."

Riley's phone buzzed a text, and she scanned the schedule for the day. "I don't know any of these people, Toby, but maybe I will after a few weeks."

She stuck her lunch into the backpack and put on her coat then grabbed her work backpack on her way out the door.

After she started her car, she pulled out her gloves from her pockets and shivered while she waited for the engine to warm up. "It's colder than yesterday, but thankfully the wind is light and not blowing out of the north."

Toby yipped, and she nodded. "I agree completely: it's still cold, but maybe we'll eventually adjust to the weather. I don't remember it being this cold when we lived in Pomeroy, but the only time I spent outside was going to and from my car."

Before she left the driveway, her phone rang. *Lizzie.*

"I have a question for you: do you have any long johns?"

"No, and I didn't even think about them for this winter because I've never spent much time outside."

"That's what I thought. I have two pairs of long johns that fit me years ago, but not anymore; I'm not sure why I still have them other than I hate to throw away anything. I'm sending them with Ned. Put on a pair for today before you leave the office this morning. If you don't like them or they don't fit, don't send them back because I don't need the reminder of how much weight I've gained."

"I layer my shirts; it never occurred to me that my legs would appreciate an extra layer too."

"My long johns are warm but not bulky because I bought them during my phase when I was more concerned about whether I looked heavy than I was about being cold."

"I don't like being cold, and my Aunt Millie always told me that curvy women ran in our family, so I've never been all that self-conscious about my weight. Pamela Suzanne told Ben when I wasn't in the same room with them that I was chubby, and he called out to me that Pamela Suzanne was jealous of my chest. She left in a huff; can you imagine?"

Lizzie laughed. "From what I saw of Pamela Suzanne, she could use a sandwich, bless her heart. I'll let you go, so you can leave for work."

After they arrived at the clinic, Riley and Toby hurried inside.

Hope hugged Toby. "How can you stand to be out in this cold, Riley? I can barely face climbing into my cold car to get to work."

"I think the secret to life is layering," Riley said.

"Did you get your schedule okay this morning?" Hope asked.

"I got the schedule, but it had only the name of the farm, and I'm too new to know what to expect for the appointment."

"That's my fault; I should have explained how to see the details. Pull up your schedule on your phone, and I'll show you."

After Hope showed her how to find the details, Riley said, "This is great, thank you."

"I'm glad you mentioned it; Toby and I have an overnight guest to check. Stay warm." Hope locked her computer screen then hurried to the hallway that led to the kennels; Toby licked Riley's hand then raced ahead of Hope.

While Riley read the details for the first appointment, Doc Ned came in the back door and handed Riley a plastic grocery bag. "I left the truck engine running, so we won't freeze when we leave. These are from Lizzie. I'll wait for you while you try them on. If these fit you, Lizzie has some flannel-lined jeans she bought but never wore because they were too warm to wear indoors, and she always found an excuse to avoid going outdoors longer than it took her to get to her car."

Riley hurried to the rest room and tried on a pair of long johns then dressed and stuffed the second pair in her work backpack.

"These are great, Doc. I'll let Lizzie know they're perfect."

"Send her a text; she's on her way to a meeting at the library, but she'll see it later."

Riley sent Lizzie a text. "Long johns are perfect; thank you."

After they were on the road, Riley said, "I'm a little confused by the three years of medical history for a miniature pony, but the appointment is marked 'new client', and the purpose of the visit is to evaluate two new miniature ponies."

"Our new clients bought the horse farm and the pony from former clients of mine who retired and moved to a condo south of Atlanta. The new people have experience with horses and burros and plan to board horses and rescue miniature ponies and burros."

When Doc Ned rounded a curve, a large tree was across the road. He slammed on the brakes then swerved into the ditch. After he came to an abrupt stop in the soft dirt, he dropped the truck into four-wheel drive and slowly eased forward.

Riley glanced into her side mirror then lowered her window to get a better look. "Doc, two men with rifles are standing on this side of that downed tree."

Riley peered out her open window. "Go, Doc. They've aimed their rifles at us; we need to get out of here."

"Hang on; if I can't get out of this ditch, I have two rifles on the floorboard of the backseat."

Riley raised her window as Doc Ned slowly increased his speed then accelerated, and the truck violently lurched. While Riley leaned over the seat to grab the rifles, the front tires reached the shoulder, and Doc Ned slammed down his foot. The sudden acceleration tossed Riley upside down onto the back floorboard as they sped away.

"Are you okay, Riley?" Doc Ned shouted.

"I landed on our backpacks, so I'm fine, except I think I bruised my ego." Riley untangled herself then sat on the back seat. "Do you want me to call the sheriff's office?"

"Go ahead. Tell them the tree is across the old county line road six miles west of town."

CHAPTER FIVE

After Riley told the dispatcher what happened and the location, she hung up. "A deputy will meet us at the horse farm."

"Call Hope, so she'll be prepared if the sheriff's office contacts her," Doc Ned said.

After Riley told Hope what happened, Hope asked, "Should I call Lizzie?"

"I'll call her," Riley said.

"You're a trooper," Hope said.

"Should I call Lizzie now?" Riley asked after Hope hung up.

"Might as well; if you get her voicemail, ask her to call you, but be sure to tell her it's nothing urgent."

Before she called, Riley asked, "Will that work?"

"Hasn't yet; maybe this will be a first." Doc Ned chuckled.

After Riley left the voicemail, Doc turned onto a narrow, paved road, then ten minutes later, he slowed and turned at a driveway.

"This is definitely a working farm," Riley said.

Doc parked in front of a large barn that was next to a covered shelter that housed tractors, other farm equipment, and two horse trailers.

"You're right about that; nothing fancy here."

"Hang close to the truck with the back door open until I give you the all clear," Doc Ned said.

That tree and those two men shook me up too.

Doc Ned went into the barn then returned. "Barn's empty. I see a car and a truck near the house, but he may have a second truck; most farmers do. Do you suppose our client forgot about the appointment?"

Doc Ned honked his horn, and they waited a few minutes but still didn't see anybody.

"Let's get back into the truck. I'll call Hope; maybe she's heard something," Doc said.

After he hung up, he said, "Hope called the house, but there was no answer; she checked with the sheriff, and the deputy is less than five minutes away, so we'll wait. I'll turn the truck around."

While they waited, a pony whinnied.

"Something's wrong." Riley jumped out of the truck with a rifle and raced around the barn to a smaller barn as the pony snorted then whinnied again.

Riley gasped when she saw the man lying face down in the dirt. The back of his shirt was covered with blood and had a large tear with an open wound in the middle.

"Doc," she shouted as she threw her bulky coat to the side, "Call for an ambulance."

She knelt next to the man; his breathing was ragged, and his pulse was weak when she lay her fingers gently on his neck.

"We'll get you help," she said.

"My wife…" His voice was so weak that Riley leaned closer to hear him.

"In the house."

When Doc Ned reached the barn, he said, "An ambulance is on the way."

"We need a medical helicopter; he has a bad gunshot wound in his chest," Riley said.

"The deputy's here; I'll get the helicopter."

"Tell the deputy his wife is in the house then bring your medical kit; we need trauma bandages."

Riley ripped open his shirt and shook her head at the size of the wound. When Doc Ned arrived, he opened his medical bag and handed Riley two large trauma pads.

"I have more in the truck bed," he said.

Riley slid her hand under the man's chest and pursed her lips at the blood on both sides of her hands. "We'll need them; then we'll have to turn him onto his side, so I can see his chest."

"Is my wife…" the man gasped the words then choked.

"Easy, easy." Riley hummed her grandmother's soft tune, and the man took in a small breath then exhaled.

"The sheriff's deputy is checking the house, we have a helicopter on the way, and I have more bandages. Where do you want me?"

"Opposite me. We'll roll him towards you, then if you'll support him, I'll check his chest. Do you have four trauma pads? Put them next to me."

After Doc Ned knelt opposite Riley, she exhaled. "Your count, Doc, then pull him toward you and prop him up with your knees. Maintain the pads on his wound as best you can."

Doc nodded then put one hand on the man's shoulder and the other one near the wound and spread his fingers to hold the pad in place as he chanted, "One, two, three."

On three, they gently rolled the man to his side.

"We've got an out of control bleeder." Riley grabbed gauze pads and packed them in the wound then added a trauma pad and pressed it tightly.

"Can you keep holding him up?" Riley shivered as she leaned close and listened to the man's breathing.

"Not worse, but his skin is gray. Do we know when the helicopter will be here?" she asked.

The man coughed. "Truck keys." The fingers on his right hand that had been clutched into a fist twitched, and a set of keys dropped onto the ground.

"I'll take care of them." Riley jammed them into her jeans pocket.

The solemn deputy stood in the doorway. "The chopper will be here in three minutes."

"My wife…" The man gasped.

Riley glanced at the young deputy who shook his head slowly then left.

"We're checking," Riley said.

The whirring of blades became louder as the helicopter neared, then the deputy returned with two flight medics and their stretcher.

"Gunshot wound," Riley's teeth chattered. "Entrance wound is his chest, and exit wound is his back."

"Any ID?" One medic asked as he quickly applied an oxygen mask over the man's nose and mouth as the other one slid a sturdy backboard between Doc and the farmer.

"I see his wallet in his back pocket," Doc Ned said.

"I'll get it." The deputy hurried to Doc's side and pulled out the wallet then handed the man's driver's license to the medic who held the stretcher against the man.

The medic dropped the license into his shirt top pocket. "That's all we need."

The medics laid the board flat then strapped the man and the oxygen tank securely to the board before they picked up the stretcher with their patient.

The deputy tossed a heavy woolen horse blanket over Riley who was shivering uncontrollably, and she clutched the blanket and tightly pulled it around her shoulders.

"Can you take over here, deputy?" The medic at the foot of the stretcher asked.

The medic handed off the stretcher to the deputy to help carry the wounded man to the waiting helicopter while the medic rushed ahead to prepare for their patient. As the deputy hurried back to the small barn, the chopper took off.

"I'll put the wallet in an evidence bag; Doc, would you go with me to my cruiser to be my chain of evidence witness?" The deputy helped Doc to his feet.

After they left, Riley remained on the ground and gazed at the pools of blood around her. When the pony whimpered, Riley said, "They took him to a hospital that has great doctors, and they'll do their best."

"The wife didn't make it," Doc said when he returned. "Do you need help up?"

"I'm okay." She exhaled then struggled to her feet while she clutched the warm blanket. "What's going to happen to the ponies?"

"I called Buck; he and a couple of neighbors will be here in less than an hour; the ponies can stay at Buck's ranch until their owner is well enough to take care of them."

Riley hugged the pony. "I heard you calling for help; you made a difference, and now he has a chance."

The pony nuzzled Riley. "A nice man who understands horses will come get you and the new ponies. You'll stay with him, and I'll visit you."

After they left the farm, Doc said, "I picked up your coat and threw it into the backseat; we're going back to the office. Hope is rescheduling today's and tomorrow's appointments. We'll finish out the day in the office at the sheriff's request, so a deputy can take our statements, then tomorrow we'll to go to Buck's and check out the ponies."

"I'm glad you had the trauma pads," Riley said.

"So am I. It was Hope's idea that I keep a trauma kit in the bed of my truck in case I ever came across a bad crash on the road. Have you ever had any medical training? I mean besides your vet tech training and experience."

"No." Riley gazed at the blood on her hands and clothes. "I'll need to wash and change clothes as soon as we get to the office." She glanced at Doc. "So will you."

"That's why we carry a change of clothes. I know you turned down veterinary school, but what about med school? You are a natural-born trauma doctor."

"No more school for me," Riley said automatically.

"Good, then you'll think about it." Doc Ned grinned.

When Riley raised her eyebrows to peer at him, he chuckled.

After Doc Ned parked at the office, he shook his head. "We look like we tangled with a grizzly. Bring in your backpack; we'll go in the back door, so we don't shock any clients."

Toby and Hope met them at the back door. Toby sniffed both of them then whimpered.

"The man had been shot and was badly injured," Riley said. "The medics air-lifted him to a trauma center."

Hope handed Riley and Doc large plastic bags. "Put your clothes in these. Riley, just drop the blanket, and I'll send it to the cleaners."

Riley glanced down at the blanket and her eyes welled up. "I took off my heavy coat before I knelt next to the farmer. At first, I was too busy to notice I was freezing; this wool blanket made a difference."

Hope furrowed her brow then glanced away. "Doc, when you told the contractor to install showers in the restrooms, I thought you were crazy, but they've come in handy more than once over the years, haven't they?"

"Unfortunately, yes." Doc shook his head.

She cleared her throat before she continued. "Riley, there's soap and shampoo in the women's restroom, and I sterilized my hairbrush for you because you need to shampoo your hair. Holler if you need anything else because we're proud to be a full service spa for heroes here. After you've cleaned up, you and I are going to spend some time on the county map to orient you to where our clients are while Doc catches up on the paperwork that he's been avoiding for weeks."

After Riley showered, brushed out the tangles from her hair, and dressed, she put the plastic bag with her clothes in her car.

When she returned to the office, Hope said, "Lizzie will be here soon with her spicy chicken tortilla soup. Did you pack your lunch?"

"Yes, I have a sandwich in my backpack."

"Put it in the office staff refrigerator; you can have it with your soup or save it for tomorrow."

"I'm not hungry, but I'm starving. Does that make sense?"

"Not really, but in a Riley kind of way, sure. Would you like some hot tea? The water's ready, and we can sit in the breakroom while we review the county map."

"Hot tea would be great. I didn't realize how cold I was until the medics took over; the warm shower was a godsend."

While Hope showed Riley where the farms she had already visited were located, the sheriff joined them in the small breakroom.

"Can I interrupt you for some questions, Riley?" Sheriff Baker asked.

"Certainly, Sheriff," Riley said.

"I'll check on Doc to be sure he's doing that paperwork." Hope left the breakroom.

Sheriff Baker sat at the table with Riley. "Start with the farm, or the road incident: whichever you prefer."

"I'll start with the farm." She told him about no one meeting them when they arrived, and Doc Ned checking the large barn but not seeing anything.

"We were ready to leave when the pony that has been at the farm for a while called out for help, so I ran to find her."

"I sure am glad Sheriff Murray in Carson gave me a heads-up about you and animals, or we'd be spending the rest of the day on that one statement, but I do have a question: what did she say?"

"It was a distinct call for help, and she was frantic. I don't know how to explain it any better than that."

Sheriff Baker nodded. "It's good enough for me; sorry I interrupted you."

Riley told him about the man and his chest wound. "He was conscious but very weak. When the helicopter arrived, they put him on a backboard then left."

"What do you know about the wife?"

"Doc told me she didn't make it; I didn't go into the house."

"Tell me about the attack on you and Doc."

After Riley told him about the tree across the road, Doc swerving into the ditch, and the two men that pointed rifles at Doc's truck, Sheriff asked, "Can you describe the men?"

"They were dressed in jeans and dark ski jackets. Both of them were medium height. The younger one, who was about thirty years old and slightly overweight, had shoulder length, stringy, dark blond hair; the other one was closer to fifty, was much heavier than the younger man, and had a short-clipped haircut. They didn't look like they were familiar with rifles because the younger man held his rifle with one hand until he pointed it at us; the other one aimed his rifle with two hands but not against his shoulder. My first thought was they were coming to help us until I realized both of them had their fingers on the triggers of their rifles, so I told Doc we needed to get away."

"How did you see so much in such a short amount of time?"

"On Monday, Lizzie told me to look at individuals, not a group, so that's what I did."

"You must be a natural for that to click in for you so quickly. I'll have to ask Mrs. Halsey to join my training staff." The sheriff smiled as he rose. "I'll give my notes to our office manager after I talk to Doc; we'll have a statement for you to read and correct any errors then sign early next week. Thanks for your help."

After the sheriff left, Lizzie carried a large slow cooker into the breakroom and set it on a counter near an electrical outlet, and Hope followed her with two tote bags.

"I hope you can handle spicy, Riley, because my chicken tortilla soup is guaranteed to warm you up from the inside out. If you don't have a sandwich, I have bread; it's the only thing that tames the spicy burn. Hope, there's more than enough for the entire staff today, so you can tell them to help themselves."

Hope smiled as she set out the bags of small baguette rolls, tortilla chips, disposable bowls, small plates, and spoons. "This looks like a party in the making. I appreciate not having to go out in this bone-chilling weather to pick up something to eat for lunch that would be cold by the time I got back."

Riley's phone buzzed a text from Ben.

"I was selected to go into the field on an active case with a supervisor. Don't know when I'll be home."

Riley responded, "We'll be fine."

Toby trotted into the breakroom and laid his head on Riley's knee. "Ben's going to be late again tonight. Do you think this is how it will always be even after he's not in training?"

Toby whined.

Riley's eyes welled up. "This morning was horrible; I wanted to help the farmer, but I didn't have the right tools or knowledge. Doc's right: I need to move beyond vet tech. What do you think?"

Toby yipped.

Riley sighed. "Taking some time to unwind is a good idea; let's bake something tonight. What sounds interesting?"

When Toby grinned, Riley giggled as Hope came into the breakroom.

"Do you have a 'he's a good boy' treat recipe?" Riley asked.

Hope opened a cabinet and pulled out a recipe card and a silicon mold of mini dog bones. "A client gave us the recipe and mold three years ago when she moved to Savannah because she was certain we'd enjoy baking homemade treats for our patients. We don't have time for that; maybe we will when Doc decides we need to become a boutique doggy spa."

Riley chuckled. "I can see it now; will you wear a frilly apron?"

"Sure; one that says, 'Ask me about my tattoos'." Hope laughed. "Where was I? Anyway, I stuck these into the cabinet three years ago; you're welcome to them."

Riley dropped the card and mold into her backpack.

"Ready to get back to our map, Riley?" Hope spread out the map on the table.

After they had located the last client scheduled for the following week, Doc came into the breakroom. "Riley, you're welcome to go home for the day; according to the sheriff, neither one of us should travel in the dark for a while. We'll go to Buck's ranch for our first appointment in the morning; plan to be here by nine."

That certainly simplifies my mornings. "Thanks, Doc."

"If you leave now, you'll have plenty of time to stop by the grocery store for the ingredients, if you and Toby are planning to bake tonight," Hope said.

"We'll do that; Ben's going to be late, and I'm glad to have something fun to do."

Riley loaded her backpacks into her car, then she and Toby headed to the grocery store.

While Riley waited in the checkout line, her phone buzzed a text from Lizzie.

"Call when you are home."

On the way, Riley said, "The recipe directions say to mix the dry and wet ingredients with the beater attachment on the mixer. I'll mix the dough by hand, but I think we'll need a stand mixer if you like your dog treats."

After Riley carried in her groceries then returned to her car for her backpacks and bag of clothes, she put away the groceries and put her soiled clothes into the washer for a cold water wash while Toby was in the backyard.

Riley called Lizzie. "We're home." She turned on the burner under the tea kettle then put her serving of the Greek chicken pasta into the oven to warm up.

"Good; I actually have some information for you that gave me an excuse to be sure you arrived safely. First, remember Madge? She and her sister talked to the local banker after all; he is happy to work with Madge's sister and brother-in-law to consolidate their debt. Madge thanked me and sent her thanks to you for giving her the encouragement to push her sister to see their long-time banker, not some stranger."

"That's good news." Riley pulled out a casserole from the freezer and put it into the refrigerator to thaw for the next day. *Enchilada pie. That sounds good.*

"It is, isn't it? Do you know about the farmer in the county next to us that disappeared?"

"Doc Ned told me about that."

"I thought he did; the wife's sister told my cousin that the farmer had changed his mind about the loan and didn't sign the papers after all. The wife feels guilty because when he received several death threats, she discouraged him from calling the sheriff. The sister made my cousin promise to keep it quiet, so my cousin, who is very literal, whispered when she told me."

Riley snickered. "I'm so sorry; death threats aren't funny."

"Not at all, but I had to share the entire story with you because my sweet, literal cousin is such a delight that I can't help but laugh too."

"I wonder if they were just verbal threats," Riley said.

"I'll check with my cousin because I think she said texts. What are your plans this evening?"

When Toby scratched at the back door, Riley opened it, and Toby hurried inside. "Ben's going to be late, so Toby and I are making treats for Toby. Hope gave me a recipe and a dog bone mold."

"That shouldn't be hard: dump all the ingredients into the mixing bowl, turn on the mixer, then spoon your batter into the molds."

"Right." Riley rolled her eyes.

"You don't have a mixer, do you?"

"No, but if Toby likes his treat, we'll get one."

"I have an extra one; it's an older model and doesn't have all the extra attachments, but it will definitely help you with your Toby treats. Can Toby wait until tomorrow, so I can send the mixer to work with Ned?"

"I don't think it will take much to mix it with a wooden spoon, and we're sort of bored tonight."

"I'll still send it with Ned; you might come up with something else you'd like to make another time. Talk to you later."

Riley checked her casserole in the oven, but it was lukewarm in the center. She turned up the temperature on the oven then measured the dry ingredients for the good boy treats before she sat at the table with her hot tea and her hot meal.

After she ate, Riley adjusted the oven temperature then mixed the ingredients and stirred the batter until her right arm ached, so she switched to her left arm and continued another two minutes. "Still lumpy, but that's the best I can do; I hope it's good enough."

When she finally filled all the dog bone molds, Riley still had a third of the batter left. "I'll do a second batch if the first batch turns out okay; you'll be my tester, Toby."

Toby lay next to the stove and lifted his head. She popped out the milk bone treats onto a rack to cool then refilled the molds.

"Would you like a good boy treat?" Riley used the pancake turner to lift it off the baking sheet. While she blew on it, Toby sat and drooled expectantly; when Riley gave him his warm dog bone, Toby scarfed it down then yipped his approval.

"Okay, one more, then that's it: taste test over." Riley put the second batch in the oven.

After all the mini dog bones cooled, Riley placed them into a plastic bag then removed the air. While she relaxed on the sofa and read, Toby lightly snored as he slept by her side.

She woke with a start when Toby nudged her elbow with his cold nose.

"Nothing puts me to sleep faster than relaxing with a book; it's going to take me forever to read it, though," she grumbled as she stumbled to the back door and opened it for Toby. He raced across the yard to chase a rabbit, and she closed the door.

When he came back inside, she said, "Brr, it's gotten colder. I hope Ben's dressed warm enough."

She glanced at her phone. *It's after ten o'clock; No texts or missed calls. I'll turn on the oven in case he's hungry.*

Riley put on her flannel pajamas and wrapped herself in a soft blanket before she curled up on the sofa with her book. "Let's wait up a little longer, Toby."

Toby circled then flopped down on his favorite spot at Riley's feet.

Riley's phone buzzed a text from Ben.

"Are you awake?"

"Yes. Have you eaten?"

"No time. Be home in 20 minutes."

Riley popped his chicken casserole into the oven.

Ben burst into the house and grabbed Riley in a tight hug.

She exhaled involuntarily. "Oof."

Ben loosened his hold on her and gazed at her before he tenderly kissed her and continued to hold onto her.

"Are you okay?" Riley asked.

"No, but I'm starving and cold on top of everything else."

"I was worried that you might be cold. Take a warm shower and put on a comfortable shirt and pants. Your supper will be ready in ten minutes."

"You are so smart." Ben kissed her again before he hurried to shower.

After Ben joined her in the kitchen, Riley dished up his casserole and asked, "What do you want to drink? A beer?"

"No, I'd fall asleep and faceplant in my plate. Do we have any hot chocolate mix?"

"We have Mom's homemade mix: one hot chocolate coming up."

Riley turned on the tea kettle for her and poured milk into a pot to warm on the stove for Ben's hot chocolate.

Ben put his arms around Riley as she stirred the milk to keep it from scorching then kissed the top of her head. "What did you and Toby do this evening?"

"Hope gave me a recipe for good boy treats, so we baked."

"How were they, Toby?" Ben asked.

Toby howled then yipped.

"Where are they, babe? Toby wants me to see what a good boy he is."

Riley giggled. "In the pantry."

"How did you make mini dog bones?" Ben asked.

"Hope gave us a mold."

"They smell good; you two are very talented."

Toby sat politely, and Ben gave him a treat.

"Your supper's ready, honey," Riley said.

While Ben ate, he said, "When I was a kid, I always wanted to be a cop. I loved going on farm visits with Uncle Seth, but I was always watching for bad guys and planning what I'd do if one showed up. I'm not sure how I would have recognized them, but I was ready."

"When I was a kid, I knew bad guys always wore black hats and had stubbly beards," Riley said.

He chuckled. "You've just described half the men I see at the gas station every time I fill up."

He finished eating then pushed away from the table. "This was great. I was afraid I'd wake you."

While Riley cleared the table, Ben loaded the few dishes into the dishwasher and continued, "I never got beyond my private world of being in law enforcement until I met you and gazed into your golden hazel eyes. Tonight was a rude awakening for me because I was immersed in the real world of finding bad guys, which meant I couldn't leave until we secured the scene and documented all the evidence. I don't think the late nights will ever end because there will always be bad guys, scenes to secure, and evidence to gather, no matter how long it takes. What made it even worse for me was that I was investigating the attack on the farmer you found and the murder of his wife. I kept thinking I should have been there with you, not documenting the crime scene."

Riley bit her lip. "I didn't want to…"

Ben put his arms around her and interrupted her. "Babe, I understand. I know you're doing everything you can to support my studies, but even if you and Doc hadn't gone to that farm this morning, I still would have been in the field investigating the scene and wouldn't have been home until now; I don't like that at all."

"I felt so helpless when I found the farmer because I didn't know enough to help him. I knew I wanted to stop the bleeding, but I didn't have the skills or the tools to find the source and stop it. Doc told me I needed to get past my burnout with studying and go to medical school."

"Really? What do you think about that?"

"I'm not interested in medical school, but maybe I'm being short-sighted by refusing to look at options. I pinched pennies and struggled to pay for vet tech training and finish my degree while I worked, so I may have become stuck in the overworked, sleep-deprived, starving student mindset," Riley said.

"I think we need to figure out what we want to be when we grow up." Ben smiled.

Riley giggled. "If we really want to grow up, right?"

"You got it. What do you think about going to visit Mom and Dad this weekend? We could relax, kick around some options, and even discuss with the folks if you like."

"I'd love it. We could leave Friday when you get home and return on Sunday. I don't work on Fridays, so I can have everything packed and ready to go as soon as you get home."

"Friday will be a half day for me, since I spent today in the field and will probably be in the field most of tomorrow, but hopefully, not so late."

"I'll tell Mom in the morning that we'll be there for supper on Friday."

"I wonder if I'm burned out by the classes just like you were this summer." Ben yawned. "I thought I'd be too wired to sleep, but I'm exhausted; what's your schedule like for tomorrow?"

"Doc Ned and I will check the ponies at nine; Sheriff Baker didn't want either of us on the road while it's dark."

"There's more I don't know, isn't there? Should I wait until morning to hear about it, or do I need to sit up all night and worry?"

"Tomorrow's fine, but let me know if you're going to worry all night, so I can stay awake and stress about you being tired in the morning," Riley said.

"Let's skip all that and go to bed. What are you doing in flannel pajamas?"

"I was cold," she said.

"I'm home now; it's my job to warm you up, babe." Ben swept her up into his arms, and she nibbled on his neck as he carried her to the bedroom.

CHAPTER SIX

While they ate breakfast, Riley told Ben about the tree across the road and the two men.

"What does the sheriff think?"

"He didn't say, but Doc Ned told me there have been several incidents of veterinarians being attacked in remote locations for their drugs."

"Uncle Seth always worried about that too," Ben said. "I'd forgotten all about it, but now I'll add it to my things to solve when the class instructor is boring."

While Ben loaded the dishes into the dishwasher, he said, "I'm inspired by you working fulltime and completing your degree: I'll finish the GBI classes no matter what we decide."

After Ben left for his class with the lunch Riley had packed for him and dressed warmly enough to satisfy her, Riley pulled out her shirt and jeans from the washer, inspected them, and exhaled. *No blood stains.* She returned them to the washer and added clothes from the hamper to make a full load then started the machine before she picked up her phone and called Melissa.

"Is everything okay, Riley?"

"We're fine. Do you have any plans this weekend?"

"I was hoping you'd ask; when are you coming, and what time will you be here?" Melissa asked.

Riley smiled. *Mom always knows.*

"I don't work tomorrow, and Ben hopes to get out of class early, so we thought we'd be there for supper and spend the weekend."

"That's wonderful. I suppose you need to dash out the door for work; we'll see you tomorrow."

After Melissa hung up, Riley stood at the back window and watched Toby as he cleared the backyard of squirrels then scouted for rabbits, armadillos, or any other intruders. *It's great to see him so active.*

At eight o'clock, she called Toby inside. "Ready to go to the office?"

Toby trotted through the kitchen, straight to the front door, and waited while she put on her heavy coat then picked up her backpacks and lunch.

On their way to the office, Riley scanned the sky. "Not a cloud in sight. That must be why the temperature dropped so fast last night."

When they went into the office, Doc Ned met them at the back door. "Riley, I have news about our farmer: he made it through surgery last night. He's in critical condition, but he's hanging on."

"That is great news."

"Toby," Hope called from the kennel, "Our Pomeranian has been waiting for you."

Toby yipped then licked Riley's hand before he scrambled down the hall to see the Pomeranian.

As he rounded the corner, Riley said, "Enjoy your day, Toby."

"Ready to go, Riley?" Doc Ned asked.

"Whenever you are; I parked next to your truck and left my backpacks and lunch in my car."

"Let's grab and go." Doc put on his heavy coat, then they headed out the door. "Lizzie sent me to work with a stand mixer for you: it's in my truck."

After Doc put the mixer in Riley's car and they were on the way to Buck's ranch, he said, "After we see the ponies at Buck's ranch, our next appointment is with an old friend of mine who wants us to check her two horses that she's had for a long time because they've been agitated this week, and she's worried they are sick or the cold is bothering them. She lives near town, so Hope rescheduled the original appointment to this afternoon."

Riley smiled when they reached Buck's ranch. "I wonder if Ben and I would be better off running a business together, like Buck's."

"Is the drudge of the classroom getting to Ben?"

"Might be; that's why I turned down the opportunity to go to veterinary college, so I definitely understand. We're going to his folks this weekend; I think he wants to talk to his dad and Sheriff Dunn."

"Lizzie and I were married when I was in my first year of veterinarian college; I had to return to campus two or three times a week to finish a project or research paper and frequently didn't get home until two or three in the morning then left at seven for classes. I hated it and wanted to withdraw from the program, but we somehow stuck it out. Setting aside time together every week was a priority for us, and we've stuck to it."

When Doc parked at the barn, the pony pranced from the field to the fence nearest the barn and whinnied.

Riley hurried to the fence. "Your farmer is very sick, but his doctors and nurses are doing everything they can to help him be better."

The pony snuffled then whinnied again.

"It's nice to see you again, Bella. I'm Riley."

"Bella?" Buck asked as he strolled from the barn to join Riley and Doc. "How do you know…"

Doc interrupted Buck. "Believe me, she just does."

"Are you what they call a horse whisperer, Riley?"

"Add dog and goat whisperer," Doc said. "That's all I know, but this is only her first week; anything else, Riley?"

"I know a guinea pig named Albert fairly well." Riley's eyes twinkled.

Buck chuckled. "Anybody else might think you were kidding around, but my granny had a way with animals. My friends at school told me she was just guessing what the animals were saying, but Maw told me Granny didn't have to guess because she knew. Bella was happy to run in the field, but the other two ponies are skittish; they're huddled in the barn."

When Riley, Buck, and Doc Ned went into the barn, the ponies' eyes widened as they panicked and kicked the sides of their stalls. Riley hummed, and they settled down, and the pony closest to Riley snorted.

"Nobody's here to hurt anybody," Riley said.

"Were they in the barn with the farmer when he was shot?" Buck asked.

The pony whinnied and nodded her head.

"Is she answering me?" Buck asked. "No wonder they've been so nervous."

"Can she tell you what the shooter looked like?" Doc asked.

The second pony reared up and stomped the dirt.

"She called him a wolf," Riley said. "I don't know how to interpret it, but I think she's saying he was very dangerous, and there was another man with him. The ponies panicked and raced away to the field when the farmer was shot."

"I wonder if the investigators know there were two men; although I don't know how I'd tell them that the ponies were eyewitnesses," Buck said.

"I'm sure they already know," Doc said. "I'd like for these two to settle down before I examine them more closely," Doc said. "We'll come back next week, Buck. Show me what you're feeding them."

While the two men discussed the feed, Riley slipped out of the barn and sent Ben a text. "FYI. Ponies said there were two men; shooter described as a wolf."

Ben replied: "Thanks."

Riley waited for Bella at the fence, and Bella raced to her. Riley stroked Bella's neck. "Did you see the bad man?"

Bella shook her head as she whinnied.

Riley nodded. "I would have waited before I checked too. Did you know the ponies before they came to the farm?"

Bella shook her head.

Riley's phone rang. *Ben.*

"Are you sure there were two?"

"Positive. The two new ponies were in the barn and bolted when the farmer was shot; they said there were two men, and the shooter was a wolf."

"The most dangerous animal a pony could imagine, right?"

"I think so. I don't know if this is important, but Bella, the pony that was living at the farm, didn't know the two new ponies before they arrived. I'll ask Hope if she has any record of their owner, but from what Doc Ned said on our way to the farm, I got the impression he didn't have any prior history."

"I don't know how significant it is, either, but it's interesting. As far as the shooter, we've assumed there was only one, based on what we've found so far; thanks for the tip. I loved you first." Ben hung up.

Riley rolled her eyes then sent him a text. "You cheated, but I still love you more."

"Ready to go, Riley?" Doc Ned was next to his truck.

She hurried to the truck and jumped in. "Bella said she didn't know the ponies before they came to the farm. Do you know who the previous owner was?"

"I didn't think about that; I don't, but Hope might. Send her a text."

Riley sent the text, and Hope answered immediately. "No, but I can check around. Not many people have miniature horses."

When Doc Ned slowed, Riley's eyes widened when she saw the silhouette of prancing horses on the sign. "The bed and breakfast has horses?"

He chuckled. "The owners used to have quite a few, and guests rode horses on the trails. It's deceiving, but the Trails End B&B is on sixty acres. After Nora's husband died, she didn't have the time or energy to care for her guests, cook, keep up with the housekeeping, run the business, maintain the trails, or care for all the horses, so she sold all except for the two older ones that were her favorites."

"Didn't Ava Fleet say she rented a bed and breakfast for the weekend to discuss the Step Up program with farmers?"

"This is the only B&B in the county, so this must be the one."

"I'd love to be a fly on the wall."

"Nora could definitely use the help for the weekend too."

When Doc Ned parked in front of the grand old house with a wide porch and stately columns, Riley's phone buzzed a text.

Ben: "Call when you can."

"Doc Ned, Ben asked me to call him. Is it okay if I call him now?"

"Go ahead; I'll rearrange the truck bed a bit."

Ben answered on the first ring. "We need to talk."

"I've got time, what are we talking about?"

"Babe, the tip from the ponies expanded the case, and the senior investigators have offered positions on their teams to those from our class that are interested. When our instructor said we'd be in the field and working an active case, I realized that the classes are my ticket to becoming a crime scene investigator. That's why you stuck it out with your classes, wasn't it? My assignment is on the team that will investigate the second assailant. Unfortunately, we'll work this weekend, but I'll be home every night for supper. What do you think?"

"I think Mom will be disappointed, but she'll understand. I'll call her right away."

"What about you? Babe, just say the word, and I'll decline; it won't impact my grade for the class or my career with GBI."

"Don't decline; you're happier in the field than in a classroom and will probably learn more."

"You're right about that; I've been given permission to play hooky." Ben chuckled.

"I don't think you could walk away from an investigation any more than I could turn my back on animals. I may be cranky once in a while, and you'll be moody, but we'll bounce back as long as we set aside a little time for each other every week."

Ben snorted. "I'm never moody; I'm thoughtful."

Riley heard the smile in his voice and giggled. "Yes, dear."

Ben laughed. "No wonder I loved you first."

"Because I love you more," Riley said.

"I'll always love you, babe; don't ever forget that."

After he hung up, Riley called Melissa. "Change of plans; Ben just learned he is working this weekend, so we won't be coming after all. I'm terribly sorry."

"That's too bad; I was looking forward to seeing you, but I understand. Don't be afraid to just show up; your room is always ready for you, and I always have enough to feed you two."

When Riley climbed out of the truck, Doc asked, "Is everything okay?"

"Yes; Ben had a long day yesterday and was feeling discouraged, but he's much better. We have a change in our plans, though, because he will be working this weekend."

"If you're serious about being that fly on the wall, just let me know, and I'll say something to Nora."

"I'll think about it."

Doc Ned knocked on the front door; a slender woman who was at least ten years younger than Doc Ned and had short, curly, silver hair opened the door. She was taller than Riley, and her dimples in her cheeks deepened when she smiled.

"Thanks for squeezing me in, Ned, and it's so nice to meet you, Riley. Are you tired of everyone knowing who you are, and you have no clue of who they are? It's the curse of not only being the only vet tech who has ever made house calls with Doc but also being the prettiest redhead in town too."

"Thank you, Miz Nora." Riley felt her cheeks warm.

"Oh, dear; sorry if I embarrassed you. My husband told me once that my filters must have broken after the warranty expired."

Doc Ned nodded. "He got that right."

Nora shivered. "It's cold out there. You have to be freezing, and here I am yammering away; come on in."

When Riley stepped inside, she gaped at the wide staircase that reminded her of a switchback road on a mountain as it flowed from the third to the second then main floor.

"Unusual, isn't it?" Nora asked. "This house was built in 1887 in the Queen Anne style and has the typical wraparound porch and asymmetrical floor plan with the rooms on each floor surrounding the central staircase. This poor house was vacant for a long time and terribly rundown when we bought it; we tried to be true to the original architecture when we remodeled it."

"I've never heard of Queen Anne style homes," Riley said.

"They were popular for a short time in the 1880's, so there aren't very many left, but when my late husband and I saw the size of this old home and how sound the structure was, we realized we'd found the perfect opportunity for a bed and breakfast. It required complete upgrades to the electrical, plumbing, and heating and air conditioning systems, but the whimsical nature of the house let me renovate the style and number of rooms without breaking any preset architectural design rules. Our large barn with horse stalls was here when we bought the property and in decent shape, so we eventually branched out to hiring staff to provide riding lessons, guiding trail rides, and caring for our horses, then we expanded to boarding horses. Over time we slowly cut back as our wonderful staff moved away for school or more exciting opportunities in the cities, and we weren't able to find replacements for them."

"Let's take a look at your horses, Nora," Doc Ned said.

"They're probably in the pasture that is close to the house. I'll be right behind you; I have to stir my spaghetti sauce."

When Doc and Riley approached the pasture, the horses plodded to the fence with their heads down; Doc Ned glanced at Riley.

She whispered, "Bored."

Nora came down the path to the barn and sighed. "See, Doc? They just aren't feeling well."

Doc Ned nodded. "How often are they being ridden?"

"It used to be almost every other weekend, then I noticed the horses weren't feeling well, so I cut back on the lessons, and they haven't been ridden at all the past three weeks. I feel guilty for not noticing earlier."

"What are their names?" Riley asked.

"The Paint is Dakota, and the chestnut-brown Morgan is Fire," Nora said.

"Who was riding them?" Riley asked.

"That new special education teacher was bringing one or two of her students to sit on the horses or be led around the pasture on the weekends when her husband was home. He's an occupational therapist in Atlanta, but they would like to start their own riding school as therapy for children; they even have a lawyer who has drawn up a contract for my lawyer to review."

Doc nodded. "I'm sure you have a lot to do; give us a few minutes to examine both horses, then we'll come to the house."

After Nora left, Doc Ned asked, "What do the horses think about the riding school, Riley?"

The horses snuffled then galloped around the pasture before they returned to the fence, and Doc chuckled. "I understand: riding school it is. So, how do I break the news to Nora?"

Doc and the horses gazed at Riley.

Riley stroked the necks of both horses. "If we look at the benefits of exercise, it helps their circulation, digestion, muscles, and joints."

"That's it; let's go talk to Nora."

When they opened the back door and entered a small room, Riley raised her eyebrows as she glanced at a large boot tray next to the door, a bench on one side, and hooks to hang coats on the other. "I should have realized how important a mud room with a working horse business would be."

After they joined Nora in the commercial kitchen, Riley marveled at the size and quality of the appliances.

Doc Ned said, "We checked them out, and you're right. They aren't feeling well, but it's because their joints ache, and they're having some digestion problems."

"I knew it," Nora said. "What do I do? Are you prescribing some medicine for them?"

"Old horses in particular have to have regular exercise or their leg muscles begin to atrophy, which puts more stress on their joints, and causes their digestion to become sluggish."

"I'll bet they miss having children and other horses around too," Nora said. "I'll contact the teacher to see if she and her husband are still interested in the joint business venture. I won't have any time to spend with my horses this weekend, though, because I will be busy with guests. I'll have to find someone who is willing to ride them and spend a little time grooming them, and I've gotten behind in their care too. I sure wish you were available, Riley. I heard you were great with animals."

"What do you think, Riley?" Doc Ned asked.

"I could be here tomorrow, Saturday, Monday, and maybe Sunday," Riley said.

"That would be ideal. I'll pay you double what Doc Ned pays you."

"Wait a minute, Nora," Doc Ned growled.

"I'm not trying to steal Riley from you, Doc; I'm just paying a decent overtime rate." Nora smiled.

"In that case, check with Hope; she'll have the numbers for you," Doc said.

After Riley and Nora exchanged cell numbers, Nora said, "The driveway for the horse barn is not quite a quarter mile down the road. There isn't a sign, but it's the only driveway for three miles. Text me when you get to the barn in the morning, and I'll join you. I have a UTV that I use on the trails to get there. It bypasses the pastures and is a pleasant ride through the woods. Is eight thirty okay with you?"

"Eight thirty is fine," Riley said.

As Nora walked with Riley and Doc to his truck, she bit her lip. "I'm a little embarrassed by the condition of the barn. I've taken care of the daily food and water for the horses, but when I said I hadn't ridden the horses in a while, I should have also told you that I neglected my regular routine in the barn and their stalls. I'll see if I can get us a little help catching up on cleaning out the stalls because it would be too much for you to do. I want you to be able to focus on the horses, so they'll be happy."

When Doc stopped at the end of the driveway to send a text to Hope, Riley furrowed her brow as she stared at winter's brown weeds and dried grass in the ditch. *How can I blend in?*

When Doc headed toward town, he said, "I told Hope to expect a call from Nora about your pay and to be sure to include the cost of benefits. She'll expect a full explanation when we get to the office. Riley, are you having second thoughts?"

"I was trying to figure out how I could hear what Ava Fleet tells the farmers without Pamela Suzanne seeing me."

"That will be tricky, but you'll come up with something."

Riley exhaled. "Thanks, Doc. I wish I had the same confidence in my skill to solve a sticky situation as you do."

"I've learned that when I'm stressed about a problem, and there is absolutely no solution in sight, if I relax and forget about it, the answer just comes to me. Have you ever had that happen?"

"All the time." Riley smiled. "I could get a cowboy hat to hide my hair and get some comfortable overalls from the farm store. Hope may have some ideas too."

"I'll bet she will; let's stop at the grocery store and pick up ice cream for dessert at lunch. We'll be heroes in the office."

"That's an excellent idea. I have a theory that when it's frigid outside, ice cream causes our bodies to warm up to counter the ice cream, and as a side benefit, the body wards off the surrounding cold temperatures."

"If it isn't a scientific fact, it should be." Doc Ned peered at Riley. "Now that Ben has realized he's called to pursue a career in law enforcement, what about you?"

"I don't know, except I'll always care for animals."

"That's a given."

After they arrived at the office with the ice cream, Hope and Toby met them at the back door as they hurried inside.

"What's that?" Hope asked.

"Ice cream." Doc handed the sack to Hope, who held out her hand. "I couldn't decide, so I got three different kinds."

"You're learning, Doc," Hope said as she went to the breakroom to put away the ice cream while Riley hugged Toby, and Doc went to his office.

Riley and Toby went into the breakroom, so Riley could put her sandwich in the refrigerator.

"Why did Nora ask me what Doc paid you?" Hope asked.

Riley told her about the two elderly horses, Ava Fleet renting the B&B for the weekend to conduct interviews, and Ava Fleet's son and his wife, Pamela Suzanne.

"Of course, you volunteered to take care of the horses for Nora, which means you are working every day for ten days in a row and explains why Doc Ned wanted to me to quote a hefty sum for your daily rate. Aren't you glad that old sneak is on your side?" Hope asked.

Riley snickered. "Actually, I am. There's a little more, but I won't flood you with details. The gist is that Ben and Pamela Suzanne have known each other since high school. She somehow took a family joke seriously and thought she and Ben were engaged; she was enraged when I popped into Ben's life."

"Are you saying that you were not her favorite person?"

"That would be a huge understatement, and Ben didn't help. When she told Ben I was chubby, he told me in front of her that she was jealous of my chest."

Hope guffawed. "Oh my gosh! I love your Ben."

After she dried her tears of laughter, Hope said, "So, you're going to be at Nora's while Pamela Suzanne is there. We need to deflect the fireworks, don't we? Does she know Toby? He can spend tomorrow and Monday with us here, and I'd love his company on Saturday while I work on the taxes for this year."

"I didn't think of Toby. I'd be surprised if she remembers him, but there's always a chance she might if he and I were together."

Hope furrowed her brow. "Your red hair is hard to overlook, but I can take care of that and your chubby chest. I'll have something for you when you drop off Toby in the morning."

"What do you have in mind?"

"I have a cool knit cap that has enough room for you to pull up your hair into it to hide your red curls, and I have a couple of other ideas. I'll stop by the thrift store on my way home and pick up a bulky, oversized sweater for you, so you can be all-around chubby. You'll need to layer anyway, as cold as our weather's been. Do you have a pair of Western boots that you could wear that would still be comfortable?"

Riley nodded. "They're comfortable but pretty scuffed up, so I don't wear them much anymore."

"Wear them because they'll make you look taller, and scuffed up is perfect for your new role as the eccentric stable hand. Problem-solving is my favorite hobby. Bring your sandwich to my desk when you're ready to eat lunch because I want to hear more about the horses."

Riley's phone buzzed a text from Lizzie: "Call when you have a minute or two."

When Riley called, Lizzie answered almost immediately.

"Ned told me you're going to take care of Nora's horses over the weekend. It makes sense to me, but how are you going to avoid Pam?"

"Hope has a cap she said would hide my hair, and I'll wear Western boots to be taller. I'm not quite sure how I can manage being a stable hand and snooping around the house, but I'll think of something."

"You could always help the caterer serve, or clear dishes; no, don't do that because your boots will have that unforgettable fragrance of horse barn. I'll let you figure that one out. I finally heard back from my friend who is a bank officer in Atlanta. She hadn't heard of Step Up, but she told me there have been a wave of fly-by-night businesses popping up and convincing farmers to sign over the title of their property to them, so the farmers can supposedly access their equity or avoid foreclosure; the scum immediately sell the property to foreign nationals then disappear with the cash."

"I hope that isn't what Step Up does because there are a lot of people who see them as an answer to their prayers."

"My banker friend told me that farmers who have backed out before they signed have had their barns burned down, families threatened, and worse; she thinks the criminals have become more brazen and are selling the property before they received the title, so they can make a fast getaway. She told me to contact my local GBI office, so they could add Step Up to their list of possible embezzlers; I called them this morning."

"Good. Ben is busy on a high-priority investigation, and I wouldn't have wanted to distract him with another case."

"Did Ned remember to give you the mixer?"

"He put it in my car for me, thank you. With Ben working in the field in addition to his daily class, I have extra time on my hands. I made dog biscuits for Toby yesterday, and they were a hit."

"Sounds like Ben's found his niche. What about you?"

"I don't know; after Ben finishes his courses, I can start thinking about what I want to do next; I might like to have my own business, but it has to involve animals and being outdoors."

"Like a veterinarian clinic?" Lizzie asked.

"Not really because that would mean being tied to a building. I like what both Buck and Nora are doing, except I wouldn't want the bed and breakfast business."

"It definitely sounds like you have plenty of time to consider your options and gather more information while Ben is putting what he's learned into practice, so it makes sense that you don't have to be in a rush."

"I need to remind myself that I'm busy considering options, gathering data, but most importantly, learning how to cook and bake," Riley said.

"How did you survive getting through school?"

"Poorly, in every sense of the word. I packed half a sandwich for my lunch and had plain ramen noodles for supper."

"No vegetables or protein at all?" Lizzie asked.

"Not a lick."

Lizzie groaned. "That's awful. I think you can mark off nutritionist from your list of possibilities for a career. Did I tell you Ned and I are going to a retirement dinner tonight? One of the deputies is retiring after thirty years' service, and his wife is retiring from teaching. They bought an RV and are planning to travel to all the places they've always wanted to visit. I was looking forward to wearing something besides jeans until I had to buy a new dress because nothing I have in my closet fits me; very annoying."

CHAPTER SEVEN

Riley pulled out her lunch from the refrigerator and poured hot water into a coffee cup then dropped in one of her tea bags before she and Toby joined Hope.

Hope had a cup of coffee and a T-rex lunch box on her desk. "My niece loves dinosaurs, so I bought us matching lunch boxes; I love being the coolest aunt in the world."

"I'm impressed."

When Riley sat in the visitor's chair that Hope had pulled to her desk, Toby flopped down between Riley and Hope.

"Smart guy, Toby," Hope said. "You're not playing favorites."

While they ate, Hope asked, "Do you know how long you and Ben will be here?"

"A little less than four months, then we'll go to wherever Ben is assigned."

"Can he request where he'd like to be assigned?" Hope asked. "I think you should stay here."

"I'd love it, but I don't think he can," Riley said.

"I thought of one other thing: do you have any muck boots?"

"No. I've never needed them."

"You will at Trails End; I'll have some for you in the morning."

After they ate, they carried their trash to the breakroom, and Hope asked before she opened the freezer, "Do you want vanilla, chocolate, or butter pecan?"

"I'll take chocolate." Riley peered into the freezer as Hope pulled out the chocolate ice cream. "The four gallons of ice cream filled the refrigerator's freezer, didn't they? Why are there two cartons of butter pecan?"

Hope chuckled as she pulled out the ice cream scoop from a drawer. "It's Doc's favorite; he always buys one each of chocolate and vanilla, and two of butter pecan because he says he never gets any if he brings only one."

While they ate their ice cream, the office phone rang; Elsie called out, "Hope, a call for you."

Hope hurried to her desk as Doc came into the breakroom for ice cream.

After he served himself a generous helping of butter pecan, he stood at the sink to eat his dessert. "We'll leave in about twenty minutes, Riley."

When Hope returned, she said, "Doc, the sheriff called, and the doctors rushed our farmer back to surgery early this morning when his blood pressure dropped. They found and repaired another major blood vessel. He's still alive."

"Thanks, Hope."

"The sheriff also told me that people are talking about Riley saving his life, but the rumor is that he described his assailant to her before they airlifted him to the hospital."

"But he didn't," Riley said.

"That's what the sheriff said, and he's furious. He asked me where your next appointment was, Doc; I think he wants to keep close tabs on you and Riley."

Doc finished his ice cream. "Ready to go, Riley?"

As Riley rose from the table, Doc said, "I may have found an animal that you haven't treated before. We're going for a wellness check."

Riley put on her heavy coat and grabbed her backpack. "I've never treated an alpaca before; is it an alpaca?"

"Good guess," Doc Ned said on their way out, "but no."

As Doc drove toward the farm, Riley guessed more animals. "A zebra? Is someone raising zebras?"

"That would be interesting, wouldn't it?" Doc smirked. "I might have misled you when I said animal because it's actually a bird."

"I have never taken care of geese or turkeys, but I did take care of Grandma's chickens."

Riley's eyes widened when Doc turned at the farm. "Ostriches? All I know about ostriches is that they are fast, will peck anything, have powerful legs, and I'm not sure if it's true or not, but I've heard they aren't as smart as other birds like crows or chickens."

Riley stared at the double-fenced field. "How tall is that inner fence? It looks close to twelve feet tall."

"Wally has two nine-foot adult males, so the fence has to be tall enough to contain them. A veterinarian from Augusta who specializes in ratites, flightless birds like ostriches and emus, visits the farm once a quarter to examine and vaccinate the ostriches. We're here to observe the birds for any issues and survey a field to see if there are any weeds that are poisonous to ostriches. Wally plans to expand his operation in the spring, but the field has to be certified first."

"How will I know what to look for in the pasture?"

"The Augusta vet sent me a list a couple of years ago, so I could perform an assessment of a new field to save him a special trip and to help Wally save money. It's on the dashboard."

Riley scanned the list. "There are a lot of plants here that I haven't even heard of. Are there any that are particularly dangerous for the birds?"

"Unfortunately, all the plants on the list cause systemic organ damage and death in ostriches."

Riley groaned. "I can identify with certainty only three of these plants, so any weed that I can't identify could potentially be poisonous to the birds. That's not good."

"I felt the same way the first time I surveyed a field. The Augusta vet walked the field with me and pointed out the poisonous plants and the ones that were okay. He told me he had no idea why a vet had to certify a field instead of a botanist, so he did the best he could and noted any exceptions then added the words, 'to the best of my knowledge' to the certification before he signed it, so I've always done the same. Wally won't open the field to any of his birds until the ratite vet certifies the new field too, but if we spot a problem weed, the farmer can take care of it."

As they slowly walked across the field, Riley examined the weeds as carefully as she could then stopped when Doc Ned did.

"What do you think, Riley?" Doc narrowed his eyes at the weeds in front of them, and Riley glanced at him then did the same.

She furrowed her brow. "Is that ragwort?"

He nodded. "I haven't seen anything else, but the farmer will have time to treat his field before his ratite vet's next visit."

After they walked the field, Riley asked, "What do we do now?"

"I'll give Wally an informal, verbal report of our findings, then Hope will send in my report with the exceptions listed. He may ask us to come back, so we can see that the exceptions we found have been corrected."

Riley exhaled. "So far, I've learned that a veterinarian has to be a skilled driver, a medical trauma doctor, a botanist, a master negotiator, and prepared to treat every creature known to man."

Doc Ned nodded. "Seth told me you were smart: you catch on fast."

After they told Wally about the ragwort that they found, the two men changed their topic of conversation to fishing, and Riley wandered to the fence to watch the ostriches. One of the males rushed the fence and crashed into it then squawked at Riley.

"I'm not the one who ran into the fence, bud," she said, and he raised his head as high as he could. Riley hurried to the barn then dragged a ladder to the fence and climbed up on the top rung; the ostrich ducked his head and ran away.

When she returned the ladder, Doc Ned asked, "Did you just win an argument with that ostrich?"

"He was rude," Riley grumbled.

Wally chuckled. "I'll have to tell my wife about your trick; she's been intimidated by him."

On the way back to the office, Doc asked, "So what did you think about ostriches?"

"I have a lot to learn. What is a good resource for a beginner?"

"That's out of my league; I'll give you the contact information for the ratite veterinarian and let him know we're working together, so he'll understand why you're asking him," Doc Ned said.

After they reached the office, Riley hurried inside and out of the cold.

Toby trotted to the back door and leaned against Riley.

"Ooo, you're nice and warm, Toby." Riley knelt next to him and hugged him.

"Riley, I have a surprise for you," Hope called out from her desk.

"Do you know what it is, Toby?" Riley asked.

"Don't tell her, Toby; it's a surprise," Hope said.

Toby grinned.

When Riley reached Hope's desk, Hope handed her a doggie treat bag.

Riley opened the bag and lifted out a pair of new muck boots and a black wool knitted cap then giggled at the long single black braid on the back of the cap.

"If you push up your hair into the cap, then you'll have black hair; add some sunglasses or stop by the drug store and pick up a pair of the blue light glasses people use to cut down the glare of a computer screen; you'll be completely unrecognizable. I didn't have time to go by the thrift store, so I don't have a bulky sweater for you."

Riley twisted her hair onto the top of her head then put on the wool cap. "What do you think?"

"It's cute on you. Go look in the mirror in the bathroom."

Riley examined her face and hairline in the mirror. *My face is pale; I don't look like myself at all.*

When she returned to Hope's desk, Riley said, "This is perfect, and thanks for the new boots."

"They aren't new; I just never wore them…there was this guy, but you don't want to hear about the angst of a twenty-two-year-old who finally divorced a particularly disgusting piece of pond scum after two years of being told that something was wrong with her."

"I do, but I'll let you off the hook for now. I love your idea of the computer glasses. I'll stop by the thrift store and find something I like, so I'll have a comfortable sweater to wear at home when I'm freezing and too lazy to stoke the fire in the fireplace."

Hope laughed. "That's the most pitiful thing I've ever heard. Do you have a lap blanket and fuzzy slippers?"

"What a great idea; I'll put fuzzy slippers on my shopping list for next week, and Ben needs slippers too."

Doc Ned joined them. "Riley, as soon as Hope releases me from my chains of arduous paperwork…"

Hope interrupted him. "Oh, good grief, Doc. You can finish it next week."

Doc Ned grinned. "In that case, Riley, we can go home. I'll see you Tuesday."

"Hope, I'll give you back your cap on Tuesday. Let's go, Toby. Thanks again, Hope."

"The cap is yours. My mother knitted it because she hated my hair, so I've never bonded with it. I'm glad you can use it; I'll see you and Toby in the morning."

When Riley and Toby were in her car, she patted her head then pulled down her visor to check her cap in the mirror. "The cap Hope gave me is warm; I love it."

She flipped the long braid across her shoulder to her front. "This braid looks natural."

As she left the parking lot and headed toward the drug store, she noticed a car that pulled away from the curb across the street from the clinic then made a U-turn and parked at the curb next to the office. She peered at the car in the rearview mirror.

"I think I saw two people in the car, but I'm becoming overly suspicious. They probably were waiting for someone in the clinic and got a text the person and our patient would be coming out soon, so they parked closer."

Toby yipped.

Riley nodded. "If it was important, we'd stay to watch. Let's go shopping."

Riley parked at the grocery store. "I won't be long."

Riley tried on several pairs of blue light glasses and picked a pair with a silver wire frame and a pair with a plastic tortoise-shell frame. *I'll have to ask Claire if she's heard of blue light glasses for the computer screen.*

While she searched for fuzzy slippers, her phone buzzed a text from Melissa. "Call when you have a few minutes to talk."

She paid for her glasses then joined Toby in the car before she called Melissa.

"Are you at work? This is not urgent at all, but it isn't short," Melissa said.

"Toby and I are off for the day; we're doing a little shopping."

"Good, after we talk, I'll have to call Mugsy because while Mugsy and I never participate in gossip, this is too juicy to not share. Pamela Suzanne's mother called me. Can you believe it?"

"Actually, I can't. Why on earth did she call you?"

"She started off by saying she knew how much Pamela Suzanne meant to our family. When I gagged, and she said bless you, I knew the conversation was going to be a doozy."

"You did not gag."

"I sneezed, but I wanted to gag; does that count? Are you going to interrupt this entire story?"

"Sorry, Mom."

"No, I'm sorry; I may be a trifle wound up. Anyway, Pamela Suzanne has a new job, excuse me, career, as a marketing manager. She was hired by a finance company to manage all the marketing. That's a direct quote; I can't make this stuff up."

"Nothing about getting married?" Riley asked.

"I asked if that particular rumor was true, and she blessed my heart and said the rumor was not true at all. She didn't actually say bless your heart, but I heard it in her tone."

"Ouch," Riley said.

"Exactly, so she continued and told me that Pamela Suzanne was so successful in her market management that she was promoted this week and is in the process of moving to Atlanta for a higher paying and more prestigious position with a private office that was necessary because she would be managing markets."

"I have no idea how doing the same thing could possibly be a promotion, much less more prestigious, but good for her," Riley said.

"You didn't hear the difference? Neither did I. Then she asked about Ben and you; she told me how much she sympathized with me because Ben gave up veterinarian school for you since you couldn't get in, which was no surprise to her, given your inferior education. So, I have a question: do voodoo dolls work? I know Mugsy's going to ask me when I call her."

"You're just kidding, right?"

Melissa sighed. "I suppose; anyway, tomorrow is Pamela Suzanne's last day managing the marketing for a regional Step Up program, and her mother told me you should host a virtual party for Pamela Suzanne to celebrate her promotion."

"She didn't really, did she?"

"Oh, yes; I snorted, but she didn't say bless you. I declined on your behalf and offered no excuse or apology; I did suggest one of Pamela Suzanne's many friends would be thrilled at the opportunity to organize a party for her. She had the nerve to get all huffy and told me that you should be grateful to have been considered for such an honor. I laughed, and she hung up on me. Of the entire conversation, that was my favorite part."

"Mugsy's going to blow a gasket when she hears this," Riley said.

"I suppose you're right; I'll cut back some of the details and give her the boring story."

"What's the boring version? Pamela Suzanne has a new job in Atlanta? Did her mother say anything about whether Pamela Suzanne will work the entire day tomorrow?"

"Actually, she did. Pamela Suzanne will hand out the marketing material in the morning, then she'll leave after lunch, so she can pack for Atlanta. Her mother implied the lunch was a fancy catered lunch to honor Pamela Suzanne and her skill at…"

"Please don't say it again, Mom."

"You're right; it's the stuff nightmares are made of. Let me know if you need anything."

After Melissa hung up, Riley said, "I love the way Mom can weave a story, Toby. Next up is the thrift store, then we'll go home."

When Riley went into the thrift store, the clerk at the checkout desk smiled politely with no indication of recognition that her customer was Riley.

I think the cap will work. Riley selected a gray-green sweater that was oversized and soft; she smiled when she checked the label. *Washable. Perfect.*

She paid for her purchase then hurried to her car. "Ready to go home, Toby?"

After they were home, Riley gathered their dirty clothes and started the washer with her new sweater while Toby enjoyed his backyard.

CHAPTER EIGHT

HOPE

After everyone left for the day, Hope locked the front and back doors then sat at her desk and exhaled. *Finally; I can update records without interruption.*

When she updated the last record and saved them on her computer, Hope glanced up in surprise at the clock. *It's already five o'clock; the grocery store will be crowded, as usual, and it will be dark by the time I get home.*

She grabbed a scrap of paper and scribbled a shopping list then zipped up her coat and turned off the lights except for the night security lights as she hurried to the back door.

After she locked the door behind her, she turned toward the parking lot, but something slammed against her head; she saw a bright flash, then it was dark.

* * *

"Hey!" A man shouted and roughly shook her then dragged her out of a car and dumped her on the ground. "Get up and walk."

Head hurts; what's that buzzing in my head? I gotta get up.

Hope used the car door to pull herself up. A man grabbed her by one arm and pulled her to the edge of the shoulder then turned her to face the car. Hope blinked. *Why is that car on top of another car?*

She blinked to refocus her eyes then stared at the two overweight men with stringy hair and the two obese men who were weaving in front of her. *Am I seeing double?*

"Do it already," the overweight man who had pulled her to the edge of the ditch said.

"I can't with her staring at me like that," the grossly obese man said.

"Criminy; you are such a loser," the first man growled before he shouted to Hope, "Turn around and count to one hundred. Don't move and forget you saw us, or your husband will be dead on your porch when you get home."

Hope turned around. *Do I have a husband? I don't want him to be dead on my porch.*

She counted aloud. "One…um…two, three…four…"

"When she reaches ten," the first man said.

"Okay, on ten," the second man responded.

Whatever is on ten won't be good. Go away, buzzing. We have to think.

"Seven…eight…"

Hope dived to her right on nine and instinctively doubled over at the excruciatingly loud sound of a gunshot then rolled as she fell. The searing pain in her left shoulder took away her breath and the wet, warm liquid spread across her back as she continued to slide down the slope of the hill with the aid of the dry, autumn leaves until she landed face down in the small crevice of a deep depression in the side of hill.

The second man said, "I got her."

"She's not moving; she bled as much as that farmer did."

"Want I should shoot her again?"

The first man growled, "Are you completely nuts? We're not that far from a farm. One shot means nothing out in the country; a second shot will be remembered."

"I didn't see no farm."

"Just across the road; don't you pay attention to anything? Let's get out of here."

Hope listened when the car engine roared through the muffled buzzing in her head. Her breath quickened and became shallow when the car slowed then returned. She held her breath as it crept past her then sped toward town.

CHAPTER NINE

ABIGAIL

"I've never understood why Cook doesn't expand the diner; it's crowded in here every time I come in," one of the farmers at the counter grumbled as Abigail refilled his coffee cup.

"Other than the fact that I'd quit, there's no reason at all." Abigail hurried away with her full pot of fresh coffee.

"Good enough reason for me; why do you keep coming back if it's too crowded for you?" the man next to him asked.

"Same as you: for the best coffee in town." The man ate his last bite of apple pie then used the side of his fork to scrape up every smidgen of pie filling from his plate.

Abigail rolled her eyes at their conversation then swooped through the noisy diner with her coffee pot that seemed to be bottomless as she filled cup after cup until Cook called out, "Order up."

She rushed to pick up the order and glared at the man who seated himself at a four-top table. *You better be having friends coming in pretty quick, fella, or the next group of farmers that barges in here will kick you out.*

After she picked up and delivered the order, she narrowed her eyes at his legs that were sprawled in the aisle. *Move those feet, or I'll stomp on those fancy wingtips of yours.*

As she neared his table, he tucked his feet under his chair before she reached him. *Good choice, fella, even if you did take away my fun for the evening.*

The men at the counter swiveled on their stools to watch the two overweight strangers who came into the diner then joined the lone man.

"I didn't think that guy would have any friends," the farmer at the counter said; the rest of the men chuckled as they nodded and turned back to their coffee.

The man who was less overweight took the seat next to the window, and the obese man pulled away a chair from the table and partially into the aisle before he sat across from the man with the wingtips. When Abigail stopped at their table with two cups and filled them with coffee, the man who had been waiting for the other two said, "We'll have three pieces of apple pie."

After Abigail served their pie, she quickly continued to clear a table then hurried to the cash register to take a customer's money.

"Order up," Cook shouted over the din.

While Abigail carried the order past the four top, the man who came in first asked, "Did you get her? The right one?"

"Sure, we watched all day, and when she came out of the vet's office, it was just like you said: we'd know we had the right one when we saw her hair; she was the vet's assistant," the overweight man said.

Abigail delivered the order then stopped to clear the table next to the trio.

The man nodded. "How did it go?"

The smaller man snorted. "Easy snatch and grab."

The first man tapped his fingers on the table and stared at the two men across from him.

Abigail furrowed her brow as she carried the dishes to the kitchen. *Are they talking about Riley?*

As she passed them on her way to take the order of new arrivals at a table in the back, the man said, "It better be a while before anybody finds her; the boss doesn't like loose ends."

While Abigail took the order at the table in the back, she held her phone with the same hand as her pad and quickly snapped a photo of the two men then hurried to the counter and stopped next to the man at the first stool.

"Did I show you the picture of my sister's new dog?" She held up her phone and snapped a photo of the man with the wingtip shoes then scrolled to a picture of a dog she'd taken at the park.

"Nice looking pup," the farmer said.

"Thanks," Abigail said.

I need to make sure Riley is okay.

After the men left, Abigail cleared their table then dropped off the dirty dishes before she stood near the back door and sent Riley a text. "Checking in."

She exhaled with relief when Riley responded: "Home. You okay?"

Abigail replied, "Sure am. Will call tomorrow."

CHAPTER TEN

HOPE

No one can find me here; I have to get up to the road. Hope pushed herself out of the crevice with her right arm and legs then pushed with her legs and screamed as she rolled to her right side.

Breathe slow and easy. After she caught her breath, she unzipped her coat midway and inhaled deeply before she slowly exhaled. *Go.*

She cried out in pain as she lifted her left arm with her right and half-slid, half-pushed her left arm into her jacket to serve as a sling. Tears rolled down her cheeks, and she sobbed.

Hope bit her lip. *Enough of that, old girl.*

She peered up the slope and spotted a large branch. Hope grabbed the branch with her right hand and pulled to lift herself to a sitting position; it broke and tumbled past her and crashed at the bottom of the hill. Her heart pounded, and she gasped for breath. *If it hadn't broken right away, I would have gone down with it.*

She dug her heels into the dirt and pushed, so she'd be pointed up the hill, then she dug in again and pushed. *Two inches; good enough.*

After her third push, she groaned and paused to rest.

This hill won't climb itself; keep going.

When Hope reached the level surface, she gasped for breath, and her legs twitched from the effort. Tears streamed down her face. *Please don't cramp.*

She forced herself to relax then glanced at the sky. *Still dark. I thought the sun would be up by now.*

She exhaled a long breath then stared at the two-lane road in front of her and sobbed. *I can't push myself across the rough road, and if I try, I couldn't get out of the way of an oncoming car, and no driver could see me.*

After her tears ran dry, she sniffled. *The only way to get across is to walk.*

Hope pushed herself up onto her right elbow then straightened her arm, brought her knees under her, and rose to her knees. Her head spun and her stomach churned, so she sat back on her heels then lowered her head. *I need to take it a little slower.*

She smiled. *Low and slow. I can do a three-point crawl.*

She listened, but all she heard was the buzzing in her head. *If I hear a car, I'll have to get off the road. Go.*

Hope focused on the other side of the road and moved as fast as she could with her awkward three-point crawl. When she was across the road, she narrowed her eyes at the fence in front of her and gritted her teeth as she crawled to it; after Hope pushed herself under the fence, she curled on her right side. *I'll rest just a bit.*

She listened to a coyote yip and howl then answering howls. She tried to push herself up with her right arm, but her muscles failed to lift her, and the howls became louder. *Are the coyotes getting closer?*

Tears ran down her face when a wolf barked and growled then grabbed her by the back of her jacket and tugged on her. *He's dragging me to his den.*

She listened to the approaching hoofbeats. *Unicorns are coming to save me.*

She exhaled in relief and closed her eyes even though the wolf continued to drag her across the field because the hoofbeats were louder. *Unicorns will be here soon.* The buzzing in her head stopped as the darkness enveloped her.

CHAPTER ELEVEN

At six o'clock, Riley gazed out the bay window in the living room as the sun went down and the orange sky turned dark. She started the fire in the fireplace then called in Toby and fed him. She smiled when her phone rang.

"I'll be home in twenty minutes, babe," Ben said.

"That's exciting news," Riley said.

She turned on the oven and put their enchilada casserole in to warm.

When Toby yipped, Riley and Toby hurried to the living room to watch for Ben's truck. Toby rushed to the door; Riley hurried to join him when she saw the truck's headlights coming down the driveway. She opened the door, and Toby raced to the truck after Ben parked.

"Hello, Toby; what a welcome."

Ben hurried to the house with Toby behind him, and the three of them went inside.

Ben hugged Riley then kissed her. "You feel good, and the house is warm."

"The enchilada casserole is in the oven. What would you like to drink? A beer?"

"Maybe later. How about coffee? Is that too much trouble?"

Riley wrapped her arms around him. "Not at all. I'll get to it right after I give you a good squeeze."

When she released him, Ben asked, "How much time do I have until we eat?"

"Thirty minutes."

"Good; I need a warm shower to take off the chill. It was cold and windy today."

After Ben's shower, he carried his uniform with his thumb and one finger to the kitchen. "My clothes are filthy. I spent most of the day crawling around in the dirt, which makes my job any boy's dream."

Riley giggled. "We have a bottle of prewash solution. Spray them, then we'll start the washer after we eat."

"You're so smart."

"I'll pour you a cup of coffee, then we can sit in front of the fireplace."

While they snuggled on the sofa, Ben asked, "Do you want to hear about my day?"

"I'd love it." Riley rested her head on Ben's chest and relaxed as she listened to his soft drawl echo in his chest while he went on about his day.

When the stove timer went off, Riley said, "Supper's ready."

She heated hot water for her tea while she served chicken enchilada casserole onto their plates.

After they ate, Ben loaded the dishwasher while Riley started a load of laundry.

When her phone rang, Riley stared at the caller ID: Tossin' Broncos Ranch.

"Buck's calling me." Riley answered.

"This is Buck. Is your husband home?"

Riley put her phone on speakerphone. "Yes, did you want to talk to him?"

"No; make that yes. I can't find Bella and the two other ponies. When I called Outlaw to come inside, he came to me, barked, then raced off. I need your help because I think Outlaw was trying to tell me something. I was going to call Ned because I was certain something must be wrong with Outlaw, but I remembered he and Lizzie were going to the retirement dinner, and I realized I needed you to help me."

Riley glanced at Ben, and he nodded. "We'll leave right away."

"Dress warm," Ben said when Riley hung up.

"You too." Riley grinned. *I love instant retaliation.*

Ben chuckled. "Touché."

Toby yipped.

"Yes, you can go too," Ben said. "I've got two good flashlights in my truck."

"We need a good one here at the house. I'll add it to my list."

As Ben drove to Buck's ranch, he asked, "What else do you have on your list?"

"Gardening tools."

"I need a few tools too; maybe we can shop at the hardware store next Saturday."

"Spending a day together sounds glorious," Riley said.

Toby yipped.

"Of course, you're included," Riley said. "Nobody loves a hardware store more than you do."

"For the dog treats," Ben added.

When they reached Buck's ranch, Ben said, "I love the space he has, don't you?"

"He raised horses for the rodeo circuit for years. He has two horses that retired, and the owner offered them to Buck. He was happy to get them back because they were his favorites and the two of them had always been together. Buck took in the three ponies when Doc Ned asked for help."

"Didn't you say the older pony was Bella?" Ben asked.

"Yes; the other two were new and skittish, so I don't know what their names are yet. Outlaw is his black Lab."

When Ben parked, Buck and a short woman with soft brown hair were waiting for them at the barn.

Ben opened Toby's door, and Toby hopped out; when the three of them reached the barn, Ben and Buck introduced themselves and shook hands.

Riley held out her hand. "I'm Riley."

"Sharon. I'm so happy to finally meet you." Sharon held out her mitten-covered hands then hugged Riley.

"Should have warned you that Sharon's a hugger," Buck said.

"Some of my best friends are." Riley smiled. "Where's Outlaw?"

Toby raced down the driveway then disappeared.

"Did Toby go to look for him?" Buck asked.

"Probably," Ben said.

"I should have known he'd start searching as soon as we were here," Riley said.

"I'm afraid Outlaw is lost; isn't this Toby's first time here? What if he gets lost too?" Sharon asked.

"He won't," Ben said. "Toby will always make his way back to Riley."

"If we can't do anything besides wait here, I can fill a thermos with hot coffee," Sharon said.

"You'd have to make a fresh pot, and you might miss out when Toby returns," Buck said. "Let's give Toby a little time."

"Okay, but I'd rather be doing something," Sharon said.

Ben peered into the barn. "We'd like to see the stalls for the ponies."

"I'll show you," Buck said. "My two horses are in the barn, so I had the three ponies in my old isolation shed for new horses. I haven't modified them for ponies yet; I think they just slipped out."

When they went into the shed, Ben and Riley nodded.

"The ponies could easily step out of either of these two stalls; my plan for tomorrow was to put boards in between the bottom boards and the ones above them," Buck said.

Riley stood in the doorway to watch for Toby; when she heard him barking in the distance, she said, "Outlaw and the ponies found someone. Do you have a UTV or something that we could use to bring someone from a field to the house?"

"I have a four-seater with a cargo haul."

"Toby sounded like he was southwest of the house," Ben said.

"I'll stay here, so you'll have room if you have a passenger," Sharon said. "Honey, do you have your cell phone?"

"It's in the house."

"You get the UTV, and I'll get your cell," Sharon hurried to the house.

Buck returned with the UTV seconds after Sharon handed the cell and a heavy quilt to Riley at the barn.

Buck drove to a gate, and Ben hopped out and opened then closed the gate.

Riley whistled for Toby, and he barked, then another dog barked.

"The second dog was Outlaw," Buck said.

Ben pointed to the southwest. "That direction."

As Buck pushed the UTV to a questionably safe speed across the field, Ben and Riley tightly clutched the grab handles for passengers when the vehicle went airborne. After they passed through another gate, Riley whistled again, and Toby barked.

"We're close. Head south," Ben said.

"Hang on," Buck said.

Ben and Riley held onto their straps. Toby met them and ran alongside then raced ahead and barked. Outlaw barked.

"Hurry," Riley said.

Before Buck stopped, Riley leapt out of the UTV and raced to the ponies who were lying partially on their sides in a circle around a form. Outlaw stood at the head. When Riley was close, Outlaw whimpered, and the ponies rose to their feet.

"That is so scary, Outlaw." Riley knelt next to the figure. "Ben," she yelled, "It's Hope; she's been shot, but she's still breathing."

Ben carefully lifted Hope off the ground. "Riley, grab that quilt, and we'll wrap Hope in it. I'll ride in the back and hold her."

Riley grabbed the quilt, then Buck turned around the UTV. After Riley wrapped the quilt around Hope, she asked, "Outlaw, can you lead the ponies back to the house?"

Outlaw barked, and Bella whinnied.

"Thank you, both," Riley said.

"Toby, can you hop into the UTV? If you can lean against Hope, you can help me keep her warm."

Toby hopped up onto the seat next to Ben, and Ben positioned Hope with her back against Toby.

Buck said, "We can make better time if I go to the road from here and drive on the shoulder to the house."

"Okay; we're a little precarious back here, so take it easy," Ben said.

"I still have your phone, Buck. Call Sharon; we need an ambulance to meet us at your house."

Buck took his phone then handed it back to Riley. Sharon answered immediately.

Riley slowed her breathing to calm her voice. "We need an ambulance to meet us at your house. We found Hope; she's hypothermic and was shot in the back, but there's no exit wound. She is still breathing, but her breathing is shallow."

"Got it." Sharon hung up.

Before they reached the road, Sharon called back, and Riley answered. "The dispatcher and I made an executive decision. A medical helicopter will be here in fifteen minutes."

"A medical helicopter will meet us at the ranch in fifteen minutes," Riley said.

"We'll beat them," Buck said. "The road is up ahead. We'll have to cut the fence, but I have the tools, and I'll do it."

When they reached the fence, Buck snipped the three wires then pulled away the wires and drove to the shoulder. When he was on the flat surface, he sped to his driveway then slowly headed toward his house and parked next to the barn.

Sharon ran out with another quilt. "I've had this old quilt in the dryer."

Riley wrapped the warmer quilt around Hope, and Hope stirred. "The wolf and the unicorns kept me safe from the coyotes."

Riley pulled the warm quilt over Hope's head like a hood. "Who shot you, Hope?"

"The fat man," she said.

The sheriff's cruiser beat the helicopter by two minutes. The sheriff and Ben strode into the barn. The young deputy jumped out of the passenger's seat then assisted the paramedic with the stretcher while the other paramedic asked, "Do we have a driver's license?"

"I can give you her name, address, phone number, and employer's name and address." Sharon handed him a typed sheet of paper.

The paramedic glanced at the sheet. "Good enough."

After the paramedic climbed into the helicopter, the deputy returned and took Riley's elbow to escort her into the barn; Buck drove the UTV back to the equipment shed with Sharon as his passenger, then the chopper took off.

Buck and Sharon returned to the barn.

"Should we see if Outlaw, Toby, and the ponies need any help?" Buck asked.

"Good idea; could your deputy accompany Buck?" Ben asked.

Sheriff Baker narrowed his eyes at Ben. "Not a bad idea."

"They'll be coming through the fields," Riley said.

"You're right, Riley; we could miss them and not know it," Buck said. "We'll just wait here."

Ben crossed his arms and frowned.

When Toby, Outlaw, Bella, and the two ponies trotted to the barn, Riley hugged Toby and Outlaw, stroked Bella's neck, and cooed to the two ponies. "I'm so proud of all of you; you saved

Hope. Outlaw, she thought you were a kindly wolf; Bella, she thought you and the ponies were unicorns."

Toby and Outlaw grinned, and Bella and the ponies whinnied.

"Does that sound strange to you, deputy?" the sheriff asked.

"No, sir." The deputy furrowed his brow. "It normally would, Sheriff, but it doesn't. Everyone knows that Riley understands animals."

On the way home, Ben asked, "Is that the same deputy that was on the scene when you found the farmer who had been shot?"

"Sure was."

"What was his name again?" Ben asked.

"I don't know; do you want me to text Sheriff Baker and ask him?"

"No, it was just a passing thought; he seemed a little too friendly and stayed awfully close to you."

Riley stared at Ben. "What are you talking about?"

Ben shrugged.

Toby whined, and Riley nodded. *I think Ben sounds cranky too; he must be tired.*

"What are you and Toby going to do tomorrow?" Ben asked.

"I'm helping Nora at the bed and breakfast by taking care of her horses; Toby was going to stay with Hope, but I'll take him with me."

"Isn't Step Up having their meeting at the bed and breakfast on Saturday? Are you helping Nora then too?"

"That's the plan," Riley said.

"I'm not sure it's a good idea for you to be there during those meetings. You don't know who might just walk in like they are on the schedule, or someone might recognize you, then the entire county will know where you are."

"I'll be at the stable, not the house, so I'm not likely to run into anyone. In fact, Lizzie told me not to go into the house straight from the stables."

Ben smiled. "She may be right about that; as long as you're carrying and have Toby with you, I can pretend I'm not worried."

As they went inside the house, Ben asked, "How about a glass of wine and a snuggle in front of the fireplace, babe?"

"I'd love it, sexy cowboy," Riley said.

"While you change into warm, soft clothes, I'll fix a snack, pour your wine, and grab a beer." Ben kissed her before she headed to the bedroom to change.

* * *

Ben left early the next morning with his lunch that Riley had packed for him.

While Toby roamed the backyard, Riley pulled out a casserole from the freezer and put it in the refrigerator before she moved the laundry from the washer to the dryer.

Before she started the dryer, she was interrupted by a call from Abigail.

"Riley, I heard three men talking in the diner last night, and I thought they were talking about you, but I heard about Hope, and I think they were talking about her. I've already talked to the sheriff, and I sent him a copy of the photos I took of the three men. I'll send you copies too because I'm not sure Hope was their target."

After Abigail repeated what the men said, she added, "I'm scared they made a mistake with Hope and should have kidnapped you instead, which would have been just as horrible. Did you ever meet that Mr. Clausen from Step Up? He allegedly died of a heart attack in his motel room outside of Atlanta Wednesday night, but according to my family who live in the area, the cause of his heart attack was a knife in his chest."

"No, I hadn't heard; that's shocking news," Riley said. "Do you think they'll cancel this weekend's Step Up meetings? Their staff may be shaken, and I know people around here are nervous enough after the attack on Hope."

"It may take a while before the news gets this far south, but now I'm worried about you. I have a cousin who would be a great bodyguard. He's a sweet guy, but he has a very intimidating appearance."

"I'll be fine; I'll have Toby with me," Riley said.

"These men aren't messing around; they use guns and knives."

"Would you feel better if I told you I'd leave in a flash in any situation that I don't feel safe?"

"If I thought you would, yes." Abigail snorted. "I'll see if Nora could use my cousin at her bed and breakfast. Derek has worked around horses before at rodeos, but he didn't like traveling all the time, and the work wasn't steady. He's a good man to have around."

"Does he know I understand animals?"

"Honey, this whole county knows you understand animals. He won't be surprised."

Riley exhaled. "Okay, but tell him I'm the girl in the stable. Don't try to describe me because I'll be wearing a knit cap to cover up my hair."

After they hung up, Riley's phone buzzed a text from Abigail. "Here are the photos."

Riley stared at the photos. *I've seen these men before.*

She called the sheriff's office and was surprised when the sheriff answered. *I expected to leave a voicemail.*

"Sheriff Baker, this is Riley. I recognize the three men in the photos that Abigail sent you."

"Who are they?"

"The two men sitting together are the same men who tried to attack Doc Ned and me; the other man was at the Methodist Church meeting."

"What are your plans for today?" Sheriff asked.

"I'm taking care of Nora's horses."

"Will Abigail's cousin be working with you?"

Riley narrowed her eyes. "You already know about Derek?"

"I suggested him when Abigail called me earlier; I haven't seen him in a long time, but he dropped by my office for a visit earlier this week, so I knew he was around."

"There's more to Derek than what you're saying, isn't there?"

"Did you know you have a suspicious side for someone who is as kind-hearted as you are?" Sheriff chuckled as he hung up.

Before Riley called Toby inside, so they could leave, her phone rang. *Lizzie.*

"Buck called Ned after you left his ranch. We're so relieved that you found Hope. The trauma surgeon removed the bullet last night, and she's doing fine, or at least she's patched up and will be home in a week, which probably means back to work, if I know her, assuming there are no complications."

"Thanks for letting me know; I've been worried."

"Ned felt guilty about not being available to go along until Buck told him that Ben was with you. I'm working at the office until Hope returns. The staff is pitching in too, so we'll keep the doors open and our patients happy; no guarantee on whether we'll even try to keep the clients happy, but don't tell Ned I said that. One thing about working at the office is I'm hearing the news firsthand instead of weeks later when Ned remembers to tell me. Elsie keeps me up to date. There was a big barn fire last night at one of the farms that a family had abandoned, and a volunteer firefighter just happened to be driving past it not long after it started. He called it in then went into the barn to rescue any animals; instead, he saw two men on the ground through the flames and dragged them out. The barn burned to the ground less than five minutes later. The bodies still haven't been identified; most people think the two men were vagrants just trying to keep warm."

Riley called Toby inside, and they left for the Trails End B&B.

After Riley passed the B&B, she slowed down, so she could watch for a driveway. "I don't know how far not quite a quarter of a mile is, so you'll have to help me, Toby."

Toby stared out the window then yipped.

Riley squinted. "That must be it."

After she reached the barn, she parked next to a truck then sent a text to Nora to let her know she was at the barn. "I guess Nora found somebody to clean the stalls. I'm surprised."

When she opened Toby's door, he bounded out and disappeared into the barn. *Evidently whoever is here is not a threat.* Riley slipped on her muck boots then followed Toby into the barn.

Whew," she said. "This is one ripe barn."

A tall, muscular black man in his mid-thirties who was built like a linebacker and had a jagged vertical scar on his cheek strode out of the tack room. Toby wagged his tail, and the man reached down and scratched Toby's ears. When the man stood up, Toby wandered off to explore.

Riley raised her eyebrows. *He has law enforcement written all over him. I wonder which department.*

"Hey, there, Riley. I heard you had red hair, so I wouldn't have known you if I hadn't been warned in advance. Your cap looks warm; I'm Derek."

Riley put out her hand, and Derek wiped his on his overalls then shook her hand.

Warned him? Abigail didn't know about my cap.

"I want to thank you for finding Hope; she's an old friend."

Hope told him; they're more than old friends.

He cleared his throat. "I fed and watered the horses and turned them out to pasture, but their hooves need to be checked. Nora told me the stalls hadn't been cleaned very well lately, but I don't think they've been cleaned at all for quite a while. I know you want to get to work, so I won't keep you. When you're ready for lunch, Nora left her UTV here for us. Mice have invaded the tack room, so we'll need to see what we can salvage. The horse blankets aren't chewed, just soiled; I want to take them with us to the Trails End because they need to be cleaned. We'll have to inspect the saddles, saddle blankets, bridles, and halters before you ride the horses. Let me know if you need any help."

"I'll pick their hooves first."

Derek nodded. "I'll give you my cell number in case you run into any problems."

Definitely a cop.

While Riley entered his phone number into her contacts, Derek said, "I've heard that you understand animals; you must have keen observation skills, and that's a real talent."

Riley side-glanced him. *He's being polite, but at least that's a kinder interpretation than what people said about Buck's granny.*

Riley slipped her phone into her coat pocket and gathered the tools she'd need then dropped them into her work backpack and called Toby. When he dashed to her, she said, "Let's go find the horses."

They went through the pasture closest to the barn then continued to the next pasture. Toby trotted ahead of Riley then waited until she joined him and the horses. Riley hummed as she neared the horses then stroked their necks.

After they relaxed, she laid her tools out on a mat. "I'd like to check your hooves. Do you have any that hurt?"

Dakota lifted her left front leg, and Riley moved her tools close as she checked Dakota's hoof.

"I can see why it hurts; I'll pick out those rocks and smooth your hoof."

Riley sang a healing song she had learned from her grandmother; Fire swayed, and Dakota relaxed.

When she finished her work, Riley put down Dakota's foot. "Shall we do your other front foot now?"

The Paint nodded then picked up her other leg.

"There are a few rocks but nothing like your other one, so it won't take long at all."

When Riley finished cleaning Dakota's hooves, she asked, "What do you think, Fire? Are you ready to have your hooves cleaned too?"

After she cleaned Fire's hooves, she said, "Both of you take it easy today. There were a few rocks that had been there for a while. I'll see how your hooves are doing tomorrow. I'll clean your blankets for tonight because it's going to be colder than it has been lately, but your stalls will be comfortable because Derek is cleaning them."

Dakota whinnied, and Riley smiled. "He is a nice man. I didn't know you were staying in the pasture at night, but I understand because the barn was pretty stinky. You'll be able to rest tonight."

Riley picked up her tools then put them into her backpack. As she and Toby walked back to the barn, she checked her phone. "It's noon, Toby. This morning went by fast, didn't it? We'll get you a drink before we go to the Trails End."

Riley pulled out Toby's water bowl from her car then carried it to the faucet at the barn and filled it. When she went into the barn, Derek had scooped up the manure in the aisle, swept the cobwebs from the ceiling and light fixtures, cleaned the first stall, and was working on the second stall.

"The barn's starting to smell better and look habitable," she said.

Derek straightened his back and groaned. "I still have a ways to go. Did you have any problems?"

"Thank goodness Dakota and Fire cooperated; their hooves were pretty bad. I have more to do, but I stopped because I had to dig deep for some of the rocks and hardened clay; I'll work on them more tomorrow."

"Are you ready for lunch? I texted Nora to let her know I'd like to clean out both stalls and let them air before I put down fresh bedding; she'll pack a lunch for me, if you don't mind bringing it back with you."

"I don't mind at all, but couldn't I help?'

"I appreciate the offer, but not really because I don't want the horses in here until the bedding's down. While the stalls are airing, I'll work on the tack room."

When Riley gathered the horses' blankets, Derek asked, "I'll carry those to the UTV for you, I pulled out the saddle blankets that were too badly damaged to use, but if you'll collect the few that are left, they need to be cleaned too."

After Riley and Derek loaded the blankets, Riley climbed into the UTV and headed toward the B&B. Toby passed her then ran in front of her.

Riley smiled. *He either knows where he's going, or he thinks I do.*

When Riley parked the UTV behind the B&B, Nora came out the back door. "Let's get those blankets in the washer; I'll take them to the barn this evening because we're supposed to get a hard freeze tonight."

Riley admired the industrial-sized washer and dryer. *I didn't think about how much laundry a B&B would have.*

CHAPTER TWELVE

After Nora loaded half of the blankets into the washer, she said, "I made a big pot of gumbo and homemade dinner rolls for us since the caterer will use the entire kitchen all weekend. The chef and his team will be here around two. Ava Fleet told me I was welcome to any of the meals the caterer prepares, but it didn't feel right to me to eat food I hadn't prepared or paid for, especially since she's my customer."

As Nora dished up two bowls of gumbo, she said, "I should have asked you if spicy was okay because the sausage is not mild."

"I love spicy," Riley said.

While they ate, Nora said, "Tell me about your morning."

"I planned to start with their hooves and took the tools along with me to pick and clean them. Toby and I walked across two pastures before we found them; the wind was light, so we enjoyed the chance to stretch our legs." Riley took another bite of the homemade roll to counter the burn on her tongue.

"I'm so glad you focused on their hooves right away; they must have been in terrible shape. I thought Dakota was limping a little yesterday when I filled their water and fed them. If you weren't coming today, I don't know how I could have possibly managed getting ready for the weekend and taking care of the horses. I did find someone to help me straighten the bedrooms and keep the common rooms clean."

"I'll work on their hooves some more tomorrow, but I want to give any swelling a chance to go down. After lunch, I'd like to brush them unless they are tired of being handled."

"I wouldn't have thought of that, but it makes sense; they might be extra skittish tomorrow if they didn't get a break."

When the doorbell rang, Nora rose. "Right on time. I'll give Ava and her crew a quick tour then let them decide where they want to set up. I won't be long."

Riley listened as Ava introduced Orson and his wife, Pam, to Nora.

"Where do you want me to set up, Ava? I could do that now before I leave," Pamela Suzanne said.

"Pam's going to Atlanta to take care of some loose ends for us; she'll be back late tomorrow," Ava said. "Pam, honey, just bring in your boxes while Ms. Nora shows us where we can hold meetings. We can decide later."

"Would you like to see the bedrooms first?" Nora asked.

"Excellent suggestion," Ava said.

"We have three restrooms downstairs. The first one is the first door to the left of the kitchen, and the other two are at the end of the hallways," Nora said.

Nora told Ava and Orson about the history and architecture of the house as the three of them went up the stairs.

The front door clicked as Pamela Suzanne left then creaked when she returned.

"So, where do I set the box? Just anywhere?" Pamela Suzanne mumbled. "Right here's good. I'm ready to get out of here. Restroom first, now where was it?"

Riley froze.

When Pamela Suzanne opened the kitchen door, she said, "Excuse me, where is the restroom?"

Riley kept her head down and motioned toward the left.

Pamela Suzanne strode to the kitchen table and whispered, "Riley? I heard farmers talking about you Tuesday night. What are you doing here?"

Riley shook her head, and Pamela Suzanne jerked off the knit cap.

"We have to talk, but not here. Where can we go without being seen?" Pamela Suzanne hissed.

"There's a woodshed on the side of the house; follow me." Riley rose and hurried out the back door with Pamela Suzanne right behind her. Toby joined them when they reached the woodshed.

"These people are evil, and they scare me," Pamela Suzanne said. "You need to get away as fast as you can."

"What about you?" Riley asked.

"I'm supposed to go to Atlanta. I'll leave the rental car in Macon like I'm supposed to, then my aunt will pick me up. I don't even know what's going on, but it's not good."

"You aren't married to Orson?" Riley asked.

"Not hardly, and that's just one tiny lie they're telling. Bad things happen to anyone associated with them, and I'm afraid I'm next."

"Why are you telling me?" Riley asked.

Pamela Suzanne's eyes welled up. "You were nice to me even after I wasn't nice to you. You're my only friend, and I don't want to see you hurt."

Riley blinked. *I didn't even know I was her friend.*

"What can I do to help?" Riley asked.

"Don't tell them who I am because I used my cousin's last name; I'll go inside then leave immediately. Don't go inside until I'm gone."

"Is there anything I can do to stop them?"

Pamela Suzanne furrowed her brow. "I have a copy of the master list with the names of people they'll meet with this weekend. I don't know if you'd have any use for it, but where can I leave it?"

"Stop at the mailbox at the road on your way out, and I'll get it as soon as you're on the road."

Pamela Suzanne pointed to the knit cap. "Wear it; it hides your hair and suits you much better than a collection of overpriced rugs like a certain backstabbing, overweight, obnoxious person I know." Pamela Suzanne hugged Riley then hurried into the B&B while Riley gaped at her.

"As Grandma would say, Toby, don't that beat all. What do you think? I think Pamela Suzanne knows more than she is saying."

Toby yipped.

Riley nodded. "She did say she was afraid; I guess I believe her too."

Riley listened intently as a car drove away from the house on the driveway.

Riley furrowed her brow. "I didn't think this through, Toby. How do I get to the mailbox without being seen?"

Toby whined.

"Okay, I'll follow you in the UTV."

Toby raced ahead of Riley away from the house and in the opposite direction of the barn then turned at a gated lane. *Is this a service road?*

Riley drove around the gate then she and Toby sped down the wide lane to the road. Riley smiled when she looked to her left. *We came out only a few yards away from the B&B driveway.*

Riley held her breath as she opened the mailbox then exhaled. "I guess I still don't quite trust Pamela Suzanne, but a bomb in a mailbox isn't her style."

She peered inside then pulled out the contents. "Toby, this is more than just one sheet: she left a packet of papers. She's one surprise after another, isn't she?"

Riley shoved the papers down her shirt; Toby ran alongside the UTV as she raced back to the house.

She strolled through the mud room and into the kitchen; after she sat at the table then polished off her gumbo, she heard footsteps coming down the hallway from the bedrooms to the front door.

"Thanks for your time, Ms. Nora," Ava said. "Oh look, Orson, Pam already brought in all the boxes from her car. She's very energetic and a real go-getter, isn't she?"

He chuckled. "I feel the pressure to get our luggage inside just as quickly."

"I need my briefcase and my file box; I'll come with you," Ava said.

"I'll let you get busy then." Nora came into the kitchen and closed the door behind her then waited until the front door clicked.

"We have chocolate chip cookies for our dessert. I'll fill a thermos with gumbo and put it and the sandwich I made earlier into a lunch bag for Derek," Nora said.

She narrowed her eyes as she glanced at the closed door and lowered her voice. "There's something slimy about those two, but I can't put my finger on it. They tried to give me a check for the balance of what they owe me after I specifically said I had to have cash so I could pay my staff over the weekend. Give these handwipes to Derek and ask him to come to the B&B when he's at a stopping point."

"I will," Riley said.

"Feel free to leave whenever you like; you have a lot to do tomorrow."

After Nora gave Riley the lunch bag, a thermos of coffee, and a bag of cookies, Riley and Toby headed toward the barn. Riley stopped at her car, removed the packet of papers from her shirt, and shoved them under her car seat before she went into the barn.

Riley gave Derek his handwipes, lunch bag, and thermos then took out two cookies for herself before she gave Derek the sack with the cookies. "Nora would like for you to go to the B&B."

Derek nodded as he cleaned his hands. "Nora's calling is hospitality. She's always loved horses, but her husband managed the care of the horses and worked alongside his stable hands."

While Derek ate his lunch, Riley cleaned and conditioned two leather saddles and inspected the other equipment in the tack room.

"Did you finish?" Derek asked when she joined him in the barn.

"I've done what I can for today. I'll have to see what I can salvage tomorrow; I'll probably need to use more saddle soap and elbow grease to clean and moisturize the saddles. The leather was super dry, but I feel good about what I've done so far."

"The floors in the stalls are dry; I'll put down their bedding then call it a day before I go to the B&B," Derek said.

"I'll help, then Toby and I will leave. Will you be here tomorrow?"

"Sure will. If we're both working at the barn, it will be my turn to pick up lunch." Derek smiled.

After Riley and Derek spread out the fresh bedding, Riley said, "I'll check on Dakota and Fire and let them know they can come to the barn anytime."

Derek narrowed his eyes. "Are you saying they stayed away, so we could clean their stalls?"

"Of course, they did." Riley tilted her head as she stared at Derek. "Otherwise, wouldn't you have thought they'd have come to their stalls to see what we were doing?"

Derek shrugged. "I'll work on the tack room tomorrow."

Riley strolled across the pasture while Toby roamed the grass with his head down. When a bird flew up from the field a few yards from him, he chased it across the pasture until it landed on a fence post in the next field; Toby sat next to the post and peered at the bird.

Dakota and Fire trotted to join Riley, and the three of them headed toward the barn; Toby abandoned his intense bird surveillance and raced across the pasture to catch up with them.

When Dakota and Fire went into the barn, Dakota whinnied, and Fire tossed her head.

Derek smiled. "I'm glad you're pleased."

Riley turned toward the door as she rolled her eyes. *Good guess, Derek; not at all bad for a skeptic.*

"See you tomorrow." Riley opened the back door of her car, and Toby jumped in.

"Let's go to the hardware store; I need geraniums, pots, soil, and tools."

Toby yipped.

"No, I am not getting a shovel, so I can dig up the koi pond."

Toby flopped down on the back seat and pouted.

After she parked, Riley asked, "Are you going in?"

Toby closed his eyes.

"I may be a while," she said.

Toby huffed then stood on the backseat; Riley opened the car door and picked up his leash before they walked together across the parking lot and into the store.

Riley grabbed a shopping cart, then they headed to the garden center. "Geraniums, pots, soil, and whatever else," she muttered. "Should have made a list."

When she found the geraniums, she picked out three and put them into her cart. An elderly woman, who was shorter than Riley, said, "Nice choice. You can leave them outside if you have a porch on the south side of your house."

"I don't; my back porch faces west."

The woman nodded. "The afternoon sun is warm; cover them if we have a hard freeze warning. You don't want to take them into the house then put them back out because the drastic change in temperature would shock them. Get the soil in the blue bag; it's best for flowers."

Riley added three large bags of soil, three pots, a trowel, garden hose, water sprayer, and garden gloves to her cart.

The elderly woman reappeared and inspected Riley's cart. "Do you have rocks at home for the bottom of your pot?"

"Not really; should I pick up a bag?"

The woman nodded then stood behind Riley when a woman's voice called out, "Mama, are you in here? It's time to go."

Riley glanced at the middle-aged woman who stood in the doorway to the main store. The woman glanced around then went back into the store.

"You're Riley, aren't you? I'm Cora; thanks for not busting me. I haven't finished helping everyone yet. You're set now."

Cora glanced at an aisle on the other side of the flowers. "That young man on the other side of the fencing display must have a rat problem. I have work to do."

Riley peered at the aisle but couldn't see anyone because of the shelves of bird feeders and seeds. *She must have radar.*

Riley unloaded the lighter items from her cart at the checkout then knelt down to read the codes for the heavy bags of soil and rocks on the underneath rack to the cashier. When a man hurried past her, she caught a glimpse of his feet before he disappeared.

Wingtip shoes. She quickly rose and glanced around, but he was gone.

"Your friend must have been in a big hurry," the cashier said.

Riley nodded. "Seemed like it."

After Riley and Toby left the store, Riley rolled her cart across the sidewalk; Toby barked then pushed her onto the sidewalk as a car slammed into her cart. The cart careened then crashed into the side of the building before the car sped away.

Cora stood near the curb in the front of the store as her daughter, another woman, and a man hurried to help Riley.

"Are you okay?" Cora's daughter asked as the man assisted Riley to her feet. "That car would have hit you if your brave dog hadn't kept you from stepping into the street."

The daughter motioned to Cora. "Mama, you're too close to the road; come here while we help Riley."

"I called nine-one-one," the other woman said. "My sister is a dispatcher at the sheriff's office. A deputy is already on the way; I'll wait with you because I saw everything. I tried to get a photo of the license plate, but it's pretty blurry."

"You scraped your cheek when you fell," Cora's daughter said. "It's only an abrasion, but you'll want to wash it with soap and put a little antiseptic cream on it when you get home. What's your dog's name? He's a hero."

Riley smiled. "This is Toby."

"I have treats in my bag for my German shepherd. Can I give one to Toby, or would you rather give it to him?"

Toby dropped into his most polite sit in front of the woman, and she giggled. "I guess it's okay if I give him one then."

After Cora's daughter gave Toby a dog biscuit, she asked, "Do you want a second cookie, Toby?"

Toby grinned, and she gave him another treat.

When the sheriff's deputy car pulled to the curb next to Riley, the daughter said, "Oh, good, it's Clay. He's young, but one of the smartest men you could meet."

Cora stood close to Riley and whispered, "His wife is six months pregnant, and they just moved here to be closer to her family; they're good people, Riley."

"That's nice to know, thank you," Riley said. *Why would Ben want to know the name of a deputy who is soon to be a dad?*

"Is that your receipt from the store, Riley?" Cora pointed to Riley's right fist where her knuckles were bleeding.

Riley stared at her hand then opened her clutched fist. "Of all things to do, I saved the receipt."

"I saw the driver," Cora said. "He had wingtip shoes."

Riley nodded. *It fits, but I don't know what it means.*

"Oh, for heaven's sake, Mama; you didn't see the driver, and nobody wears wingtip shoes anymore. You're confused."

The daughter took the slip of paper from Riley's hand. "Let's take Riley's receipt into the store, Mama."

Clay strode to Riley. "Sheriff Baker is on his way. Do you need an ambulance, Mrs. Carter?"

"No, I'm fine. I scraped my cheek a little when Toby pushed me out of the way of the speeding car."

The woman who took the photo joined Riley and the deputy. "I snapped a quick picture, but it's not as clear as I expected."

She handed her phone to the deputy. "I sent my sister a copy."

The deputy glanced at her phone then returned it and nodded. "Sheriff saw it before he left the office. The GBI investigator will be here soon, and she will want to talk to you, if you don't mind waiting."

Riley exhaled. *At least it isn't Ben.*

"Not at all, I'll sit in my car until she arrives; it's getting colder, isn't it?"

"That's fine, and you're right about the cold. Mrs. Carter, let's sit in my cruiser, and I'll take your statement, so you don't have to wait."

"I'm okay." Riley furrowed her brow and glanced at Toby. "I didn't see much. I had my head down while I pushed my cart out of the store because of the gusty wind; when I reached the curb, Toby knocked me down to keep me from going into the road."

"Good boy, Toby." Clay patted and stroked Toby. "Anything else you noticed, Mrs. Carter? Did anyone follow you to the store? Did you see which way the car went after it hit the cart?"

Riley bit her lip to keep from rolling her eyes. "No, I was face down on the pavement, so I didn't see anything."

Clay nodded and finished taking notes as the sheriff sped into the lot and parked behind the deputy's cruiser.

"Do you have Riley's statement?" Sheriff asked.

"Yes, sir."

Sheriff Baker read Clay's notes then narrowed his eyes as he inspected Riley. "Riley, I think that your eye may turn black. The ambulance will be here in two minutes. I'd like for them to check you; I don't want you to drive if you have any signs of a concussion."

Riley grumbled, "I don't need an ambulance."

"I do," Sheriff Baker said.

Cora and her daughter came out of the hardware store with a young clerk pushing a cart behind them.

"I talked to the manager, Riley, and the store has replaced all of your items," the woman said.

Riley gaped at the smashed cart and her pots. "Can't we salvage the geraniums?"

"I can give it a try, ma'am," the young clerk said.

"We'd like to get some pictures first," the sheriff said.

The clerk shrugged. "Can I load your car for you?"

"That's an excellent idea," the woman said.

"I won't be far." Riley glared at the sheriff before she and Toby headed toward her car with the woman at her side and the young clerk following them.

"How are you doing?" the woman asked.

"I think I'm going to be stiff tomorrow," Riley said.

"Mama would tell you to have a hot toddy before bed." The woman smiled. "Mama visits me every weekend because the retirement home won't fix her a hot toddy at bedtime."

After the clerk loaded her car, he pushed the cart back to the store as the ambulance parked behind the sheriff's cruiser.

When Riley and Toby reached the deputy's car, the ambulance crew had their stretcher out of the back of the ambulance and were waiting for her.

"We'll take you to the hospital," the paramedic said.

"No, thank you. Is there anything else you need from me, Sheriff?" Riley asked.

The sheriff shook his head, and Clay smiled.

"You know where to find me." Riley turned toward her car.

"Riley, I apologize; I misunderstood and came off as a bossy jerk. Can I buy you a cup of coffee sometime, and you can tell me what an idiot I am?" the paramedic asked.

"Sure." Riley kept walking while the sheriff chuckled, and the paramedic laughed.

On the way home, Riley said, "I hope we run into Cora again, Toby. She sort of reminded me of Mrs. Smythe who stalks the grocery store in Barton; I miss being around our friends, but wasn't it nice of Cora's daughter to ask the store to replace all of our purchases that were smashed along with the cart?"

After Riley finished carrying the bags of soil to the backyard, she sat on the porch to catch her breath from the exertion. "We need a wagon, so I can load it up then haul things from one place to another. Am I getting so much stuff we're going to have to rent a truck to move us?"

Toby yipped at the same time as her phone rang. *Ben.*

"Where are you? Are you okay? I heard you were hit by a car, but the sheriff didn't call me, so what happened?"

Dang, news really spreads fast in small towns.

"We're at home, and we're fine. Toby and I went shopping at the hardware store, and a car hit my shopping cart."

"Bumped it?"

"More like smashed," she said. "Toby pushed me away from the curb, so I have a little road rash on my cheek, but that's all."

"Would the sheriff corroborate your story?" Ben growled.

Riley stared at her phone then continued to listen. *I'm beyond cranky to angry, and I'm not talking to you.*

"Babe? Are you there?" Ben's tone softened.

"I haven't decided yet," she said.

Ben hung up, and Riley gaped at the phone.

"He hung up on me, Toby."

Her phone rang and she narrowed her eyes. "He's calling back. Do I answer, so he can hang up on me again? Or should I answer, so I can hang up on him?"

Toby snorted and left the porch; Riley answered.

"Hi, Babe. I need to start over."

"Go ahead." Riley's tone was flat.

"I planned to call you earlier, but the day got away from me. We've been invited to a big barbeque at my instructor's farm tomorrow; he's going to roast a pig. The whole class has been invited, actually. I know you aren't crazy about crowds, so I can decline gracefully…"

Riley snorted.

Ben chuckled. "I stand corrected: I can decline. Our instructor made a point to tell us it wasn't fancy; we'll be in his barn, and he said no one would freeze. What do you think?"

"I think it would be good for us to go somewhere together, and I've been a little lonely because I've been used to being around a lot of people all day. A big bonus is it will be particularly refreshing because none of your classmates are likely to try to run over or shoot either one of us."

"That would be different, wouldn't it?" Ben groaned.

Riley giggled. "Do we take something?"

"Right; I almost forgot; we take a dessert or an appetizer, and we're supposed to be there around five. I know it sounds early, but the class is taking turns helping with the pig tonight and most of the day tomorrow. I'm working, so I'm excused, and I didn't want to drag you out tonight then again tomorrow night, so I didn't volunteer for a shift."

"You can, if you want; Toby and I will be fine."

"Excuse me?" Ben exhaled. "I was going to snap at you again. Let's just leave it at I definitely don't need a break from my wife like some of the other guys. I'm going to have to get back to work. Do you need for me to pick up anything on my way home? Bread? Milk?"

"We could use a utility wagon, but we can get that later."

Ben laughed. "I love you, Riley; you are so full of surprises. We'll add getting a utility wagon to our list of things to do on a date."

"We have a list?"

"If we don't, we should. Do you want to hang up on me this time?"

"I love you. I loved you last." She hung up and laughed.

Her phone buzzed a text from Ben. "You are hilarious."

Riley smiled. "I guess I can go back to work."

She stared at her phone then sent a text to Claire. "Call when convenient."

Claire replied, "Now or after work?"

I can always count on Claire. "Take your coat off and return to your desk. After work."

Claire: "So you're psychic now?"

Riley giggled. "Yes."

Riley's phone rang.

"We'd text back and forth the rest of the day, wouldn't we?" Claire snickered. "What's up?"

"I miss everybody. I met a woman in the hardware store that reminded me of Mrs. Smythe; she introduced herself as Cora."

"I love her name. Tell me more about Cora."

"She was in the store with her daughter who was looking for her mama, and Cora hid behind me. She told me she couldn't leave because she had more people to help. Her daughter thinks Cora has dementia, and maybe she does, but she had some very lucid moments when I was with her."

"I have very few lucid moments, according to Thad. He's being a total knucklehead lately. He and Doc Julie Rae are working a lot of extra hours, and both of them are downright miserable to be around."

"Ben hasn't come home until close to bedtime most of this week; being a knucklehead must go with along with overwork. I think I'll fire him and replace him with a scorpion."

"A scorpion would be a big improvement over Thad or Julie Rae as far as personality is concerned; I'll tell Zach our latest assessment; he's been caught in the crossfire too."

"We need scorpion repellent for Zach."

Claire sputtered then coughed. "Sorry; I should know better than to take a quick sip of water when we're on the phone. Thad and I couldn't agree on what we'd like to do this weekend, so we have absolutely nothing planned; we'll probably mostly snap at each other, then late Sunday night I'll stress over the hundred things I should have done. What does your weekend look like?"

"Ben's instructor invited Ben's class to a pig roast at his farm tomorrow, and we're supposed to take a dessert or appetizer. You know my culinary abilities. Can you suggest something?"

"I'll look through my recipes this evening and send you suggestions for an appetizer and for a dessert, then you can decide which you want to make. Do you work tomorrow?"

CHAPTER THIRTEEN

"I'm working half days at a B&B this weekend and Monday to care for two older horses that have been neglected for a while. I cleaned and picked their hooves today, but I have more to do tomorrow."

"Oh my, two days to clean their hooves? Did you have to stop to give them a break?"

"Exactly."

"If you fire Ben, come here and bring the horses with you. You can stay with Lindsey at the horse farm. Nobody would think of looking there for you and the horses, and Lindsey has so many horses, she'd never even notice."

Riley giggled. "I love that you always have a wild suggestion of where I could stay if I leave the scorpion here and come back to Barton. I bought geraniums today; after I plant them in pots, I'll put them on the back porch. Cora explained how to care for them in our close to freezing temperatures."

"Sounds to me like you've discovered the cure for feeling down: make a friend, preferably one with dementia, at the hardware store," Claire said.

"You're exactly right." Riley sighed. "I do miss having friends around."

"Excuse me? I'm only a phone call away, and I'll bet you don't even realize how many friends you have all around you. Your friend Cora gave me the idea for the perfect appetizer if you don't have time to make either of my recipes: peanut butter and jelly pinwheels. Mrs. Smythe would be very proud."

"That is so tempting." Riley giggled. "Claire, thanks for calling."

"It's what friends do. You let me know anytime you have another scorpion emergency, and I'll do the same. Pinky promise."

"Pinky promise."

After they hung up, Riley said, "Toby, Claire always brightens my day; let's plant geraniums."

Toby watched while Riley put some rocks in the bottom on one pot then returned to the porch, flopped down, and closed his eyes. Riley added some soil before she frowned at the bags of soil and the pots. "I should put the pots on the porch before I add rocks and soil, shouldn't I?"

Toby swept the porch with his tail when he wagged; Riley tugged and dragged the already heavy pot to the porch. "I can't lift it; I should have taken out the rocks first instead of now."

She removed the rocks then positioned the three pots where they would have afternoon sun but still be close enough for the house to shelter them.

After she lined the bottom of the pots with rocks, filled the pots with soil, and planted her flowers, she dropped onto her chair. "I'm guaranteed to be sore tomorrow from my fall topped off with all the heavy lifting I've done, but I have my geraniums."

The late afternoon sun dipped below the trees, taking the warmth of the sunbeams on the porch with it, and the light, refreshing breeze became stronger and cooler; Riley shivered. "Time for me to go inside, Toby."

She refilled the tea kettle then put it on the stove to heat for a cup of tea. While she waited, she turned on her laptop and found the recipes Claire had sent to her. *I could make the peanut butter cookies now, so I'm not stressing tomorrow; the oven will warm up the kitchen, and I can try out my new mixer.*

When she opened the pantry to pull out flour, sugar, and peanut butter, she smiled. *Mom brought a tablecloth and napkins for us. We could have a fancy dinner at home as soon as Ben gets over being a knucklehead.*

While she creamed the butter, peanut butter, and sugar with the mixer, Riley's phone rang. *Abigail.*

Riley turned off the mixer then answered.

"Did you hear about the barn fire and the two men?" Abigail asked.

"The fire from last night?"

"That's the one; the local television news flashed the photo I took of the two men in the diner on the TV screen when their on-the-scene reporter stood in the middle of a road and talked about the fire, but the reporter didn't mention the picture or even indicate whether the murdered men had been identified. I have no idea how the station got my photo; do you suppose pictures sent to the sheriff's office are public record? I thought about calling the sheriff but decided I was just being nosy. I was wondering if you'd heard anything." Abigail sighed. "I admit it: I'm just being nosy."

"I haven't heard anything, but I'll let you know if I do. As far as the photos you took being public record, seems like a valid question to me."

"I have a friend who works in law enforcement; I'll ask him. Thanks, Riley; you're brilliant."

After Abigail hung up, Riley shuddered. *Pamela Suzanne said the Step Up people were evil. Is Ava Fleet behind all this?*

Riley put her first batch of cookies into the oven then drank the last of her lukewarm tea. *Is Derek Abigail's friend who works in law enforcement?*

After Riley pulled out her last batch of cookies from the oven and slid them onto a rack to cool, she stared at her phone. *It's getting late. I expected to hear from Ben by now.*

She put on her warm coat and her knit cap, stuck her phone into her pocket, and went outside. "Let's go for a walk in the woods before it gets dark, Toby."

As Riley pushed deeper into the woods through the thick brush and fallen logs, the daylight slowly dimmed until it was dark.

"I guess we better head back, Toby."

As Toby led her toward the house, Riley squinted at the ground to watch her foot placement. "I should have brought a flashlight; the woods are creepy in the dark."

After they were close enough to the house to see the kitchen lights, Riley rolled her eyes. "I just remembered I could have turned on the flashlight on my phone. Don't tell Ben or Claire."

When they went into the house, Riley inhaled. "The house smells like peanut butter; that will be a nice surprise for Ben."

Riley's phone rang, but she didn't recognize the number; she shrugged then answered.

"Hey, Riley. It's Shelby, you know, the audio tech. I got your number from Nora. She called me in a panic because so many of the people who will be at the meetings tomorrow are hard of hearing, Mrs. Fleet decided she needs microphones set up in all the rooms at the B&B, can you believe it? I think she should have thought of that earlier, but the money's too good to turn down. Nora told me you're taking care of her horses this weekend. Want another freelance job? I have to set up the system early tomorrow morning, like five o'clock. I need an extra pair of hands and ears to help me set up and test the equipment, and nobody's available."

"I'm your last choice?" Riley asked.

Shelby snickered. "Pretty much the bottom of the barrel. What do you say?"

"You make it sound so attractive; how could I say no?"

"Good. Nora's promised us breakfast, so wear your stretchy pants."

After she hung up, Riley smiled. *Claire was right; I have people all around me that I didn't even realize were my friends.*

When Ben called a few minutes later, Riley turned on the oven as she answered the phone.

"I'm finally walking to my car in the parking lot. Where are you?" Ben asked.

"You want the real answer or the answer you deserve?"

Ben hesitated then said, "Your choice."

"I'm in jail, and I'm allowed only one phone call. You just snatched my one chance to call my boyfriend out of my hands."

"Was that the real answer or the one I deserve?" Ben asked.

Riley burst out laughing. "You are so good. Come home, and Toby will chase the boyfriend into the woods."

Riley smiled as she put the casserole into the oven. *We will get through this together.*

Ben burst in through the front door with his hands on his hips like an old-time Western gunslinger. "Where's that varmint of a boyfriend?"

Toby snarled then grinned.

Ben laughed. "Well done, Toby; I can count on you to have my back." Ben inhaled deeply. "Do I smell peanut butter cookies?"

"Sure do, and you'll have to taste-test them for me after we eat supper because I'm planning to take them tomorrow night to the barbeque."

Ben hugged Riley. "I missed you; nobody can make me laugh like you do."

He kissed her then cupped her face with his hands as he carefully examined her cheek. "Would it be in my best interest to refrain from calling you Scarface?"

"It depends on whether you'd like to have cookies for dessert," Riley said.

"You got it, Doll Face; I'll lock up my hardware and change out of this uniform."

"Beer with your casserole or with your cookies?" Riley asked.

"I'm too tired to decide; make it both."

While Ben changed clothes, Riley put the tablecloth on the kitchen table then set the table with the cloth napkins and plates.

Ben came into the kitchen and stared at the table. "Wow, babe; you sure know how to brighten my entire day."

While Ben opened two beers, Riley set the casserole on the table.

"Do we need glasses for our beer?" Ben asked.

"That's too fancy for our budget," Riley said as they sat at the table.

Ben chuckled while he tapped Riley's bottle with his. "Cheers."

After they dished up their food, Riley said, "Tell me about your day."

She smiled and nodded while Ben waved his fork and told her about the case, his teammates, and the investigation problems that weren't included in their studies.

"I'm a little stressed because we're taking what the instructor called a preliminary final. The word is that it's more like a midterm test, and anyone who fails it will be released from the class. I'd like to go in a little early, so I can do a quick review of what we've studied so far."

Riley told Ben about Shelby's last-minute call for help in the morning.

"You're meeting her at five at the B&B? I'll follow you; I'll have plenty of time to go to the coffee shop and review my notes before the test and won't have to stay up late tonight to study. The coffee shop is famous for their breakfast burritos, so we won't have to have breakfast before we leave in the morning, and don't make me lunch; our team made plans to go to the new pizza shop tomorrow."

"This is working out all the way around. Shelby told me Nora was planning to have breakfast for us, so you and I don't have to get up extra early or worse, skip breakfast."

"I appreciate working on a field case instead of studying an old case in the classroom. Our instructor told us the classroom gives us the basics, and the field tests our skills. What about you? How was your first day at the B&B?"

Riley told him about the condition of the stalls and the horses and Abigail's cousin. "I quit picking at the horses hooves to give them a chance to heal. I'm glad Derek cleaned and sanitized their stalls because there's no way I could have finished cleaning them before Monday. The horses have been staying outside because of the conditions inside the barn. Do you know Derek? He has that law enforcement vibe. I asked the sheriff about Derek, but he ignored my question."

Ben smiled. "Sheriff Baker doesn't know you as well as Sheriff Dunn. Sheriff Dunn would have just told you because he knows you'll figure it out before the weekend's over."

Riley raised an eyebrow. "So, you're ignoring my question too, even though you know I'll practice my skills. Blink twice if I'm right."

Ben covered his eyes with his hand. "Not saying."

Riley giggled. *He might be a knucklehead, but he makes me laugh.*

After they cleared the dishes, Riley said, "I almost forgot that I wanted to show you our geraniums. They're on the back porch. It's too cold to be out there, but you can take a quick peek."

Ben turned on the porchlight before he opened the back door and peered out at the large pots and flowers. "Those are nice. Will they be okay in this cold weather, or do I need to bring them inside?"

"They're supposed to be okay because they are sheltered on the porch."

On their way to the living room, Riley selected two cookies, and Ben picked up four and crammed two others into his mouth before he started a fire in the fireplace.

While they relaxed on the sofa in front of the fire, they munched on cookies and finished their beer; Riley told Ben about Cora.

"Did you feel like Mrs. Smythe had followed us here?"

"I really did, and I realized how lonesome I've been for our Barton friends, so I called Claire."

"I understand exactly what you're saying because even though I'm around people all day, I miss our Barton friends too. As soon as I finish this class, we'll have to spend a few days at the cabin; when I need a break from listening to a lecture, I daydream about the projects we could do there."

"Grandma and I always had a food plot for the deer, rabbits, and racoons, then we planted peas that were winter-hardy in the fall as ground cover and to build up the soil."

"Did your grandma ever talk about adding on to the cabin? That might be something we could do," Ben said.

"Grandma told me one time that she had big plans to build a house closer to the road for me and Dad, so he could retire in Barton; she would live in the cabin, then after she was gone, Dad could move into the cabin, and I could live in the house with my family."

"I love her plan." Ben kissed Riley's forehead after she yawned. "If we're going to leave around four thirty, we should think about going to bed. I plan to dream about that house near the road and our family."

* * *

When Ben slipped out of bed to start the coffee and take his shower, Riley glanced at the time then pulled up the covers around her neck. *No sane person gets up at three thirty in the morning.*

Ben tiptoed into the bedroom to dress.

"My turn." Riley stumbled to the bathroom and turned on the water Ben had prewarmed for her with his shower.

After she showered and dressed, she hurried to the kitchen.

"I fed Toby, and he's been outside. I found frozen biscuits in the freezer. Mom used to keep a supply in her freezer, so I thought she might have sneaked a bag of them in for us." Ben poured a cup of coffee for Riley and refilled his cup.

Riley smiled at Toby, who lay next to the warm stove.

"I knew something was in the oven before I even smelled the biscuits because Toby is being a devoted oven guard, and a biscuit before we leave is perfect for me; I'm not sure when Nora plans to have breakfast ready."

While they ate their biscuits and jam, Ben said, "No rain in the forecast for today, but it will be colder and windier than yesterday."

"When we're not at the B&B, we'll be in the barn, so we'll be sheltered. Nora hired me to ride the horses, but I think a little attention is all they've wanted."

Before they finished eating, Riley's phone buzzed a text from Nora.

"Hope this isn't too early. Park at the barn. I'll pick you up in the UTV."

Riley read the text to Ben. "I was wondering where I should park because there isn't all that much spare parking at the B&B."

"Sounds perfect since after you help Shelby, you'll be working at the barn," Ben said.

After Riley put on her warm coat and her knit cap and slung her backpack onto her shoulder, she and Toby hurried to her car while Ben locked the house then followed her.

When she reached the driveway to the barn, she pulled in and parked before she hurried to talk to Ben, who had pulled onto the shoulder.

"I was wondering if you'd missed your turn when we passed the Trails End B&B sign. Is this the service road to the barn?" Ben asked.

"Sure is; the barn is not far down this lane." Riley stood on the side bar at the driver's door and kissed Ben. "What's the saying for good luck when you're taking a test? Break a pencil?"

Ben laughed. "Must be. I love you, pretty girl, whoever you are."

Riley giggled. "Glad you like my hat. I do too because it keeps my ears warm."

Riley hurried back to her car and hopped in. As she headed toward the barn, she said, "Ben's still frustrated with being in a classroom and not in the field, and I'm still lonesome, but everything is tolerable because we are talking, and neither one of us has to face our problems alone and in silence."

Toby whined.

Riley shrugged. "It was a good thought, but I'm not convinced either."

When they reached the barn, Nora waited in the driver's seat of the UTV; she wore gloves and a heavy coat with the hood pulled up.

As Riley and Toby hurried to join her, Nora said, "Perfect timing; I just pulled up. I was glad the UTV has a windshield; the wind is harsh."

On the way to the B&B, Nora added, "Shelby will be at the B&B in about fifteen minutes. Would you like a hot cup of coffee to warm your hands?"

Riley smiled. "I'd love it. Ben asked me once if I was waiting for the coffee to cool before I drank it."

"My husband used to tease me by asking me to hold his coffee with my cold hands, so it would cool faster." Nora chuckled. "Shelby asked for a small room where she could set up but not be noticed. I guess she's been interrupted quite a bit in the past by well-meaning people who either wanted to chat and ask questions or wanted to give her their not-so-helpful advice on how to do her job."

"I don't know if it's because she's young or because she makes it look so easy, but I saw several people stand around her table at the Methodist church meeting. I thought she was very patient," Riley said.

"I don't have the patience that she does; I'd chase them out of the kitchen with a cleaver."

"Let me know when that happens because I'd love to see it," Riley said.

Nora chuckled. "I have a small dining room that we use for our honeymoon guests; it has a small restroom, so our lovebirds don't have to walk down the hall to the main restroom, a door to the kitchen, and a second door to the main hallway, which we can lock. There's a small, round dining table in there, but I have a larger table that would be easy to move into the dining room. I asked Shelby what I could do to help her before she arrived, and she told me you two would have plenty of time to set up. Derek will be here around ten, so you don't have to worry about him doing all the work before you get to the barn."

After they went inside, Nora said, "You can hang your coat and backpack here in the mud room."

"I have some tools in my backpack; I'll keep it with me." Riley hung up her coat but didn't take off her knit cap.

Nora peered at Riley. "You may find the house is too warm for your knit cap, or you may decide you stand out too much with the cap on. I can put up your hair for you then cover your hair with a scarf."

"I didn't think about how conspicuous wearing a warm cap might be; maybe it would be smart to put up my hair, if you don't mind; it would be less obvious that I'm hiding my red hair, and I won't break out in a heat rash," Riley said.

While Riley sat at the table and warmed her hands on her cup then sipped her coffee, Nora quickly braided Riley's hair into a single braid before she wrapped the braid around Riley's head and anchored the braid with two flat clips.

Riley went into the restroom that was set up for the kitchen staff and examined her hair. "I like it, Nora; too bad I need to hide the color of my hair because this is cute."

Toby yipped, and Nora smiled. "It does suit you. I can teach you how to do that braid yourself. I'll be right back with that scarf."

After Nora headed down the hallway to her room, Riley heard Ava's voice as she shouted from upstairs. "No coffee until six is unacceptable. Nora has to be in the kitchen, or at least, she better be. Tell her we need coffee upstairs now."

"Okay," a man replied.

Riley and Toby slipped into the mudroom, and Riley closed the door to the kitchen slightly then sat on the bench behind the door. Toby ducked under the bench then lay behind Riley's feet.

"Nora?" the man called out as he opened the kitchen door.

Riley peeked through the crack as the man with the wingtip shoes grabbed her cup of coffee from the table. She raised her eyebrows when he poured her coffee into the pot then rinsed the cup. *That's Jim.*

He hurried out of the kitchen and called out while he went up the stairs. "I've got a hot, fresh pot and a cup for you."

When Nora returned, she said, "It took me a little longer than I expected because I wanted to find my wild mustangs scarf, and it wasn't where I thought it was. Did I hear shouting? What was that all about?"

"Evidently Ava has to have coffee first thing in the morning, and six was too late. Jim came into the kitchen to talk to you then took the full coffee pot and my cup. Toby and I went into the mud room before he came in."

"Your cup?" Nora quickly wrapped the scarf around Riley's head.

"I was a little startled when he picked up my cup and poured my coffee into the pot then rinsed out my cup and took it," Riley said.

Nora snorted. "That Ava must run one heck of a tight ship; okay, see what you think."

Shelby came into the kitchen from the mudroom and set a box on the counter as she peered at Riley. "I didn't know you were a fashionista too, Nora; the scarf looks good."

"Thanks; okay, Riley, you can check it," Nora said.

Riley hopped up and rushed to the mirror. "This is perfect. I love the blue-gray background and the pale buckskin horses; I look like a stable hand ready for work."

"Or a really nerdy audio tech." Shelby snickered. "Where do we set up, Nora?"

The three of them went into the small dining room. Nora asked, "Will this work? That other door goes into the hall, but you can lock it from the dining room. I have a large table with folding legs that you can use."

"This will be a great place to set up. Where's the table? Is it something Riley and I can carry?" Shelby asked.

"It's in a hall closet." Nora led Shelby and Riley to a storage closet that was between the small dining room and the large meeting room.

"This is perfect," Shelby said. "If I could have half of a shelf near that electrical outlet, Nora, I have some equipment I don't need to monitor that would work better in here."

"You got it, Shelby. It won't take me long to clear you a shelf. I expect the caterer's assistants at five thirty, and they will be here all day. I set up the coffee machine in the meeting room to start at four, so the assistants wouldn't have to be here quite so early. They will put out the fruit and warm the pastries for the gathering in the meeting room and keep the coffee flowing."

Riley and Shelby carried the table to the dining room and centered it in the middle of the room, so they could walk around it. Shelby ran outside to bring in the rest of her equipment while Riley carried the box from the kitchen to the dining room.

Shelby pushed a flat cart with large boxes stacked on it into the dining room; she put a small box on top of a medium-sized box. "I'll ask Nora to show me all the meeting rooms, so I can do a preliminary installation for the systems in the rooms before I set up these boosters in the storage closet."

When she returned, Shelby said, "We're in luck; there are only two rooms besides the large meeting room, so you and I can monitor all the rooms and the hall outside each room."

"Why are we monitoring the hall?" Riley asked.

"I'll explain later." Shelby pointed to a box. "Unpack the equipment from the boxes while I set up the microphones. Ava Fleet specified two microphones in each room, so it won't take me long.

I'll explain how to operate the microphones to her before the meetings begin, but that's only so she feels like she's in control."

While Riley unpacked boxes, she paused when she heard the front door open.

"You're right on time; I'll show you the meeting room before we go to the kitchen. The tables for people to sit in small groups for the meals are in place, and the coffee and drink stations are set up too," Nora said.

When Nora and the assistants returned from the meeting room and walked past the dining room on their way to the kitchen, she asked, "Do you have everything you need? There is the kitchen; if you have any questions or need something, I'll be in the meeting room."

After the assistants went into the kitchen a woman whispered, "I didn't expect a commercial kitchen, Don."

"Certainly makes it easier for Chef, which means it will be easier for us. Let's unpack the food that needs to be refrigerated first then get organized," Don said.

"Don't you love that there's plenty of room in the refrigerator? I wish all of Chef's clients had kitchens with enough room to work."

Riley crept to the door to the kitchen and slowly closed it.

CHAPTER FOURTEEN

When Shelby came into the dining room, she locked the door behind her.

Riley whispered, "Sound carries from the kitchen. One of them whispered, and I very clearly heard what he said."

Shelby grinned. "Where were you standing?"

Riley side-glanced her. "Next to the table; why?"

Shelby pointed to a headset on the table. "You have great hearing; you heard them through that. We can hear what's going on almost anywhere on the first floor; if I'd had an extra day's notice, I could have set up the second floor too. I have signed releases from Nora and Ava Fleet to monitor the sound system for quality control through Monday morning. I need to be sure no one is complaining about the system; I hate to be blindsided with complaints I could have taken care of before anyone else noticed."

Riley rolled her eyes.

"Skeptical? Mrs. Fleet asked me to record all the meetings, and I told her I didn't have the equipment. She was very put out and claimed it was in my contract but couldn't tell me where; I offered to release her from the contract if that was a critical requirement for her, so she could find someone else. She turned all sweet and nice when she told me it was not necessary at all. I think she's a bully, at a minimum."

After Shelby finished setting up the equipment, she pointed to the equipment on the table that was closest to the meeting room. "You're set up to monitor the large meeting room, the kitchen, the hallway near us, and one of the smaller rooms. I have the master console, so I can monitor everything else. If you would like a break, I can take over your stations from my console; it would just mean even more flipping from one room to another for me. If you hear something that I need to hear, push the green button, and my console will pick it up, and both of us can listen at the same time. I can add you to a room to listen the same way; it overrides whatever you are listening to at that particular time, so I doubt I'll be doing that. You can't break anything, so feel free to change the volume and to change from one room to the other. Put on your headset, and I'll show you."

Riley sat at the table in front of the console and adjusted the headset while Toby lay down next to her.

"Volume first," Shelby said, and Riley nodded.

Shelby clicked another dial to three positions. "What did you hear?"

"Typical kitchen noises, but no talking; Nora was humming, so that was the main meeting room. I didn't hear anything on the third setting, so that must be the smaller room."

Shelby nodded. "It gets a little tricky when people are talking in all four of your areas, but you'll get the hang of it. Let me know if you get bored, and I'll add another room for you to monitor."

Not going to happen.

Riley listened to the prep work in the kitchen. *They are doing what needs to be done without any chatter.*

When she turned her dial to the large meeting room, Nora asked, "Is there something I can do for you, Ava?"

"Not at all; everything's been perfect. Is it okay if I help myself to a cup of coffee? I need a little jump starter in the mornings. It's my one indulgence." Ava chuckled.

"I'll pour it for you. We have cream, creamer, sugar, and artificial sweeter."

"Aren't you sweet? You've thought of everything. How long have you been here, Nora?"

"My husband and I bought this house thirty years ago."

"You must know everyone, then." Ava's voice turned somber. "One of my very dear, longtime friends lived near here her entire life. She was married to a farmer, but she was tragically murdered earlier this week. Do you happen to know someone named Riley? I heard she saved my sweet friend's husband's life."

"I've heard of her; she's new to the area, but I don't know much more than that. I'm sure the sheriff knows her: he knows everyone," Nora said.

"I don't want to bother the sheriff; it would be such a pleasure to meet her and thank her for saving that man's life."

"I'll ask around; some of my friends might know her," Nora said.

"That would be wonderful; I'd love it if we could invite her here for dinner this evening. I wouldn't want to embarrass her or anything like that, but maybe she has a favorite charity that I could send an honorarium in appreciation for her quick action."

"Are you ready to test the microphones?" Nora asked.

Riley pushed her green button.

Nora continued, "Our audio technician will explain the operation of the handheld microphone and the one on the table."

"I don't think that's necessary; I'd hate to bother him." Ava continued, "Test, test. I wonder if these microphones work. Have you used this particular audio technician before? Did he come with good references? Maybe the volume is set too low."

Shelby rushed out of the door that led to the hallway.

"I think you have to…here's Shelby."

"All of the microphones work the same…" Shelby began.

Riley turned the dial to listen to the larger meeting room then the kitchen; she gave the dial a turn to the hallway and heard men's voices. *I recognize Jim's voice; I'm not sure who the other man is.*

"What are you doing here, Jim?" a man asked. "What were you doing upstairs? You better not have been in Ava's room."

"Where is she, Orson? I have a report for her to pass on to Chief."

"You can tell me," Orson said.

"Naw, I'm in no hurry," Jim said.

"What the matter? You don't trust me or something?" Orson growled.

"I'll be back to talk to her before the clients show up. You could tell her that, if you don't forget." *I can hear that sneer, Jim.*

Jim's shoes creaked as he strode to the door. After the front door closed, Orson hissed, "You'll be sorry you walked out on me like that, Jim."

Riley switched her dial to the kitchen.

"This platter is ready for the large meeting room. I'll carry it if you'll bring the fruit, Diane," Don said.

"I'll come back for the plates and napkins while you set up," Diane said.

Riley switched back to the hall as the two assistants left the kitchen. *This is fun.*

"Is that platter for the large meeting room?" Orson asked. "I'll take it."

"Thank you, sir, but we have additional set up to do too. I appreciate the offer," Don said.

"Ingrate," Orson mumbled as he headed toward the stairs.

I hope I'm not about to make a horrible mistake. Riley hurried to the door and peered at the large man who had reached the stairs then lumbered up them. *If that's a toupee, it's definitely expensive because it looks real to me; he is overweight.*

She quietly closed the door and returned to put on her headset to listen to the meeting room.

"Thank you, Shelby," Ava said. "I'm just all thumbs when it comes to all this technical stuff you young people understand."

Shelby snorted.

"Bless you," Ava said.

"You're all set, and a very quick student," Shelby said.

When Shelby hurried into the small dining room, she asked, "Did you happen to catch what Ava said? I thought I'd gag."

Nora came into the dining room before Shelby could lock the door. "Lordy, what a two-faced liar; now I know to watch my back."

"We'll keep our ears open too." Shelby locked the door.

Nora smirked. "Good thing I didn't know that Riley person because I don't believe anything Mrs. Fleet has to say."

Riley switched her dial to the hall as Nora left through the kitchen door.

The front door creaked as it opened, and the latch clicked when it was closed.

"Ava?" Jim called out.

"I'm in the meeting room."

Riley changed her dial to the meeting room.

"Job's done; do you have anything else?" Jim asked.

"Did you take care of it personally? Those last two bumbling fools were a joke."

"Orson recommended them; yes, I took care of it myself and waited to be sure you would have your desired effect."

"In that case, I'm sure it will be fine. Thanks for putting in the extra time and effort. Take off the rest of the weekend and go fishing," Ava said.

Jim laughed. "Fire and water? That was funny, Ava. You have the greatest sense of humor. Thank you for the work; you know how to reach me if there's anything else I can do for you."

After Jim left, Ava tapped on her phone to make a call. "Chief? We're a go."

She paused for a few minutes. "Yes, Jim apologized for his lapse in judgement with those two and assured me it was a good burn."

She swore quietly under her breath. "I agree; we can't afford mistakes, but maybe he can take care of our problem. I'm certain she's undercover too because there's no way an uneducated dog groomer would piece together any of this."

Ava's next breath was a sharp intake. "Orson? Of course, he could handle it. We finish up our assignment here late Sunday night. I'll let him know right away; he'll be excited."

After she disconnected, Ava mumbled as she headed toward the meeting room, "Time for me to take over, Chief."

When Ava reached the meeting room, Riley switched her dial. "Jim? We're moving up sooner than we planned; I have an assignment for you after all."

After Ava hung up, she hurried to the front door.

Riley's phone buzzed a text from Ralph. "Call when you have a few minutes."

"My landlord wants to talk to me. Is there somewhere I could talk to him?" Riley asked.

"How about in my old truck?" Nora asked. "It's parked behind the B&B in a shed, so no one will see you. If you wear your coat, you won't have to turn on the engine, which wouldn't do you any good because it takes over thirty minutes for the heater to kick in with actual heat."

Riley giggled. "Sounds perfect; I know I won't be long."

Nora handed the truck key to Riley; after she put on her coat, Riley headed toward the kitchen door then stopped. "Are you coming, Toby?"

Toby closed his eyes.

"Smart boy, Toby; no sense in both of you freezing," Shelby said.

Riley nodded then hurried through the empty kitchen to the mud room and out the back door. Her teeth were chattering by the time she unlocked the truck and hopped in.

Ralph answered immediately. "The investor is anxious to see the house. What's your schedule like today and tomorrow?"

"I'm working today and tomorrow. Ben might be available sometime tomorrow afternoon; I can let you know."

"That sounds good; my investor told me he'd heard a lot about you and was looking forward to meeting you, but he could see the house if Ben's home and you aren't. You and Doc are putting in long hours these days, aren't you?"

Riley's eyes narrowed. *Is Ralph supposed to find out where I am? Am I being overly suspicious?* "We sure are. I'm certain it will be just this weekend. Maybe we can come up with something that will work with your investor. What was his name again? I've forgotten."

"I have trouble with names myself." Ralph chuckled. "It's Porter Lewis."

"That's right; I'll talk to Ben this evening to see when he thinks would work for him."

"There's an idea; could we come by this evening sometime?"

"We have a prior engagement and won't be home; I'm sorry," Riley said.

"It was just a thought," Ralph said. "I didn't mean to take up so much of your time, so let me know about tomorrow when you can. Has the house been warm enough for you in this cold weather?"

"We've been fine; we love the fireplace; it takes off the chill."

"That's all that counts, isn't it?" Ralph said. "I'll talk to you later. Thanks for calling back so quickly."

Riley locked Nora's truck then rushed back inside. She sighed with relief when the kitchen was still empty then hurried to the dining room.

Shelby glanced at her and motioned toward Riley's chair. Riley put on her headset and listened to Ava, who was speaking in the meeting room.

"Welcome everyone, and a warm thank you for coming, particularly in this cold weather. I'd like to thank Nora, too, for her kind hospitality and allowing us to meet in her beautiful, comfortable establishment." Ava was interrupted by applause.

Riley rolled her eyes. *I can just imagine how self-satisfied Ava must be with orchestrating her audience.*

"I might also point out that Chef has provided us with coffee and a little something to nibble on while his helpers prepare a warm, hearty breakfast for us. If you care for more coffee or another pastry, please help yourself. We don't stand on ceremony here," Ava said. "Orson will…"

Orson interrupted. "I'm handing out your contracts to sign."

Ava cleared her throat then added, "A mere technicality, so we won't take any more of your valuable time than necessary before we enjoy our celebration breakfast. Bring them with you to our private meetings, so we can answer all your questions and go over your personal schedule that will give you the details of when to expect your money."

"They're going straight for the throat, aren't they?" Shelby asked. "I don't like this at all: sign first, then we'll skip any details and tell you what we want you to hear."

"It certainly was blatant and doesn't seem ethical at all; how could it possibly even be legally binding?"

Shelby growled, "I'm tired of their nonsense; let's pull the plug. Give me four minutes then call nine-one-one and report a fire here. As soon as the fire alarm goes off, flip all the breakers except the kitchen in the mudroom electrical box to the off position."

Shelby grabbed her backpack then stopped at the door to the hall. "Pack up all of my equipment and take everything out the back door. We want to be out of here before the fire department arrives."

Riley carefully packed equipment into two boxes in the allotted four minutes then called the emergency number and reported the fire while she packed the remaining equipment in a third box. She quickly carried the boxes through the kitchen to the mudroom then carried two of the boxes out to the UTV before the harsh claxon of a fire alarm filled the B&B.

Shelby spoke over a loudspeaker in a mechanical-sounding monotone. "We have a fire. This is not a drill. Please exit the building quickly and safely. Active Fire. Exit safely and quickly."

Riley flipped all the circuits on the board, except the one marked kitchen, to their off positions; she listened until the heater blower stopped then put on her coat and knit cap over her headscarf and carried the third box outside.

When Shelby came out of the back door with a medium sized box, she asked, "Where did you put the boxes?"

"In the UTV; do you want to take everything to my car at the barn?"

"I like how you think, stable girl; let's go."

Toby raced in front of the UTV as Riley sped along the path to the barn.

On the way, Riley asked, "What about a fire?"

"I had exchanged the electrical cord on a lamp for a frayed one in one of the smaller meeting rooms when I set up the microphones, just in case we needed to disrupt the meeting. It seemed like the right time to break up Mrs. Fleet's scheme, so I went to the room and turned on the lamp; it immediately sparked, melted the cord, and gave off a nice burned plastic and electrical-type fire odor in the room. I set off a small smoke bomb then carried it back with me, so there's a little light smoke in the hallway too."

Riley side-glanced Shelby. "All that stuff can't be part of your audio tech tools."

Shelby shrugged. "It has been for quite a while; my brother has a novelty and party shop and gives me samples. I have all kinds of stuff just waiting for the right opportunity. Brothers are handy to have when they aren't being annoying."

"I never had a brother; I'm not sure if I feel left out or grateful," Riley said.

Riley parked the UTV close to her car; after she and Shelby moved the boxes to her trunk, her phone buzzed a text from Ben.

"Are you okay? Did you start the fire?"

"I have an annoying husband, does that count?" Riley showed her text to Shelby.

Shelby laughed. "That's the kind of man I need to find. Does he have a brother?"

Riley texted Ben, and Shelby leaned over her shoulder and watched. "Do you have any single classmates interested in a supercool, nerdy techie? She might be my clone."

Riley's phone rang, and Riley put it on speakerphone as she answered. "What on earth are you talking about?" Ben asked.

"I didn't start the fire, and I'm okay. The audio tech here today was at the Methodist church. We're a lot alike."

"Are you sure you didn't start the fire? Invite her to go to the barbecue with us. If she's like you, she'll have her pick of single, upright, law enforcement officers that will have no clue what she's talking about. Love you, pretty pyro girl. Call me if you need bail money."

Ben chuckled as he hung up.

"He's been annoying lately, but he makes me laugh," Riley said.

"We need to head back to the B&B as soon as we put the boxes in your car; was he serious about inviting me to a barbeque?"

While they loaded the boxes, Riley said, "Of course. We're supposed to be there at five, so you can come to our house a little after four, or we could meet you somewhere."

"This is crazy and sounds like fun."

"Give me one minute to talk to the horses, then we can go back to the B&B."

Riley hurried to the fence where Dakota and Fire waited. Dakota whinnied and shook her head.

"Sorry the sirens bothered you, but everything's okay." Riley stroked both horses and hummed a tune, and they relaxed. "I'll be back later this morning."

Riley climbed into the UTV where Shelby waited for her.

Toby trotted toward the path to the B&B then raced ahead as Riley and Shelby followed him in the UTV.

"You talked to the horses like you understood what the Paint horse said, and you acted like they understood you."

"They do," Riley said.

"I don't see how that's possible; is that what all veterinarians do, and I never realized it?" Shelby asked.

"I don't know anyone else who understands quite as well as I do, except my grandma."

"Do you think it's something you learned when you were young?"

"Did you have a cat, dog, or guinea pig when you were a kid?"

Shelby furrowed her brow. "No, but my neighbor had a chicken. When I told Mama what Chicken said, she told me I was pretending and had a wonderful imagination; now I wonder if I'm skeptical because Mama was."

When they reached the B&B, Nora hurried to the UTV. "Did you get your equipment out, Shelby? We have a crowd of people standing in the front yard; thank goodness most of them grabbed coats on their way out. Ava and Orson didn't, so they're huddled in Ava's car with the heater running full blast."

"We grabbed as much of the more expensive equipment as we could and took it to Riley's car at the barn; I didn't want to put it in my van in case the fire became too hot. Did the fire department put out the fire?" Shelby asked.

"I asked the fire captain for a status earlier, and he told me they pulled a line but hadn't charged it, which I did not understand at all. After he went back to his vehicle, one of the farmers' wives who had been standing close to me told me that meant they took a fire hose into the B&B but hadn't filled it with water. I'm actually glad the fire crew planned to investigate rather than flood the B&B before they found the fire. He told me just a few minutes ago that his fire crew was still investigating, and he was grateful that several people called the fire department on their way out of the B&B, so they could get here before the fire could spread."

"That is good news," Shelby said. "The equipment that we weren't able to take with us would have been ruined by water."

"I'm going to stick close to the captain's car to be a reminder for him to keep me posted," Nora said.

Riley, Toby, and Shelby followed Nora to the front of the building.

While Riley and Shelby stood near the crowd, a nearby man said, "I told the fire crew to check the small meeting room. When the fire alarm went off, I smelled an electrical fire and followed my nose to the small meeting room. I saw an electrical cord sparking and it melted a spot in the rug. It was awfully close to those frilly curtains, so I stomped it out. My wife found me and dragged me out here; I'm glad she brought my coat."

"Can you imagine being out here without a coat?" another man asked.

"I don't know why Ava and Orson didn't grab their coats like everybody else did," the first man said.

"City folks; they must never go outside, but you would have thought they would have figured out it was a smart thing to do," the second man said.

"I'm starting to get this feeling they think they're smarter than the rest of us. I have yet to hear them say anything that wouldn't be on a TV commercial or a newsfeed ad."

People around the two men nodded their heads and murmured assent.

Shelby elbowed Riley, and they nodded along with everyone else.

"The fire engine didn't block me in, so I'm grabbing the missus; I've got work to do before I call my banker on Monday," a man said.

As the farmers and their wives headed toward the parked farm trucks, Orson climbed out of his car and called out, "Wait, we haven't had a chance to go into your details yet."

A few farmers glanced back at Orson but kept walking.

"Now what, Ava?" Orson growled as he held onto the frame of the car and lowered himself into the passenger's seat of Ava's car. "This was your bright idea."

"Shut up, you fool," she shouted as he slammed the car door.

"Family argument; let's check our status with Nora," Shelby said.

When they joined Nora as she stood close to the captain's car, Nora asked, "How quickly can you get us back into operation? I think I can wrangle permission for you two to go inside and set up. We should be back in business long before the next appointments, but Ava will need to call all of them to let them know their appointments have not been canceled."

"After we return from the barn with my critical equipment and carry it inside, we can be operational in less than twenty minutes," Shelby said.

"Go ahead; I'll lean on the captain then see if I can motivate Ava to pull herself together and get busy. I've already talked to Don and Diane, and they are game."

"We're on it." Shelby glanced at Toby. "Are you going?"

Toby sat behind Nora.

"Did Toby really answer me, or was it a coincidence that he stared at me then tried to hide?" Shelby asked as Riley headed the UTV toward the barn.

Riley side-glanced her. *What would the chicken say?* Riley cleared her throat. "What do you think?"

Shelby laughed. "Were you about to tell me to ask Chicken?"

"We're at the barn," Riley said.

"I was right, wasn't I? Let's get busy."

Fire snorted and stomped her feet as Riley and Shelby loaded the boxes onto the UTV.

"It's been a long morning for me too; see you soon." Riley locked her car then joined Shelby in the UTV.

On the way back, Shelby said, "I've figured it out; I read Toby's body language, but how did you get that the brown horse was complaining about a long morning? Don't tell me he told you."

"She: Fire is a mare, and what did you think she said?"

"Seeing as how I didn't even notice the horse was a female, I thought a bug was bothering her."

Riley parked, then she and Shelby rushed to carry the boxes into the mudroom. Shelby stayed with her equipment while Riley searched for Nora. When she passed the Fleet cars, Ava and Orson were on their phones, smiling and gesturing. *They're back in their element.*

"There you are," Nora said. "If you go into the house through the mudroom, you can set up, but the captain told me we won't be able to use the room where the lamp failed. Unfortunately, I still have to tell Ava. She doesn't seem to be very flexible or have any ability at all to roll with the punches, does she?"

"I'll let Shelby know, and you have my sympathies." Riley hurried to the back door, and Toby followed her.

CHAPTER FIFTEEN

When Riley went into the mudroom, she wasn't surprised that all the boxes and Shelby were gone. She and Toby hurried through the kitchen and into the small dining room.

"Good, you're here. I expected to get the okay, so I set up everything," Shelby said. "I assumed we wouldn't be allowed to use that one small meeting room, but other than that I've got everything in place to test. I'll start at the hallway then take a quick trip up the stairs before I continue to the meeting room and end with the small meeting room."

"Up the stairs?"

"I added one at the top of the stairs. I'll show you all the positions on your console, so you can track me. I hope you like poetry."

After Shelby went into the hall, Riley chuckled as she listened to Shelby softly recite, "Mary had a little lamb."

Riley switched channels as she followed Shelby and listened intently when she heard a light creak on the stairs. After Shelby tiptoed back down and past the small dining room, she continued through the hall to the main meeting room. "All the kings horses and all the kings men."

Riley flipped to the channel for the small meeting room. "And that's the way the cookie crumbles."

Shelby rushed into the small dining room and quickly closed and locked the door. "One of these days I'm going to be goofing around at the wrong time; Ava and Orson would have caught me mumbling in the hallway on my way back from the meeting rooms except they stopped to argue at the front door. I got the impression they hadn't been given permission to come inside yet, but Ava wanted to make sure no one had touched anything; she seemed particularly worried about the unsigned contracts. The door to the small meeting room with the shorted lamp was locked though, so she won't be able to check in there. How clear was I?"

"Very poetically clear."

"Good." Shelby sat at her console. "Take the four channels to the right of the meeting room channel that's in the middle on your dial, and I'll take the four on the left. We'll take turns monitoring the large meeting room. You first. When Ava's audience begins arriving, I'll join you."

"Don and Diane came into the kitchen from the back door," Shelby said.

Riley nodded as she listened to Ava and Orson in the meeting room.

"Count them again," Ava hissed.

"I've already told you; they're all here," Orson growled.

"Give them here; I want to count them myself." Ava muttered as she counted. "Thirty-two? There are supposed to be thirty-five. Where are the other three?"

"We only printed thirty-two." Orson carefully enunciated each word.

"Don't speak to me in that condescending…"

Ava was interrupted when the front door opened, then Nora called out, "Ava, are you in here?"

Ava stepped into the hall. "Orson and I are in the meeting room. Are people ready to come inside out of the cold?"

"Everybody left, Ava; you may want to call all of your next group to let them know that the bed and breakfast is still ready for their meeting and their lunch."

"Exactly what I was saying to Orson," Ava said.

"Good; the kitchen staff will wait for a bit if you want to give them a count of how many people will be here for lunch, so your money won't go to waste."

"That's so kind of them; what about our microphones? Will they be ready in time?"

"It wasn't necessary to remove the microphones, so they will be ready when your next group arrives."

"You certainly have found the best possible staff to keep everything running so smoothly."

"I think so," Nora said.

After Nora left the meeting room, Orson asked, "How do you plan to call all those people?"

Ava snorted. "I have to save my voice for the meeting, but I'll help you out and call the first page while you call the rest. You better get busy, Orson."

While Ava and Orson made phone calls, Shelby said, "Remember the locked door to the small meeting room? I slid three of the contracts under the door."

Riley furrowed her brow. "Why three? Why not just one?"

Shelby shrugged. "I thought it might cause a little dissension."

"I could get those three contracts into the right hands," Riley said. "I'm not all that great at picking locks, so I'll ask Nora."

"Meeting room," Shelby said. "Listen."

"I'm not going to sit here and listen to you yammer while I'm making calls," Ava said. "I'm going to my room."

"First time you've had a good idea," Orson sneered.

Orson hurried to the stairs and bounded to his room.

"Good riddance," Ava muttered as she headed to the stairs.

"I'll be right back," Riley said. "Nora's in the kitchen."

When Riley went into the kitchen, Don and Diane were discussing lunch while Nora took notes.

Riley said, "Nora, Shelby wants me to check the equipment in the small meeting room. We're getting some feedback that Shelby didn't expect."

"Of course, will you need a little help?" Nora pointed to the keys dangling from a clip on her jeans belt loop then winked.

"Actually, I will," Riley said.

After they reached the first meeting room, Nora asked, "What shall I do?"

"You go into this meeting room, and I'll go into the other. You talk for thirty seconds, and I'll talk while you are, then I'll join you while you're still talking. I don't understand all the techie pieces, but that's what Shelby said she needs to determine where the feedback is coming from."

"Thirty seconds? Will that give her enough time to capture what she needs?"

"That's what she told me; my uneducated guess is either there is feedback or there isn't, and I have no idea what I'm talking about."

Nora removed the key ring then gave it to Riley as she dangled the ring from one key.

"This one," Nora said.

After Riley unlocked the door, she said, "Okay, Nora."

"Once upon a time," Nora said as Riley quietly closed the door.

Riley folded the papers into quarters and slipped them into her back pocket that was hidden by her long sweater before she left the room and quietly locked it behind her. When she joined Nora in the other meeting room, Riley handed Nora the key ring, and Nora said, "And they lived happily ever after. The End. How was that, do you think?"

Riley touched her ear like she had a tiny earbud in it. "Perfect, thank you."

"Good; I'll go back to the kitchen and see what else I can learn from Don and Diane. They're amazing."

After Riley returned to the small dining room, Shelby asked, "Success?"

Riley put the papers into her backpack. "Yes. Did you notice how much Nora loved being a part of a conspiracy, even though she had no idea what it was?"

Shelby nodded. "I think I'm set here, if you want to go to the barn and take care of Dakota and Fire."

Riley narrowed her eyes. "How did you know her name is Dakota?"

Shelby snorted. "You told me."

Riley raised one eyebrow. "No, I didn't; you asked Nora."

"Four o'clock, right? I have a great audio tech who takes over for me after I set up. He'll be here at one, so I'll have plenty of time to go home and get presentable, and now I'm nervous. What are you wearing?"

"Jeans, my Western boots, and a plaid flannel shirt, but I haven't decided which one," Riley said.

"Oh, good. I think I had a minor panic attack; for a second there, I forgot this is a barbeque, not a prom," Shelby said.

"I'm glad you're going with us," Riley said. "I don't know anyone who will be there, and Ben will know practically everyone, and all of those he doesn't know, he will before we leave. If he can be himself and not have to hover because I'm terrified, I'll be happy."

"I can't imagine you being terrified of anything; I'll be at your house at four," Shelby said.

While Riley put on her coat in the mudroom, Nora hurried in from the hall. "Good, I caught you. Take the UTV because Derek will come here after he's through to help me with a few things around the B&B. I can't tell you how much I appreciate that you were willing to pitch in with something that I'm sure must have been out of your comfort zone."

When Riley and Toby reached the barn, she frowned. "I expected Derek to be here. What time is it?" She pulled out her phone. "Ouch. It's only nine thirty. Why did I think it was almost lunchtime? Let's find Dakota and Fire. I'll leave my tools here; I don't feel like carrying them."

As Riley crossed the field, Toby dashed ahead and zigzagged through the pasture to clear it of small birds. He trotted back to Riley for a face rub then raced to the fence closest to the road and returned with Dakota and Fire following him at a trot.

"That was impressive," Riley said. "I'm glad your hooves are feeling better; are you ready to go back to the barn?"

Dakota snorted.

"No, I'm not going to run back; you three can, and I'll be there when I get there."

Fire whinnied, and Riley rolled her eyes. "No, I'm not a sissy; you're just too fast for me."

The three of them took off for the barn.

When Riley reached the barn, Derek was brushing Fire. "They had a nice run; you did a good job with their hooves yesterday."

"I still have a little more to do, but I'm sure I can finish them in a fairly short time."

"While you're busy, I'd like to go to the feed store. We're lower on feed than I expected. I sure hope those folks decide to buy the equine business from Nora because it's too much for her to handle on top of her B&B."

Riley furrowed her brow. "Won't that put you out of a job?"

"I can always find work. I'm kind of like you right now; this is my second job."

"What's your other job?" she asked.

"Nothing exciting; it's mostly indoors, but it pays the bills. I better get out of here; the feed store sometimes closes early on Saturday." He chuckled. "Their Saturday hours depend on whether the fish are biting."

After Derek left, Riley asked, "Who's first?"

Dakota nudged Riley with her head.

Riley laid out her tools. "I'll start with your back legs."

After she picked out small rocks and cleaned Dakota's hooves, she said, "I need a short break, then it will be your turn, Fire."

Riley pulled out the thermos of sweet tea from her car then sat on the bench in the barn. Her phone buzzed a text from Abigail. "Can we talk?"

Riley immediately called her.

Abigail answered, "Give me one second, sugar; I'll call you right back. Love you too."

Riley stared at her phone. *Did Abigail just pretend she got a call from a boyfriend?*

After Riley returned her thermos to her car, Abigail called.

"I guess that sounded goofy to you, but I didn't want anyone to know I was talking to you. I've had this imaginary boyfriend for a while. He gives everyone something to talk about, so I can go about my business without having to deal with any meddling matchmakers. Are you working?"

"I'm at the barn with the horses, but I'm kind of taking a break," Riley said.

"Good; where's Derek?"

"He went to the feed store. Did you need to talk to him? What's up?"

"I needed to talk to you, but I didn't want you to have to pretend you have a boyfriend; he's such a worrywart. The wingtip guy came into the diner for breakfast and asked for a table that was quiet and away from everyone else. I came this close to telling him we're a diner, not a fancy supper club, but I figured he wanted to have a private conversation, and I wanted to eavesdrop. The Saturday counter crew keeps me hopping, then five or six couples who were supposed to have breakfast at the B&B showed up, so I was super busy. I didn't catch all the details, but I did hear wingtip man tell the man he kept calling Chief that he wasn't convinced Ava and Orson had the right target because they were relying on gossip with no facts to back up any of the stories they'd heard."

"Target for what? Do you know?" Riley asked.

"No, he didn't go into any specifics, at least not that I caught, but he made arrangements to meet Chief here for lunch at one. Do you already have lunch plans? Could you get away that fast?"

"I can try," Riley said.

"Let me know, and wear something to hide that red hair of yours; it's beautiful, and I love it, but it's a neon sign that announces Riley is in the house." Abigail cackled as she hung up.

Why would Derek worry just because Abigail called me? Is that just my suspicious side like the sheriff said?

Toby slumped as he looked at Riley with his sad eyes.

"I really don't think you could go into the restaurant, Toby. We aren't exactly established here like we are in Barton and Carson."

Toby whined, and Dakota and Fire hung their heads then turned their backs to Riley.

"It's a diner; even Chef has to wear a hairnet," Riley said.

Toby yipped then grinned, and Riley snickered. "I don't think they make hairnets for dogs, either, and if they do, I don't want to know; your plan for a quiet afternoon at home, so you can nap before the barbeque sounds like a wonderful idea."

Riley went into the tack room, and her eyes widened. "I planned to clean up saddles and harnesses, but it looks like Derek beat me to it."

Toby went to the barn door and stared at the driveway; Riley listened. "I hear the truck now too."

The four of them met Derek after he parked, and he chuckled as he lowered the tailgate then pulled out a pumpkin. Dakota and Fire followed him as he took it to the nearby pasture. He slammed it on the ground, and it split open.

Dakota whinnied, and Derek said, "You're welcome; enjoy."

When Riley smiled, Derek shrugged. "I've always talked to horses; they're my favorite people."

After Dakota and Fire polished off the pumpkin, Fire came into the barn. While Riley picked out stones and cleaned out Fire's hooves, Derek unloaded the feed into the tack room then scrubbed the water buckets.

When Riley finished, she asked, "Are you having any problems with your teeth?"

When both of the horses nodded, Riley continued, "I'll check them to see if I need to arrange for an appointment for you with Doc."

After she checked their teeth, Derek asked, "What did you find?"

"I think it's been a while since they've had a dental checkup; both of them have tartar buildup and ragged spots that need to be filed down."

Derek nodded. "When I asked for the large bags of senior feed at the store, the clerk told me Nora always buys the feed for pleasure horses."

"They'll be better off with the senior feed you got. I'll ask Doc Halsey if we should recommend a specialist."

"What are your plans for tomorrow?" Derek asked.

"I'm going to check in with Nora before I leave because I've done everything I can for Dakota and Fire; I'm not sure what I could do tomorrow that she couldn't do in a half hour."

"I was thinking the same thing; there's no reason for her to pay me if there isn't anything I can do that will be productive," Derek said.

"I'll give her a list of what to do, so she won't feel like she should be doing more," Riley said.

"Great idea; I think that's why she hasn't been taking care of them: she's been so overwhelmed that she didn't know where to start, just like an old mule that won't budge." Derek chuckled. "Don't tell her I said that."

Riley smiled. "I won't, but it was the perfect description."

"If you'll pull together your list, why don't we talk to her together? I'll text her and ask her to come here, so she won't have any distractions; while we wait, I'll write up a list of recommended food for the horses then you can check it."

After they finished their lists, they exchanged them.

"I think you might want to add recommended treats to your list," Riley said.

"Good catch."

When Nora arrived, she said, "Thanks for giving me an excuse to walk away, Derek. Ava and Orson Fleet are trying my patience more than any other guests I've ever had. While I was in the kitchen,

Orson barged in and demanded fresh coffee and more pastries in the meeting room. Mind you, there is no one there other than Ava and Orson. Diane told him not to get his shorts in a wad, and he told her she'd never cater any of their events again."

"Did she thank him?" I asked.

Nora smiled. "It was beautiful, and I'm so glad I didn't miss it: Diane said, 'Bless your heart, Mr. Fleet; I appreciate it.' Orson's face got so red I thought he was going to have a stroke, then he rushed out of the kitchen."

Riley laughed. "What are you going to do if Don and Diane walk out?"

"I've got it all planned out. Baloney sandwiches, and for dinner, fried baloney sandwiches."

Derek laughed. "Those are my favorites. Can I crash those gourmet meals? Speaking of meals, Riley has a couple of lists to go over with you."

Riley stared at Derek, who smiled at her.

That was slick; now I'm convinced you're law enforcement.

After the three of them talked about each item on both lists, Nora said, "This makes it easy for me. You've broken it down into tasks I can do in less than an hour each day. That's do-able." Nora furrowed her brow then gazed at them. "Does this mean you've done what you can?"

Derek nodded. "We don't see what else we could do for Dakota, Fire, or in the barn. Dakota and Fire shouldn't be ridden for a while at least, to give their hooves a chance to heal."

"I'm going to talk to Doc Ned about their teeth; they might need a dental veterinarian, but that's normal for older horses. You can call his office anytime if you have any questions or need help with anything else," Riley said.

"This is wonderful," Nora said. "Riley, are you still going to help Shelby?"

"If she needs me; she'll let me know if she does."

"I've got your car blocked in, Riley, so I'm clearing out," Derek said.

As Riley, Toby, and Derek left the barn, Derek said, "I'm available anytime you need help; my work is flexible, and you've got my number."

Riley side-glanced him. *He said Hope was a good friend; does he feel guilty about the attack on her?*

On the way home, Riley said, "I can't figure out Derek, Toby. He has that law enforcement aura, but Nora said he knew horses because he worked the rodeo circuit, which makes sense to me because of how quickly he cleaned the barn and the equipment. He must be hiding something, and the sheriff is in on it; do you suppose he is investigating Ava and Orson Fleet undercover? That must be it. I don't think I messed up anything for him because no one has yelled at me for interfering with an investigation yet."

When they reached home, Riley said, "I have time for a quick shower; did you want to go out?"

After Riley opened the back door of her car, Toby bounded around the house to the backyard, and she hurried inside to shower and change.

She called Toby inside when she was ready to leave. "I should be back in an hour or so. Enjoy your nap. I plan to join you before we go to the barbeque."

When she reached the diner, there were more cars than she expected, but it wasn't full. She held her breath as she walked inside. Abigail gave her a nod to motion toward a table near the back. Riley exhaled. *Nobody recognized me.*

Riley sat at the small table for two.

Abigail brought her a menu. "What would you like to drink, Miss?"

"I don't know; something hot," Riley said.

"You got it; I'll be back with your hot chocolate and will take your order when you're ready; no hurry."

Riley furrowed her brow as she pretended to study the menu.

When Abigail served her hot chocolate, Riley said, "I'd like the grilled ham and cheese sandwich with fries."

"Cheddar, Swiss or pepperjack cheese; whole wheat, rye, or white bread?" Abigail asked.

"Can I have Swiss and pepperjack on rye?" Riley raised her eyebrows as she glanced at Abigail.

"You got it."

When Jim, aka wingtip man, came into the diner, he spoke quietly to Abigail, and she led him through the diner toward Riley.

Riley glanced out the window and watched Jim's reflection as he followed Abigail to his table that appeared to be isolated from any others; he didn't even glance at her as he passed by. Riley's table was around the corner and out of sight but within easy listening distance.

"What would you like to drink?" she asked.

"Coffee with cream and sugar. I'm expecting someone," Jim said.

"I'll bring you two menus and your coffee while you wait."

Two couples came in together; Riley recognized them from the meetings at the churches. Abigail motioned toward a large table on the other side of the diner, and Riley exhaled. *I need to relax; no one will recognize me.*

Abigail carried a coffee pot, cup, and the menus to the man's table. "Cream and sugar are on the table."

When the sheriff came into the diner, Riley's heart stopped. He glanced around the diner then sat at the counter.

She looked at the clock over the cash register. *One o'clock exactly.*

A slim man in his forties came into the diner and glanced around.

"Were you meeting someone?" Abigail asked.

The man nodded. "Man with a scar on his face."

"Right back here; follow me."

Abigail led the man to Jim's table.

"Coffee for me too," the man said.

The two men were silent until after Abigail poured their coffee, took their order, and left.

"So, how's it going?" the man asked.

"A little rough; she's a little slow getting things moving, and he's making mistakes. They definitely don't want any help; I offered."

"That's too bad; you have more experience than both of them put together. You mentioned their target earlier; what other mistakes are they making?"

I wouldn't trust that guy if I were you, Jim. Sounds like he's buttering you up.

Abigail brought Riley her lunch and a glass of water then hurried to the cash register where a customer waited.

"Their biggest mistake is that they are focused on the wrong target. Ava's too steeped in the local gossip and is obsessed with the redhead; she is relying on what she calls her 'gut' instead of looking at the hard facts. She's headed straight toward failure of the entire project." Jim's voice rose in anger.

Why is Ava obsessed with me?

The man cleared his throat then spoke softly. "What is it she's missing?"

Jim lowered his voice. "There's nothing to support that the redhead knows anything; just because she stumbled across the man on the farm, and according to the locals saved his life, doesn't mean she knows anything about the operation. What's being totally overlooked is the technical side. The one person who is always in the background and listening."

The hair on the back of Riley's neck rose, and a chill ran down Riley's spine. *He's talking about Shelby.*

Abigail delivered the men's food and refilled their coffee.

After she left, the man asked, "What about him? What's he missing?"

Jim snorted. "He's all caught up in being a bigshot; he's throwing his weight around and drawing the wrong kind of attention to himself."

"What's your proposal?"

"I'll stop the target for you and save the operation from failing," Jim said.

"I need for you to work closely with Ava and Orson and keep me informed; they have to be successful and it's up to you to make sure they stay focused on their assignment, especially Orson. I want to pull the plug at the right time, and I'm relying on you."

Riley twirled a french fry in the small pool of catsup. *Jim doesn't like that idea, but he's afraid to say anything.*

"Is that a problem?" the man asked.

"He's a bullheaded blowhard; we didn't part friendly-like. I'll have to mend some fences; I can do it, but it will take a while."

"Why don't I take care of that part for you? What else can I do to help you?"

"I can handle it from there; thanks, Chief."

"You don't have to wait for me; I'll pay the bill on the way out," Chief said.

After Jim left, Chief spoke quietly.

He's on his phone.

"You were right. He's outlived his usefulness and has gone on a tangent. Do what you need to do."

After Chief paid the bill and left, the sheriff rose from his counter seat and spoke softly to Abigail then paid his bill and left.

When Abigail came to Riley's table, she asked, "Care for anything else? We have fresh blueberry cobbler, Miss."

"I don't think I can eat another bite; I'll take my bill."

Abigail whispered, "I don't know how, but the sheriff recognized you and bought your lunch. Do you think we're in trouble?"

Riley exhaled. "Probably."

"I have bail money set aside; just call me when you need me."

Abigail's serious. "We'll be okay; at least he didn't bust me when he came in."

"That's true; I wonder why not." Abigail furrowed her brow. "I don't know what's going on with wingtip man, but I don't trust him."

When Riley stepped outside, the sheriff waited for her next to her car.

"So what did you hear, anonymous young woman?" the sheriff asked.

"How did you recognize me?"

"I'm a master detective, but besides that, I recognized your car and was curious. You had to be up to something to come here for lunch by yourself; I'll bet Abigail is in on it too."

"I'll tell you what I heard if you'll forget about Abigail."

"What if I don't agree?"

"I could burst into tears."

Sheriff laughed. "It would almost be worth it to see how you pull that off. Fine, Abigail is off the table."

"I recognized one guy, Jim: he wears wingtip shoes and works for Ava. I don't know who the other man is, but it sounded like Jim wanted to quit because he and Orson had a falling out. The other man told him he'd smooth things out with Orson because Jim has more experience than Ava, and she needs his help."

"What was your impression of the whole conversation?" Sheriff asked.

"I think the other man was either Ava's and Jim's boss or someone high in their organization, and he was here to keep the weekend from derailing from an internal power struggle between Jim and Orson."

"That's interesting."

"What do you think?" Riley asked.

"You glossed over a few details, but I think you gave me the meat of the conversation."

Riley rolled her eyes as she climbed into her car and headed toward home. *He didn't answer my question.*

After Riley went inside, she removed her knit cap and scarf then loosened her braid. "What do you think, Toby? Should I leave the braid in?"

Toby grinned then trotted to the back door, and Riley let him out. She picked up the book she'd been reading then stretched out on the couch.

Her phone startled her when it rang. She sat up in a groggy haze then fumbled for her phone on the table that was next to her.

"Hey, cousin has plate of huge chicken. Wanted to go to party for two weeks but can't. Apologize to Derek."

"Wha…"

Shelby coughed and hung up.

Riley furrowed her brow as she walked slowly to the back door and opened it. Toby lay on the porch in the sun; he raised his head and stared at Riley.

"Do you want to come in or are you enjoying the sun?"

Toby closed his eyes, lay down his head, and was soon softly snoring.

"Sunbeam wins." Riley went inside and poured herself a glass of iced tea then took a big gulp.

Shelby said to give Derek her apologies. She wouldn't have confused Ben and Derek's names.

Riley called Derek, and he answered on the second ring. "What's wrong, Riley?"

"Shelby was supposed to go to a barbeque with Ben and me this evening. She just called me and told me she couldn't go to the party; she wouldn't have called a barbeque a party, but more than that, she said to give Derek her apologies and hung up before I could say anything or point out her mistake."

"Got it. Anything else?"

"She said her cousin showed up with a big plate of chicken, and she'd been looking forward to the party for two weeks, but I just told her about it today, so that didn't make any sense."

"You're sure she said two weeks? Never mind, of course you are. Thanks." Derek hung up.

He didn't give me a chance to tell him about the papers. Oh no, Pamela Suzanne's papers! I forgot all about them.

Riley hurried out to her car and removed the packet from under her driver's seat. She put them into her backpack when she returned to the house. *We'll probably have time for me to give these to Ben when he gets home, but if not, I can tell him about them on our way to the barbeque.*

CHAPTER SIXTEEN

SHELBY

While Shelby listened to the private meetings, she sent photos of the clients from the security cameras in the meeting rooms to a shared cloud for her team to catalog then forward for identification. To keep herself entertained, she compared the amount of time it took for Ava and Orson to close each one of their deals.

Shelby tapped her pen while she reviewed the numbers. *Ava's much faster because she's so slick; Orson has closed all of his too, but he's slow because he likes to talk about himself. I think people sign just to get away from him.*

After Diane and Don set up the lunch buffet in the large meeting room, and everyone was eating, Ava and Orson went into the small meeting room and closed the door.

Shelby turned up the volume slightly because Ava whispered.

"I got a call from Chief; he asked me how you and Jim were getting along because he heard one of our clients tell the cashier in the grocery store that there was definitely tension between you two. I told him you and Jim were old friends, and maybe not everyone understood the bantering was all in fun. Chief reminded me that we want our clients to talk in the grocery store about how great our program is not about how much you and Jim argue; you need to settle down and make a show of what good friends you and Jim are. You are not taking me down because you can't control your temper, ego, or whatever your problem is. Where is Jim?"

"He had something else to do; I got a text from him," Orson said. "He offered to help us tomorrow. I didn't answer."

"Make sure he's here, and get him here today if you can; you two need to act like the old buddies I've said you are. Let me know if Jim balks."

Orson raised his voice. "Nobody was around when we had our little discussion before Jim left."

"You don't know that; somebody could have been in the restroom for all you know, and if you're going to argue about it, you might as well just steal a boat because you'll end up wet."

"Is that a threat?" Orson growled.

Ava whispered, "No, it's a fact, and you have to dump that attitude fast and realize you're in the spotlight all the time. Everyone is watching you, including Chief."

Ava closed the door as she left. Orson exhaled. "Okay, boss. I'll text Jim and be nice."

I'd bet against you, Orson; I don't think you can pull it off.

"Be nice or die, is the way I heard it, chump. Pocket full of posies, we all fall down," Shelby muttered. *I love those morbid nursery rhymes from the times of the Black Plague; probably says something about my attitude, doesn't it, Orson?*

When Nick came into the small dining room, Shelby smirked. *He'll always have that fresh-faced look of a nerdy high school student.*

"What do we have, Shelby?"

"Orson and Jim clashed, and someone overheard them. The best news from their banty rooster fight is that we were right: there is someone higher up that is calling the shots. Ava told Orson to settle down because Chief heard about the argument in the grocery store. Besides that, I've sent the photos of the people who have attended the private meetings and a list of those who signed up. It shouldn't be hard for the fraud team to intervene."

"Doesn't sound like I'll be bored with all the fringes of drama. What are your plans this evening?"

"I'm sticking close to Riley. She invited me to go with her and Ben to a barbeque hosted by one of Ben's instructors. I can't tell you why I thought it was important for me to be there because you'd think she'd be perfectly fine with all those upright guys and gals around, but my radar tingled, so I'm going."

"A barbeque? Dang, I'll get myself a fill-in and go as your back up."

"Wonder how many there will think we're criminals. You always remind me of a serial killer."

Nick bowed before he sat in front of the console. "Thank you kindly for that compliment."

"I have some papers that need to be shredded." Shelby pointed to a folder on the desk. "Can you take care of that?"

"Consider it done."

Don stopped Shelby before she reached the mudroom. "Take a sandwich with you, Shelby."

"Thanks, but I brought my lunch and already ate earlier."

"Don't bring your lunch tomorrow," he said.

Shelby grinned and saluted him.

While she put on her coat, Diane handed her a sack. "One for the road."

Shelby groaned at the cold wind and rain when she went outside; she flipped up her hood and put down her head as she hurried to her car. *One for the road.* She chuckled. *Do I have to field test myself before I can drive home?*

Something slammed down on her head.

* * *

Shelby gritted her teeth when she woke to intense pain in her head. She opened one eye. *Dang it, I let the weather distract me from paying attention to my surroundings. Rookie mistake. I'm in a broken-down shed.*

She was on her left side with her arms behind her and her legs crossed at her ankles. *I'm bound at the wrists and ankles.* When she tried to roll to sit up, she bit her lip from the pain in her head.

Shelby realized men were speaking outside of the shed. She took slow, quiet breaths.

"Why'd ya have to hit her so hard?" a man asked in a deep southern drawl.

The second man snorted. "You want I shoulda just gave her a little tap and asked her to pretty please come with us?"

"No. What do we do now, Gus? Just wait for Jim to show up?"

"He said he'd call with instructions as soon as he could get a minute alone," Gus said.

"I thought he was going to meet us here."

"So did I, but he said Chief had other instructions; I don't know who Chief is, so don't ask me, Ike," Gus said.

"Should we see if she's breathing?"

"I guess; Jim said he had to talk to her before he decided what we'd do."

Shelby blinked at the abrupt change of light when the door flew open.

"Get her up; let's go into the old cabin. I don't want to stand out here in the cold with rain running down my collar until Jim decides to show up," Gus said.

When a large man with rough hands and scraped knuckles jerked her off the ground, she heaved. He quickly held her away from his body, and the other man gagged.

"Cruds, Ike. You almost got me," Gus said.

Ike headed toward the cabin as he continued to hold her off to the side with her head down. "I've tossed out more drunks into alleys than you can count. I ain't never been got by any puke yet."

The angle of her head made her headache rage even worse than before, but the dreadful bile in her throat drained out.

Ike dumped Shelby onto her side on the floor. "It's cold in here; want I should start a fire?"

Shelby blinked as she tried to focus, but the room was a fuzzy blur.

"And announce where we are to the world? I don't think so."

"Did you hear them ostriches squawk?" Ike asked. "At least they don't screech like peacocks."

Gus snorted. "I'm not that well-acquainted with bird calls."

"Birds are fascinating, Gus. Their ancestors were dinosaurs."

Shelby couldn't stifle a cough.

"You ain't going to puke again, are you, girl?" Ike lifted her with one hand and sat her up with her back propped against the rough-hewn bare boards of an outer wall.

Shelby squinted to see Ike, but everything was still a blur; she shook her head slowly and carefully.

"I think she understood what you said," Gus said.

They aren't being careful with names. They don't expect me to be alive very long.

"Hey, you. Is there anybody who would report you missing anytime soon?" Gus asked.

"Good question, Gus; you've always been a smart guy," Ike said.

Thanks for the opportunity, guys.

Shelby cleared her throat as well as she could. "What time is it?"

"A little after three; what does that matter?" Ike asked.

"I'm supposed to be at a girlfriend's house, so we could go to a party together."

Ike grabbed Gus's arm and whispered in a loud voice, "What do we do, Gus?"

"Where's your phone, girl? You need to call her and tell her plans changed," Gus said.

"Back pocket." *I hope it didn't fall out.*

Ike jerked her aside, and Shelby pursed her lips to keep from moaning.

"Got it," he said. "Dang, girl. Your hands are blue and cold as a witch's…"

The zip tie must have cut off the circulation in my hands. Shelby wheezed and coughed repeatedly.

While she caught her breath, Ike handed the phone to Gus. "She's in bad shape, Gus."

"How do you unlock this phone, girl?" Gus asked.

"Seven-seven-eight-eight," Shelby said.

Gus asked, "What's her number, and we'll dial it. Oh wait, tell me her name: she must be in your contact list." He frowned. "Can't find the contact list."

Shelby gritted her teeth. *Must stay focused.* "Speed dial. Hold down two."

"Hunh. I never heard of nothin' like that before," Ike said. "What does tapping on one do?"

"Mother." Shelby coughed then controlled herself by breathing slowly and forcing herself to relax.

Gus handed the phone to Ike, who was closer to Shelby. "Phone's ringing; you hold it."

When Riley answered, Shelby fought to find the words and to speak as clearly as she could. "Hey, cousin has plate of huge chicken. Wanted to go to party for two weeks but can't. Apologize to Derek."

Ike hung up.

"That was good; you musta graduated from high school." Ike dropped her phone onto a table somewhere across the room from her.

Shelby stared to see her phone through the fuzzy blur. *Might as well be on the moon. I'd never have a chance to grab it with them around anyway.*

When his phone rang, Gus went outside, but Shelby listened.

"Okay. Does one of us have to stay?"

"Just making sure."

Gus was silent for several minutes before he said, "Cabin's pretty cold, and she don't look so good."

"Yeah, I smell woodsmoke," Gus said.

He was silent again then said, "We can do that, boss."

When Gus came inside, he said, "It's still raining, and it's getting colder. Jim said we can start a fire in the woodstove because if everybody else around us has a fire going, we won't be noticeable at all. He said we could get us some dinner if we wanted to, and maybe we should get some blankets or something because he doesn't expect to be able to get here until late tonight."

"We just leave her here while we get dinner? Is that what he said?" Ike asked.

Gus shrugged. "He told me she couldn't go anywhere and even if she could there's nothing close to us at all except for your squawking ostriches, and he said they are dangerous killers like alligators. He said that farm is huge, and he's not even sure where the farmhouse is, but it's not close at all."

I'm close to the ostrich farm. I still don't know where I am, but I'll bet Riley would.

A wave of nausea washed over Shelby. *And the cow jumped over the moon.* Shelby slumped over into the dark that came from the crippling pain in her head.

A rough hand shook her shoulder; Ike shouted, "Hey, girl. You can't fall out like that. You gotta stay awake, so Jim can talk to you."

He's right; I need to know what Jim wants from me.

"Why does Jim want to talk to me?" she asked.

Gus snorted. "Like I would know; I'm going to see if the wood in that shed is dry enough to burn. One thing I do know is setting fires."

After Gus left, Ike said in a quiet voice, "People think I'm a big dumb guy, so they talk around me all the time; Jim thinks someone in his organization is undercover, and he's positive you know who it is."

"Are you undercover?" she asked.

Ike chuckled. "I ain't never been accused of being undercover. I'm a security guard at strip joints when I can find work, like what they used to call a bouncer. Security guard is a fancy title, but the pay was better when I was called a bouncer because I could empty wallets and nobody complained."

Gus brought in firewood. After he split a piece of wood into kindling, he started a fire in the woodstove. "Why don't you go get us something to eat, and I'll stay here and take care of the fire."

He split firewood; that means he has a hatchet.

"I don't have no money for food or blankets. You going to give me some cash or your credit card?" Ike asked.

Gus grunted. "Guess we'll both go then, like Jim said. I've got a list of stuff we need to buy, and I've got Jim's credit card."

How about if I go and the two of you stay here? Shelby leaned back to rest then straightened up. *Ike's right; I need to stay awake.*

"I could stay and keep the fire going," Ike said. "She needs to be warm."

Gus headed toward the door. "She'll be cold later anyway, what does it matter? Let's go."

Ike shook his head as he followed Gus out.

Shelby listened as their car drove away. *I think I can get my hands free if I can get them in front of me.*

She bent forward and was almost overcome by the pain and accompanying wave of nausea that swept over her.

She took deep breaths until the pain subsided then shifted her weight and pushed with her knuckles as she grunted and slid her hands under her bottom until they were under her legs. Sweat from the exertion rolled down her forehead. *That was the easy part; here's where I channel my inner gymnast.*

She brought her knees as close to her chest as she could and quickly rolled onto her back and grabbed onto her shoe soles at the heels. When the explosion of pain in her head blinded her, she pulled her knees closer to her chin and inched her hands past her heels. She pointed her toes toward her chin and pushed her hands past her feet before she rolled to her side and vomited. *I am not in good shape.*

She wiped her face against her shoulder then brought her wrists close to her face and found the end of the tie. *Good; the lock is facing me. I can do this.* She raised her arms overhead then forcefully brought them down past her chest as she pulled back her elbows and shoulders and slammed her wrists against her body; the zip tie snapped open.

Feet are next. She slowly lowered herself and sat on the floor; after she slipped her feet out of her boots, she pulled her boots out of the zip ties then put on her boots. *I should have done that first, so I could run if I had to; I guess my brain's in a blurry fog too.*

She staggered to where Ike had placed her phone. *This is a counter, not a table.* She peered at the wavering counter then saw her phone; when she reached for it, it wasn't there.

My perception's off. She carefully felt where her phone might be then found it and stuck it into her back pocket.

Shelby reeled as she headed toward the door. She reached to open it, but when she bumped against something, it clattered to the floor. She kept her head straight as she carefully bent down to pick it up. *Bonus! I found a broom. Only fair, right, Ike? I'll ride out of here on my broom.*

When she stepped outside into the cold, the rain had turned to a drizzle, and in the distance, an ostrich squawked.

Everyone needs a friend. "Let's get away from the cabin, Chicken, then we can call Riley."

After she had stumbled across three fields and climbed over three fences, Shelby clutched her broom with both hands. "We're not going to make it, Chicken."

She leaned against a fence post and slid to the ground. She reached for her phone and pulled it out of her pocket then unlocked it with her finger and put it on the brown grass next to her.

"Call Riley," she said.

When the phone rang, she said, "Ostrich. Chicken, we have to tell Riley ostrich."

Not far away, an ostrich squawked, and Shelby smiled as she closed her eyes.

CHAPTER SEVENTEEN

"I thought Shelby would already be here," Ben said when Riley and Toby met him in the front yard.

"She called and told me something came up, but she sounded confused. She sent you her apologies for not going with us after all, but she called you Derek. I called Derek and told him, and he seemed very concerned. I didn't realize they were close friends, but I guess they are. I have a lot more to tell you about today, but let's go to the party, I mean barbeque. That's something else: Shelby called the barbeque a party. It was a strange call."

"Sounds like it," Ben said as they strolled into the house with their arms around each other. "I'll change, then we can leave, if you're still okay with going."

"Of course; I'll grab the cookies and a plate for them, then I'll be ready too."

"Did you make more cookies? I thought they were all gone."

"Did you now?" Riley raised an eyebrow.

"Well, you know, I was just going to have one more, but they were all gone; I don't know how that happened."

Riley chuckled. "Did you look in the freezer?"

"Just briefly; I have to change."

"Are you going to change your wicked cookie-snatching ways too?" Riley called out as she removed the bag of cookies from the cold oven.

She giggled at his silence while she selected a plate from the cupboard then put the plate and cookies into a tote.

"Do you want supper now, Toby, or would you rather wait?"

Toby grinned.

Riley smiled as she dished up his food. "It was a silly question, wasn't it?"

While Toby gobbled down his food, Ben came into the kitchen and pointed to the tote. "You made more, didn't you?"

"Nope, but I knew you'd check the freezer, so we still have the cookies that I planned to take today."

Ben hugged her and nuzzled her neck. "I love your braid and your devious mind. I think we'll see rain soon; we'll be in the barn, so we don't have to take any rain gear."

"I wouldn't mind having it along." Riley put her rain gear with her backpack.

Ben nodded. "I'll get mine; do we need to take anything for Toby? I have a water bowl for him in the truck."

"I think that's it." Riley put on her warm coat. "I'm ready."

"Rumors are already starting about where everyone is going. At least three of our guys have been approached by the FBI. What would you think about that?"

"It depends. I've been free to explore farm visits, and I love them so far, but if something feels right for you, I'm game. What about you?"

"I was one of the three, but I wanted to talk to you, so we can decide together. It would be more money and more opportunities for me from the career standpoint, but I like Georgia and the small towns we've lived in, and it's been nice to be relatively close to family and friends, although you make friends wherever we go. The money is almost a negative because we'd probably live in areas with higher costs of living."

"I'm not hearing any compelling reason from either of us for you to change agencies," Riley said. "Are you?"

"Not at all, but I'm glad we talked it over and agree."

Toby yipped.

"Thank you, Toby; it's unanimous," Riley said. Ben turned at a driveway then stopped. "I know you were looking forward to Shelby going along with us. Are you going to be okay?"

"If you don't hover, I'll be fine. You just said I make friends wherever we go; maybe I'll make a friend."

"If you don't see me, and you're ready to leave, text me," Ben said. "We'll leave immediately."

After Ben parked alongside all the other trucks, Riley gulped as she saw the crowd of men huddled around a barbeque pit and a large group of women chatting near the barn.

Several men hailed Ben and motioned for him to join them. Ben hung back and stood next to Riley.

"They're calling you, Ben. Aren't you going over there?" she asked.

"I will in a minute. I thought I'd see if I can find some people to introduce you to first." Ben took her elbow.

"You're hovering," she said.

"Riley! Over here!" a woman called out.

"Evidently somebody I know is here," Riley said.

"Okay, you win." Ben strode to join the group.

Madge hurried to Riley. "I'll bet I'm a surprise," Madge said. "My husband is the instructor's older brother, and we love barbeque, so we crash all his get-togethers; he loves to entertain"

Riley smiled. "How's your husband?"

"We had a long talk, and a lot of his stress was worrying about money and our future, so we've taken a few steps to downsize; he has stopped pushing himself to complete all his large projects, which was wrecking his knee. Come with me; I know everybody, but I won't try to introduce you. That's too much to absorb. Are you allergic to crowds like Lizzie? We can find somewhere to sit with a nice glass of sweet tea and let people come to us."

"That sounds great. It will give me a chance to get used to all the people and the noise."

When an old friend of Madge's sat next to her, Riley relaxed and listened to the chatter around her. *I guess that's what they call small talk.*

A young woman sat next to Riley. "Hi, I'm Shelby's cousin. I thought she was going to be here."

"She was going to come with me, but then she called me and said something came up."

"She's not a party-person."

Riley nodded. "I told her it was a barbeque, not a fancy party, but I think she would have told me if she had cold feet."

Shelby's cousin laughed. "You're right about that. I just stopped by to say hi."

After Shelby's cousin left, Riley leaned down and whispered to Toby, "Did I just do small talk?"

Toby moaned.

"That bad?"

Riley's phone rang. *Shelby?*

Her voice was so weak that Riley covered her other ear to hear her. "Chicken, we have to tell Riley ostrich."

In the background, a nearby ostrich chirped a distress call, and others answered, then the call dropped.

Riley didn't see Ben, so she sent a text: "Need to go to the ostrich farm. Can I take the truck?"

"I'll take you. Meet me at the truck."

While Riley hurried to the truck, she called Derek. When his phone rang over to voice mail, she disconnected. *I'll send him a text on the way.*

Ben reached the truck the same time that Riley did. "What's wrong?"

"I'll tell you on the way."

"I don't know where I'm going," Ben said.

Riley quickly gave him directions as he drove up the driveway, then she called the sheriff.

He answered immediately. "What's wrong?"

"Shelby is near Wally's ostrich farm. I'm not sure where, but the ostriches think she is hurt very badly."

"I'll call Wally and send a deputy. I'll be there as soon as I can. More details later, right?"

"Yes, sir."

Riley sent a quick text to Derek. *I know where Shelby is.*

"The ostriches think she's more than hurt very badly, don't they?" Ben asked softly.

"What makes you say that?" Riley asked.

"I heard it in your voice. You might be an animal and bird whisperer, babe, but I'm a Riley whisperer."

"They do; they are mourning for her because she is dying."

Ben pulled out his phone from his pocket. "Shelby's near the ostrich farm and badly wounded. Get a bird in the air."

After he put his phone on the console, Ben said, "You don't know this, but Shelby's undercover. She's on one of the teams that is investigating the farm fraud that convinces farmers to sign over their deeds, then they sell the farms to foreign investors and disappear."

"Really? Shelby's an undercover cop? Is she GBI? What about Nick? Is he undercover too? You're right, I didn't know it."

"How do you know Nick?"

"He works with Shelby. I met him today."

"What?" Ben stared at Riley then went off the road, but he corrected the truck's path before the wheels dropped into the ditch.

She continued, "I told you I was helping Shelby test the audio equipment at the B&B. That was what I wanted to talk to you about: she gave me copies of three unsigned contracts to keep for her, but I'm sure her team has everything she found because Shelby told me she loved encryption; we need to find Shelby."

"How much farther is the ostrich farm?" Ben asked.

"About a half mile up the road then on the right. We'll go past some woods then the fields for the ostriches."

After they passed a second field, Toby barked, and Riley said, "Stop! Stop!"

"Hang on; there's no shoulder." Ben slammed on the brakes then pulled over with the right side of his truck in the shallow ditch. Riley jumped out of the truck, and Toby leapt over the passenger's seat and jumped out behind her.

Riley and Toby crawled between the fence crosspieces then dashed into the field.

"Wait," Ben called out as he climbed the fence.

When Riley thought her lungs would burst from running, Toby whined.

"Is that an ostrich sitting next to the fence?" Riley asked softly.

The ostrich chirped, and Riley hurried to the large bird and found Shelby curled against the ostrich. She leaned down and listened. *She's breathing.*

"Shelby?" Riley said softly, but Shelby didn't respond.

Riley took off her coat and carefully logrolled Shelby toward the ostrich then put her coat under Shelby before she called Ben. "We found her; an ostrich has been keeping her warm, but she's unconscious. There's a lot of blood in her hair on the top of her head."

Toby flopped down on the other side of Shelby and snuggled next to her.

"I'll be right there."

Riley heard the roar of a UTV headed towards her.

"The ostrich farmer is coming to take you to the helicopter, Shelby," she said.

While Riley hummed her grandmother's tune of comfort, Shelby mumbled, "Riley...target you."

Ben joined her as Wally rolled up in the UTV. Ben and Wally carefully carried Shelby to the UTV where a quilt was across the back seat. After they laid Shelby on her side on the seat, Riley wrapped her with the blanket and tucked it in as a helicopter approached the farm. Riley knelt next to Shelby; Ben put Riley's jacket around her shoulders before he jumped into the UTV passenger's seat. Wally drove with care toward his barn with the ostrich and Toby following along behind them.

After they reached the farm, the paramedic and Ben placed Shelby on the stretcher.

When Shelby struggled to get up, Riley hummed as she knelt next to the stretcher. "I'm here, Shelby."

Shelby gasped for breath in between her words as she spoke. "Chicken...called...ostrich."

"Chicken is a hero." Riley stroked Shelby's face and hummed.

"Hero," Shelby muttered.

The paramedic shook his head. "We have to leave immediately."

Riley stepped back, and Ben put his arm around her while the paramedic and Deputy Clay whisked Shelby to the helicopter.

The old male ostrich marched to Riley and flapped his wings then lowered his head and trilled with the sweet sound of a baby chick.

Riley's eyes welled up then overflowed, and the tears streamed down her cheeks. She bowed to the old male, and her voice broke as she said, "Thank you."

The old male turned away and slowly walked back to the other ostriches that had lined up along the fence.

"What did he say, Babe?" Ben asked softly.

Riley shook her head and bit her lip.

"Babe, Derek called me and said thanks, and that makes two he owes you. What's he talking about?"

Riley sniffled then cleared her throat. "I think there's something between him and Hope, and he and Shelby obviously were working closely on the Step Up investigation."

"And you don't know that," Ben said.

"Not at all."

After they were in Ben's truck he asked, "What was Shelby talking about before they loaded her into the chopper?"

"You mean what she said about Chicken? I'll tell you on the way back to the barbeque."

"She was talking about a chicken? You mean you want to go back to the barbeque?"

"I'm upset about Shelby, but I'd be unsettled just as much at home; watching people will at least occupy my mind until we hear…who knows, maybe I'll meet someone who isn't undercover," Riley said.

"Think about it, babe: that's not likely," Ben said.

The sheriff strode to Ben's truck, and Ben lowered his window.

"How are you doing, Riley?"

"I'll be okay."

"Ben, we'll talk tomorrow, and your wife belongs on somebody's payroll."

"I've been trying to get her fired," Ben said.

Sheriff chuckled. "I hear you."

As they headed back to the barbeque, Riley told Ben about the neighbor's chicken when Shelby was a kid.

"The neighbor's chicken was her only pet? That's sad, isn't it?"

"In a way yes, but at least she had Chicken," Riley said. "She told me Chicken called the ostrich." Riley's voice broke. "When I reached her, she had her arms crossed like she was cuddling something against her chest, but I didn't see anything."

"Wally told me the ostrich kept Shelby warm. I don't think Shelby could have survived lying on the cold ground as long as she did without the ostrich."

Riley brushed away a stray tear. "When Shelby called me to cancel, she told me her cousin brought a plate of huge chicken. The words didn't make sense to me, so I rearranged them in my head to a big plate of chicken. She was telling me she was close to the ostrich farm; I should have caught that."

"Babe, when you said a plate of huge chicken, I reinterpreted it exactly the way you did. Shelby did the best she could, and so did you."

"Thank you, honey."

Ben parked in his same spot, and Toby yipped.

Riley inhaled. "It does smell good, Toby; now, I'm starving."

"Ready to get into line for some food?" Ben asked as they held hands and strolled together.

Toby trotted to the end of the line and lifted his nose and sniffed.

"We were walking too slowly to suit Toby," Ben said. "I'm surprised he didn't try to cut in line."

"I was thinking the same thing," Riley said.

As people walked past them with their plates loaded down with food, Ben's classmates stopped to say hello and to meet Riley; Toby sat, and each one gave Toby a decent-sized piece of their barbequed pork for being a good dog.

"He's already had plenty," Riley said repeatedly.

One of Toby's newest friends replied, "It's just a taste, and he's such a good boy."

The rest also claimed it wasn't much, and he was a good boy.

"You're going to have a bellyache tonight, and you know what that means," Riley whispered, and Toby grinned.

"Is everyone here in your class?" Riley pushed her food around on her plate with her fork. *Maybe I'm not as hungry as I thought I was.*

Ben smiled. "No, there are only fifteen of us in the class. The rest of the folks are locals. There is a loosely organized group of men from the local churches who take turns hosting a monthly get-together for the town. Farmers provide the meat from their livestock: pork, beef, goat, or chicken, and people pitch in to help pay for the meat. Everyone who can brings a side dish, an appetizer, or dessert."

"What a nice way to get everyone together."

Ben nodded. "There are a lot of families that are sent home with food that they might not otherwise have. Have you finished? Would you like some dessert? Do you want to see what they have, or take your chances that I'll pick out something good?"

After Riley ate two bites of a delicious blackberry cobbler, she put down her fork.

Ben finished eating his cobbler, then as he picked up their plates to clear their table, his phone buzzed a text. He glanced at it then put it into his pocket. "A couple of my classmates are leaving. Are you ready to go?"

Riley nodded.

On the way home, Ben said, "Thanks for going, Riley. I know this has been a rough day for you. What did the old ostrich tell you?"

Riley's eyes welled again. "He told me that all the ostriches were sorry for my loss of my good friend. Ben, Shelby died on the way to the hospital, but no one has told us yet."

Ben sighed. "The text I got right before we left was from the sheriff. He wanted to know if he could talk to us. He'll meet us at our house. Maybe the ostriches were wrong."

Riley nodded and stared out her window. *You don't believe that, and neither do I.*

When they went into the house, Ben asked, "Would you like a cup of hot tea?"

"You don't have to make it; I can do that," Riley said.

"You went with me to the get-together; let me fix you some hot tea." Ben kissed Riley on her forehead then helped her take off her jacket and hung it up for her. "Kick off your boots and put on a warm sweatshirt and your wool socks, and I'll get a fire going in the fireplace."

Riley came out of the bedroom. "This helped; thank you. I didn't realize how cold I was."

"You're welcome, babe; I made a fresh pot of coffee."

"The sheriff will appreciate it."

When the sheriff reached the porch, Ben opened the door. "I have a fresh pot of coffee, Sheriff, come in."

The sheriff's face was somber as he sat on the chair near Riley then accepted the hot cup of coffee that Ben offered.

"The hospital called, Riley; I am so sorry to bring you the sad news that Shelby died before she reached the hospital. I've worked with her for over five years; she was a talented young woman with a great future ahead of her. She will be sorely missed."

Toby put his head on Riley's knee, and she stroked his back. She glanced at Ben as he put his arm around her and leaned close to whisper, "Are you okay?"

Riley nodded.

Sheriff drank half of his coffee then gazed at Riley. "I have more, but I'll be breaking every rule I've laid down for my deputies and staff. Ben, I'd like for you to leave the room, so I don't put you in the difficult position of being forced to report me."

Sheriff finished his coffee, and Ben refilled both of their cups then took his coffee outside with Toby following him.

Sheriff waited until Ben closed the door. "Both Derek and Shelby have worked closely together for the past three years and had a stellar record of success. I think Shelby would want you to know that Derek turned in his resignation with the GBI; his official reason for resigning was a change in careers. He was undercover for over fifteen years and was one of the best. Very few people know that Derek and Hope had plans to marry this summer; Derek kept it private for Hope's protection. Shelby's death so close to the attack on Hope…" The sheriff sighed. "I think he's bent on revenge."

Riley nodded. *I'm right there with him.*

Sheriff strode to the back door. "I just realized I didn't give you a chance to grab your coat, Ben; come inside where it's warm."

After the sheriff left, Ben said, "All I need to know, Babe, is whether the sheriff told you that you were in danger because of Shelby's death."

"No, he didn't. It was just…sad."

Ben kissed Riley's forehead.

"I knew Shelby for less than a week, but we had a level of trust…"

After Riley's voice trailed off, Ben said, "That's rare for anyone, even after working closely with someone for a long time."

Ben rinsed the coffee pot and set it up for the next morning's coffee. "I'd like to take my shower tonight while the house is toasty rather in the morning."

"Good idea; I'll take mine after you, so I can put on my pajamas and jump straight into bed later."

While Ben showered, Riley picked up her phone. *Derek said he was available anytime I needed help.*

She sent him a text. "I need help tomorrow."

Riley stared at her silent phone then put it on the table while she stoked the fire.

When her phone buzzed a text, she rushed to read it. *Derek.*

"Be at the barn at nine."

She stuck her phone into her back pocket. *Maybe I have someone else I can trust.*

Ben opened the bathroom door. "Shower's free."

Riley rushed to the bedroom and pulled out her warm, flannel pajamas from the drawer; Ben stopped her with a hug in the hallway, then he sauntered to the living room while she showered.

After Riley joined Ben and Toby in the living room, Ben asked, "Do you want to talk about anything special?"

"Not really; I just want to sit with you and be warm; what are your plans for tomorrow?"

"I'll go in early, but I'll be home around two."

"Ralph has an investor who is interested in the house; the investor would like to see the house tomorrow, but Ralph wants you to be here," Riley said.

"I can't promise a time tomorrow, but I can text you before I leave."

"I'm sure that will be fine with Ralph; I got the impression that he wasn't all that sure he wanted an investor, but he's willing to listen."

"What about you? What are you going to do tomorrow?"

"I'm going to check on Dakota and Fire. I want to be sure they were comfortable in their stalls overnight, and I'll recheck their hooves then brush them down. They are beautiful horses, but their manes could use a good brushing."

"Will Derek be there?"

"Probably; Nora had some things she wanted him to do at the B&B this afternoon, so he probably didn't finish cleaning the equipment today like he'd planned." Riley yawned then sighed as she closed her eyes.

"Bedtime, babe." Ben strolled to the back door then opened it for Toby to go out.

Ben checked the fireplace. "Mostly ashes." He brushed ash from the hearth into the firebox then closed the fire curtain and glass doors.

Riley opened the door for Toby, then Toby flopped down on his favorite rug while Riley and Ben went to bed.

CHAPTER EIGHTEEN

When Riley woke to a sizzling sound, she opened her eyes and inhaled deeply. *Bacon!*

She quickly dressed and hurried to the kitchen.

Ben set her cup on the table. "I just poured our coffee, so it's hot." He kissed her cheek then smiled. "What got you up so early?"

"Like you didn't do that on purpose." Riley snorted as she pointed to the bacon then held her cup with both hands to warm them.

"I thought I'd surprise you with my version of a chuckwagon breakfast: bacon, scrambled eggs, biscuits, and Mom's peach jam."

After breakfast, Ben kissed Riley and smacked his lips. "Mmm, peach kiss."

On his way out, Ben said, "Loved you first, babe."

"Love you more, cowboy," Riley said before he closed the front door.

When Riley opened the back door to let Toby outside, a gust of wind chilled her. "Brr. It's going to be another cold day, Toby."

Riley poured herself more coffee then pulled out Pamela Suzanne's packet of papers from her backpack. She organized the papers into emails, photos, and hand-written notes that were on five by seven sheets of lined paper from a notepad. She glanced at the photos then sorted the notes by date and matched them with the emails with the same date.

The earliest note was dated a little over a month ago. Riley squinted to read the tight scrawl. "Pam, print out two copies of my emails, so I can read them in meetings. I don't like to read them on my phone. It makes me look disorganized and unfocused. A."

Her eyes widened as she read an email with a date two weeks earlier that was from Chief@stepup.org to Ava. "You are doing a fine job of keeping the spotlight on yourself in South Carolina while my team works behind the scenes, and you can congratulate Orson for serving so well as your foil. You have definitely more than earned your generous bonus, as we discussed. I know I had promised you some time off, but I may ask you to forego your vacation because we've had a few problems with Mr. C and some of his hand-picked team members; if adjustments aren't made fairly quickly, I will need you to step in at the last minute."

Riley read the handwritten neatly printed note. "I printed an extra in case the others got lost. Be careful. P.S. Talk to you later."

Riley stared at the note. *Great move, Pamela Suzanne; your initials are a perfect post script, but are you really going to call me?*

The rest of the emails were instructions on how to conduct meetings and manage Orson from Chief or details about farmers from Ava to Chief.

Riley read a short email from three days ago from Chief to Ava. "J plans a takeover. Move now."

When she read the email from two days ago, she shuddered. "You have two days to take care of J or you're finished. R is getting too close. I'm taking over in two days if you fail that too."

That's today. Riley put the papers, a backup pistol, and extra ammunition into her backpack and her rifle on the kitchen table.

Riley hurried to the bedroom and put on her long johns and a flannel shirt. After she put on her knit cap and warmest coat and picked up her backpack and rifle, she and Toby left.

On the way to the B&B, Riley peered at the clear sky as the sun lightened the horizon. "I don't see any clouds; maybe we won't get any rain after all. We're going early, but I want to talk to Nora."

When they reached the barn, Riley went inside to check on Dakota and Fire. Dakota exhaled through her nose, and Fire whinnied when they saw her.

"Good morning. Have you eaten yet?"

Dakota shook her head.

"I'll take care of that." Riley propped her rifle in the tack room and left the door open.

When Toby cocked his head, she said, "I'm hoping you and the horses will be distracting enough for me to get to my rifle."

Fire nodded her head and stamped her feet.

"Perfect." Riley scooped up their food into their buckets then gave them their breakfast.

When Riley heard the sound of the UTV headed toward the barn on the path, she picked up her rifle and stood in the trees near the barn until she saw that Nora was alone.

Before Nora reached the barn, Riley slipped inside and put her rifle in the tack room then met Nora at the barn door.

"I didn't expect to see you today," Nora said.

"I need to keep busy. I've fed Dakota and Fire, but I haven't removed their blankets yet. I thought I'd wait a bit."

"I came to feed them, so you've saved me some time. I'm devastated about Shelby, and I'm sure you are too. I'm not sure whether Nick will be here or not, so I'll tell Ava we don't have the microphones today if he doesn't arrive before the meetings start."

Golden opportunity. "Shelby taught me enough that I can manage the microphones in the two meeting rooms. If there are any problems, though, I can't do any troubleshooting, so Ava will have to do without. Are you expecting Derek today?"

"I left it up to him; he may be here later this morning."

"He's much more technical than I am; if you don't have anything else in mind, maybe he can show me a few things."

"I think I knew that," Nora said. "Shall I text him to see…"

The sound of a truck coming down the driveway interrupted Nora.

"Shall I wait until you two are ready to come to the B&B?" she asked.

"No, you can go on back. We've got a few things to do, and the walk along the path is nice."

Nora nodded then left before the truck reached the barn. Riley hurried to the tack room and picked up her rifle. She stood next to the barn door and held her rifle out of sight.

Derek parked his truck next to Riley's car and waved as he climbed out with a rifle. Riley waited for him with her rifle at her side.

"We had the same thought," Derek said. "What's up?"

While they removed Dakota's and Fire's blankets, Riley said, "I volunteered to run the sound system until Nick arrives or as long as we care to stick around." Riley glared at Derek. "I need help, so I texted you. I pegged you as a cop the first time I met you. Are you?"

Derek stared at her then chuckled. "Am I that obvious? I must really be slipping."

Riley rolled her eyes. "Derek, I live with a cop. You're either law enforcement or a hardened criminal, and you aren't a criminal of any kind because Toby, Fire, and Dakota would have told me."

Derek snorted. "Do you have something else in mind besides the sound system?"

"Is that an official question?" Riley asked. "If it is, my official answer is that I'm worried about my safety."

"No, I'm not official anymore; I resigned."

"In that case, I want to kill Shelby's killer."

Derek whistled as he sat on a bale of hay. "I'm with you and listening."

"I know Shelby took notes and sent them to the team, but I don't know if you had access to them."

"Not really. I was her backup; the data types collected and analyzed her notes."

Riley told him about the arguments between Ava and Orson and between Jim and Orson.

"Shelby put microphones all over the B&B. There are microphones in the two meeting rooms, several in the hallway, one in the kitchen, and one at the top of the stairs."

"All public places." Derek nodded. "Shelby was a great cop."

"I'm convinced that Jim was behind Shelby's murder, but that's just my interpretation of what I know and have overheard about Jim."

"We could let Nora know she can tell Ava you're working here." Derek frowned. "No, I don't like that either."

"That's a good idea. I hope Jim shows up, so I can shoot him."

"You can't just shoot Jim," Derek said. "You have to let me help. We need an airtight case against him."

Riley narrowed her eyes. *Derek's good; he's been interrogating me, which is why this information exchange is one-way. Not much help, Derek.*

"Airtight case? Even ignoring the fact that you resigned, you think like a cop, but you can't arrest them because you have no evidence other than what I overheard and some far-flung theories of 'an uneducated, kind-hearted, dog groomer' to quote Ava, except I added the kind-hearted. I think we should stir the pot and let Nora tell Ava I'm taking care of the horses."

"I don't like it, but okay, if you agree to one rule: no shooting in the back."

"If they shoot me then try to run away, can I shoot them in the back?"

Derek chuckled. "Doesn't matter what I say, does it? I lose."

"You sound like Ben, so who calls Nora?"

"I'll take that as a…"

Derek was interrupted by his ringing phone. He raised his eyebrows at Riley, and she nodded.

She strolled out of the barn; Toby, Fire, and Dakota followed her.

"We'll give Derek some privacy."

Fire and Dakota pranced into the nearest field.

"I didn't know that," Derek said a minute or so after he answered.

Not my fault I have excellent hearing.

"You knew I'd want to be the one to talk to him. You said his name was Ike?"

"No, I hadn't heard his name before; I can be in Atlanta in an hour."

When Derek hung up, Riley hurried to the fence along the field where Dakota and Fire were grazing. Toby raced into the field to check for field mice.

Derek joined her. "Riley, there might be a big break for us. My supervisor put my resignation in her drawer and didn't turn it in, so I'm still on the payroll, and she has a guy that she wants me to interview in Atlanta. The Step Up crew will still be here tomorrow. Promise me you won't do anything until I get back."

Riley narrowed her eyes as she examined his face. *You didn't resign after all, did you? Cop through and through.* "Really?"

He rolled his eyes. "Okay, you can shoot them if they shoot at you first. Happy?"

"Yes, let me know when you're on your way back," Riley said.

After Derek left, Toby barked.

"Don't nag; I didn't promise Derek anything anymore than he agreed to call me when he was coming back."

Riley called Nora. "Derek and I finished what we needed to do, so Derek left. Dakota and Fire are feeling much better; they're out in the field. Do you need my help there?"

"You must be a mind reader, Riley. I need help with the microphones, after all; I heard from Nick, and he can't be here until this afternoon. I think the microphones are turned off or need a charge or something, and I don't know what to do. Ava claims it isn't appropriate for her to shout at her audience, so they can hear her; I told her she was being overly dramatic, and there's just so much I can do under the circumstances; I topped it off by telling her I expected more compassion from her after the untimely death of the young woman who was my audio expert. I'm embarrassed because I have never snapped at a client like that before; I'll come get you."

"Nora needs my help with the microphones, Toby; maybe we'll get some of that evidence that Derek needs."

Toby gazed at Riley then yipped.

"I'm pretty sure you rolled your eyes; well done, and I get it: I have to talk to either Ben or the sheriff."

Riley sent a text to Ben. "How's your day?"

Ben replied, "Swamped; will you be able to be home by two or so?"

"I can do it."

"Ben's not available, Toby; I guess it's the sheriff."

Riley sent a text to Sheriff Baker. "This is Riley. Can you come by the B&B sometime this morning?"

He responded immediately. "On my way."

Riley glared at Toby. "I tried to make my text as lowkey as possible, but the sheriff may beat us to the B&B."

When Nora arrived in her UTV, Riley said, "I'm taking my rifle with me; I've been a little nervous since I heard about Shelby."

"I appreciate it. I'm going to sign up tomorrow for lessons at the gun range. I have my husband's old rifle and a pistol that he bought for me. We used to go to the range all the time, but I quit after he died; he'd be glad I'm going back to work on my skills."

On the way to the B&B, Nora asked, "Did you bring your scarf?"

"I have it in my backpack, but I decided I don't need to hide my hair. Everyone already knows I'm here, and I'm sure my scarf was an item of discussion. Do you suppose Ava can get by with using the microphone only in the large meeting room and not the small one?"

"I doubt it; she told me her hard of hearing clients appreciate the microphone in the smaller room too because her voice is so soft." Nora snorted. "I can't imagine who told her that because she has an irritating, whiny tone to her voice that I can hear all the way down the hall."

After Riley and Nora hung up their coats in the mudroom, Nora asked, "What do you think about my hooded sweatshirt?" Nora stretched out her arms then struck a modeling pose and smiled.

Riley gazed at the tan Trails End B&B sweatshirt with the same silhouette of prancing horses as the sign near the road. "I love it."

"My husband special ordered them as a surprise for me only a week before he died. They arrived three weeks later, and I was devastated that he never saw them, so I put the box into a storage closet. I was inspired by you and Shelby to unpack them. I have one for you."

Nora pulled out a sweatshirt from a large paper shopping bag that was on the bench in the mudroom.

"It's pale sage green; I thought it would look great with your red hair and your golden-hazel eyes, and you can flip up the hood anytime you like to hide your hair. Do you like it? You don't have to wear it if you don't want to. I have other colors if you don't like this one." Nora bit her lip and lowered the sweatshirt.

Riley's eyes welled up as she hugged Nora. "I love everything about it." She tried on her new Trails End sweatshirt.

"Does it fit okay? It looks a little big to me." Nora frowned.

"It's great; I'm still wearing my sweatshirt under it, so I know I'll have plenty of room to layer to my heart's content. The color is absolutely perfect. Does this mean I'm on the Trails End staff?" Riley asked as she removed the new sweatshirt.

"Absolutely. Don dropped off two large boxes of pastries and started the pot of coffee in the large meeting room earlier this morning. I told him I could take care of setting out the continental breakfast. I'll call him later to tell him how many to expect for lunch, but I suspect the number will be much lower than what Ava told me yesterday evening. Everyone knows Shelby was in charge of our audio; Ava's clients may assume she has canceled the meetings like any normal, kind person would do. What can I do to help you, Riley?"

Nora is definitely not an Ava Fleet fan. "I'd like to test the microphones in the meeting rooms and the sound to the console like we did yesterday."

"Have you had breakfast?" Nora asked.

"Ben surprised me this morning with a huge breakfast; he called it a chuckwagon breakfast."

Nora chuckled. "I'll have to remember that after the riding school starts. Don't you know the kids would love it? I need to clear out the old firepit too, so the groups can have s'mores. Those were the kinds of things my husband told me kids and adults would enjoy, and our original mission statement was for Trails End B&B to create memories. You're helping me pull out of my doldrums…Did you hear someone at the door?"

"I'm expecting the sheriff," Riley said. "I'm sure that's him."

When Nora opened the front door, the sheriff nodded. "Good morning, Nora. Where can we talk, Riley?"

"Nora set up the small dining room for the sound equipment. We can go in there."

"Take a cup of coffee with you," Nora said.

"Deputy Clay will be here in a few minutes, Nora."

"I'll let him know where you are."

After Riley closed the door, Sheriff Baker asked, "Do I sit?"

"Yes." Riley removed the papers from her backpack while the Sheriff turned around the chair at Shelby's console then sat.

She handed the papers to him. "Read these."

Sheriff frowned as he read the emails then growled, "Who made the copies of the emails?"

"Her name is Pamela Suzanne; she was at the first Start Up meeting. How I know her is a long story, but she was hired to be Orson's wife, so he'd look respectable, I suppose."

"Explain to me how you know her." The sheriff narrowed his eyes.

Riley exhaled. "You asked."

The sheriff raised his eyebrows as she told him about Ben's pseudo-engagement and Pamela Suzanne, and furrowed his brow when Riley continued with Pamela Suzanne's reaction to her, the papers Pamela Suzanne had from a former boss who was murdered, and how Riley helped her.

"Pamela Suzanne told me I'm her only friend, which is sad, don't you think?"

Sheriff nodded. "You're right: I asked."

Riley repeated the conversation between Jim and Chief at the diner. "My interpretation is that Jim was convinced that there was someone on their team who was undercover, and Shelby knew who it was; he wanted to go after Shelby, but Chief specifically told him not to. I think Jim had grandiose plans of taking over the entire organization."

The sheriff frowned. "Your summary of their conversation was actually pretty good because I'm not sure their detailed conversation would have meant much to me, and I would have dismissed your interpretation," he said. "I won't do that next time, but let's plan on no next time, shall we? So, does that mean you know who Chief is?"

"By sight, yes, but I don't know his name. I have a suspicion, but I don't have any facts to back it up."

"Tell me; I need to know everything that is in your head."

"Ralph wasn't impressed with Step Up…"

"Did you just jump to a different subject?"

"No, an investor contacted Ralph about supporting his work on the house, so he could have it ready to go on the market soon. I'm not clear on whether the investor was interested in buying the house or if he would take a cut of the profits after the sale. I'm always leery of vague money dealings," Riley said.

"Ralph's smart; he wouldn't fall for a scheme."

"Those people are really polished though. What is interesting and the basis of my suspicion is that the investor has insisted on examining the house. Ralph won't show it to him without Ben there, but the investor, Ralph said his name is Porter Lewis, told Ralph he'd heard a lot about me and wanted to meet me."

"Have you met this Porter Lewis?"

"No."

"I'll keep these," Sheriff picked up the papers as Deputy Clay came into the room and quietly closed the door behind him.

Riley furrowed her brow. *Jeans, flannel shirt, and boots. Was Deputy Clay off today?*

"Do you have anything else for me, Riley?" Sheriff asked. "If you hear anything else or need anything, call or text me or Clay."

"Here's my phone number, Riley." Clay gave her a Sheriff's Department business card with his number handwritten on the back.

After they left, Nora came into the room. "I guess I can put the cash for your bail back into the safe since they didn't arrest you after all."

Riley giggled. "I got time off for good behavior."

Nora snorted. "Not likely. Are we ready to test the microphones?"

Toby stood guard in the hallway while Riley and Nora went into the large meeting room. Riley examined the table-top microphone that Ava used then found the small switch to turn it on.

"One down," she mumbled after Nora tested it.

Riley checked the two hand-held microphones, but neither one of them worked after she pushed their small switches. "They must have been left on; their recharging station is with the rest of the radio equipment in the small dining room, but I don't know how long it will take to recharge them. Ava may just have to make do with the table-top."

Nora frowned. "I heard Shelby tell Ava and Orson that the microphones had to be turned off when they weren't in use or their batteries would run down. Ava claimed she and Orson were used to microphones and always turned them off, especially overnight. It didn't occur to me to check after them."

When they went into the small meeting room, Riley found the switch on the table-top microphone in the small meeting room; when she turned on the switch, the microphone still didn't work.

"Back to the wall and the basics." Riley followed the electrical cord to its outlet.

"Somebody must have tripped over the cord because it's partially out of the socket." Riley plugged it back in.

Nora tested it, but it didn't work. "Is there a volume control or something?" Nora frowned.

"I may have turned it off instead of on." Riley moved the switch back. "Now, try it."

Nora smiled then spoke into the microphone. "Works fine."

Nora picked up the hand-held mic and spoke into it. "How about this one?"

When the microphone didn't work, she flipped the switch like Riley had done earlier in the large meeting room. "How about now? Okay, still doesn't work."

On the way back to the kitchen, Riley said, "I have a friend in Carson I can call to ask how long it will take them to recharge. He'll either know or will research them for me."

"Ralph might know too," Nora said.

Riley nodded. *What a perfect way to tell Ralph that I'm at the bed and breakfast; I'll have to be ready for Chief.*

After Riley and Toby went into the small dining room, she put the three microphones into their chargers then called Ralph.

"Hi, Riley, I didn't expect to hear from you until this afternoon."

"Ben will call me this afternoon as soon as he knows when he can leave, but I called you with a technical problem."

"Right up my alley," Ralph said. "What's your problem?"

"I'm trying to help Nora by setting up the microphones for the meetings today at the B&B. All three of the handheld microphones were left on overnight, and their batteries are dead. I put them in their chargers, but I don't know how long it will take for them to charge."

"That's an easy answer: it depends," Ralph chuckled. "Do you have any paperwork with them?"

"I'm not sure; do you want me to look then call you back?"

"I'm in my truck at the diner and was just leaving when you called, so I'm only thirty minutes away. Shelby may have some back up equipment that we can put into service quicker than waiting for those batteries to recharge."

"I hate to impose…"

"No imposition at all; I'm happy to help. Does Nora have any of her cinnamon rolls?"

"No, but Don dropped off pastries earlier."

"Grab us a couple before Nora sets them out; we might need brain food."

After Ralph hung up, Riley went into the kitchen, and Nora raised her eyebrows as she placed two each of the raspberry and blueberry cream cheese Danishes, cream puffs, and chocolate eclairs on a small tray then filled a large tray from the rest of the box.

"What's the verdict?" Nora asked.

"I called Ralph, and he thought Shelby might have some back up equipment. I didn't think of checking the boxes of equipment for an alternative, but he's going to come here. Did you know pastries were brain food?" Riley asked.

Nora chuckled. "Ralph used to always snitch a cinnamon roll when he came here. I'm glad he hasn't changed his ways. I'll set aside three of each, so we'll have choices; you and I can be smart too."

"Before he gets here, we can test Shelby's monitoring system."

Nora nodded. "I'll walk from the kitchen to the meeting rooms then back."

"It was a dark and stormy night," Nora began as she headed toward the kitchen. Riley listened to Nora's rambling story as Nora continued down the hallway, into the small meeting room then the large meeting room and back. "And they lived happily ever after," Nora said when she reached the kitchen.

Nora came into the small dining room and smiled. "How was that?"

"Dee-lightful." Riley returned her smile.

"If you don't need anything else, I'll take the small tray of pastries to the large meeting room, so Ava can see that everything will be set up for the meetings."

Riley put on her headset then listened while Nora hummed on her way to the large meeting room.

"Hurry up, Orson," Ava said at the top of the stairs. "How much time does it take to plop on a toupee? I need to make sure everything is ready for our guests because Nora seems overly distracted by the death of that young woman."

Ava hurried down the stairs and to the large meeting room. She cleared her throat before she went into the room and joined Nora. *Adjusting your halo, Ava?*

"Oh, you've already brought in the pastries, and they look delicious, but there aren't very many, are there?"

"We have plenty; I have more in the kitchen," Nora said.

"I'm sorry, of course you do. I must be more stressed than I'd like to admit because I didn't mean to question your judgment. Everyone says that you are famous for your wonderful hospitality."

"I'm not myself either, I'm embarrassed to say," Nora said. "I'll pour both of us a cup of coffee, if you'd like to help yourself to a pastry."

"I just noticed your sweatshirt; it looks comfortable. Is the design on the front the same as the B&B sign at the road?"

"It is; it's our staff sweatshirt for cold weather; we have T-shirts for our hot summers."

"I think staff uniforms give a business a more professional appearance. I'll just cut one of the blueberry cream cheese Danishes in half for a sampling," Ava said. "Orson can eat the other half; he'll be down shortly. That's probably all he should eat, but he'll tell me he has to test all the others."

"I don't blame him. Chef has a very talented pastry chef on his staff," Nora said.

"Mmm, this is good. How are our microphones? I think I'll take that second half after all; Orson can fend for himself." Ava chuckled.

Pretty fake laugh, Ava. Riley rolled her eyes. *Guess I'm not an Ava fan either.*

"Riley checked the microphones, and the two tabletop mics at the front of both rooms are fine. We left the three handheld mics on overnight, and their batteries ran down. She's charging them, but she's also checking to see if we have alternatives in case the mics don't fully charge in time."

"Riley? Is she the gifted vet tech I've heard everyone talk about? She's also an audio expert? What a talented young woman."

"She has assisted Shelby with several projects in the past and offered to do what she could to help me."

"Isn't that wonderful? I've heard so much about her; maybe, I'll finally be able to meet her."

"I'll ask Riley to find you when everyone is on a break," Nora said. "I know you'll like her; she's very personable. I'll leave you to prepare for your guests."

"Thank you. I like to have a little time to meditate before a meeting. Oh, I should mention that I appreciated your suggestion to make those personal calls yesterday. We expect twenty people this morning at nine o'clock, forty for lunch, and fifty for dinner."

When Nora joined Riley, she asked, "Did you hear that? Is she laying it on thicker, or have I caught on to her? Where is she going to find all those people in our small community?"

Nora exhaled. "She certainly gets on my nerves, doesn't she? After her first meeting starts, I'll tell Don what she said, and we'll have a good laugh; he'll judge how many to plan on for lunch by the number of people who show up at nine. When Orson comes downstairs, I'll straighten and clean their rooms; they're supposed to leave in the morning, which is not soon enough for me."

Riley side-glanced Nora. "I didn't know you had staff T-shirts too."

Nora rolled her eyes. "You weren't supposed to catch that. I didn't either, but now that I've announced it, I think it's a great idea."

When Orson went into the meeting room, Ava said, "About time you made it. What took you so long?"

"I called Jim to make nice like you told me and asked if he'd help us today; he'll be here later this morning."

"What's your plan after he shows up?"

Orson yawned so loudly that Riley cringed from the unexpected loud noise. "That's your job, Ava. You wanted him here; I made it happen. When will the breakfast buffet be set up?"

"You're eating the breakfast buffet; leave some for the guests. We're having what is laughingly called a continental breakfast."

"Ugh, the coffee is weak. We leave first thing in the morning, right? I don't think I could take this hick town another day."

"We're scheduled to leave tomorrow, but if I can talk some of our more recalcitrant guests into coming back tomorrow, then we'll stay another day."

"I'm not staying; I was paid for Friday through Sunday, and that's it."

"Suit yourself, but I think you're being a pig-headed fool."

Orson snorted. "So what's the plan for this morning? Same as usual or have you gone rogue and decided to freelance?"

Riley was startled by a loud clatter.

"Don't ever accuse me of freelancing," Ava hissed. "You'd be writing the death warrant for both of us, or haven't you noticed the dwindling numbers? And leave some pastry for our guests."

"She gets more dramatic every time I work with her." Orson's mumbling was muffled as he left the meeting room.

Ava's team is crumbling. I wonder how many Danishes are left.

"Orson has completely lost it; I need to protect myself," Ava muttered.

After Ava quietly closed the meeting room door then cleared her throat, Riley furrowed her brow as she listened to the ringing of an outgoing phone call.

She's sitting at the front table, and the microphone is on. Her phone volume must be on high; I wonder if her insistence on microphones is because she's a little hard of hearing?

"Chief, Riley is here at the bed and breakfast. Would you like to drop by for lunch?"

"I'll think about it. What's she doing there?" Chief asked.

"It seems our wonder girl is also an audio tech; she's getting the sound system back into working order."

"This particular project has been messier than most because of your wonder girl. We can move forward if we know what her schedule for the day is. Do you feel comfortable handing that off to Orson? You have to be very careful to distance yourself from any involvement, so you can continue being unsullied while you're in the spotlight. It would be nice to wrap this up today, so you can move on to your next assignment, and I can finish my business before the end of this next week."

"Jim will be here later this morning. I'd rather Orson take care of Jim, and I'll chat with Nora about schedules."

"Good suggestion; Orson has a tendency toward being heavy-handed, especially when it's not his idea. No complaints; we hired him because of his style, but he's less useful now. What do you think?"

Careful, Ava; I smell a trap.

"Some of our clients appreciate his straightforward approach and prefer to meet with him in our small meetings."

After they hung up, Riley exhaled. *Sounds like I get to plan my own ambush.*

CHAPTER NINETEEN

Nora came into the dining room with a pot of coffee. "Need a refill, Riley?"

Riley removed her headset. "I've had my quota."

"I'm glad I set out only a few pastries on that small tray; they're all gone."

"What's our schedule like for today?" Riley asked.

"Don and Diane will probably be here around ten. Don had mentioned sandwiches for lunch, but as cold as it is and with the wind picking up, I'll bet he makes soup or chili. Diane sometimes makes crackers that are perfect with soup or chili, but she may make only a small batch for us. He'll decide what they will prepare for dinner after the afternoon crowd shows up. You've taken care of the horses for the day, so all I have to do is to visit them this evening, feed them, and probably put on their blankets. I forgot to mention that I have a meeting tomorrow with my lawyer and the riding camp people, so we can sign all the papers to make the agreement final, then they can start building their clientele for this spring."

"That's the best news I've heard in ages."

"What about you?" Nora asked.

"I didn't have anything particular in mind; I thought I'd stay until Nick comes and maybe check on the horses during the lunch break."

"I'd go with you, but I don't want Ava or Orson coming into the kitchen or talking to Don or Diane at all. Maybe Derek will be back by then."

Riley nodded. "Toby will go with me; he loves running in the field."

"I'll let you know when I hear from Nick."

"I think I heard a truck; do you suppose Ralph is here?" Riley asked.

"I'll check." Nora hurried to the kitchen, and Riley put on her headset.

Someone's pacing in the hallway.

"One of our clients came early." Ava hurried from the meeting room.

"No, it's an old friend of mine; he told me he'd stop by to check the hot water heater for me. Did you notice the water wasn't quite as hot this morning?" Nora asked.

Well played, Nora.

"I did; I'm in awe of your attention to every detail to make your guests comfortable. If anyone does come early, please ask them to make themselves comfortable in the meeting room. I need to have a quick word with Orson."

Ava sauntered to the stairs while Nora opened the door.

"Hi, Ralph; let's go into the kitchen."

"I smell Danishes," Ralph said.

"Help yourself; I'm glad you could make it."

When Ava reached the top of the stairs, she said, "Orson, your assignment today is to take care of Jim. Have him meet you somewhere."

"Where? It's too cold to stand around outside and wait for him. Jim's always late."

"Figure it out for yourself, but you need to do this right."

After Ava returned to the meeting room, Orson said, "Jim, this is Orson. Meet me at the roadside park outside of town on the road to the B&B at noon. Let me know if you'll be in town earlier or later; we have an assignment."

As Orson lumbered down the stairs, he mumbled, "Left him a voicemail and sent a text. He better not be ignoring me."

Riley removed her headset when Nora and Ralph came into the dining room.

"What do we have here, Riley?" Ralph polished off a raspberry Danish and carried in a chocolate éclair and a blueberry cream cheese Danish on a napkin.

"The three microphones are charging. We had two of them in the large meeting room and one in the smaller one. The instructions say to charge them overnight if they've completely lost their charge, but I couldn't find anything that mentions the minimum amount of time the mics need to recharge."

"Probably longer than what Mrs. Fleet has patience for. Where's the rest of the equipment?" Ralph asked.

"We have two full boxes of equipment. I looked in one but didn't see anything, then I realized I had no idea what I was looking for, so I called you."

Ralph looked in the first box. "I may have found something, but I've only seen two so far."

After Ralph thoroughly searched through both boxes, he said, "We have two lavalier style microphones that are meant to be clipped onto a lapel or collar, but they can be held by hand too, so we could have one in each room. I'll check both of them; they should work because all we need to do is to plug them into a USB port, and Shelby has the USB connectors to plug into a one-ten wall receptacle for power."

"You lost me," Nora said. "Let me know if you need anything."

Ralph set up two USBs for power and plugged in both microphones; they worked. "They aren't as convenient as a handheld portable microphone because they can't be passed around, but if a mic is required, they fit the bill. Are you okay with taking over from here, Riley? Do you know how to pair them with the amplifier?

You'll have to find the most convenient outlet then plug them in, and they'll be ready to go."

"I'm not sure about pairing them."

"It's easy; I'll show you." Ralph went through the simple steps and paired one of the mics to an amplifier in the small dining room. "Just do the same with the amps in the meeting rooms."

"You're right; it was easy. I've got it from here; sorry you had to come out of your way, but I appreciate it."

After Ralph took one more éclair and left, Riley checked the microphones and found a roller thumb switch. *I don't know if this controls the volume or turns it on and off.*

She tested the mic that Ralph had paired with the amplifier in the room. *Volume. I'll set it, and if someone fiddles with it, I'll know, and it will be an easy fix.*

She put the microphones and the equipment in a small box and carried it to the large meeting room.

"You must be Riley." Ava smiled. "I have been wanting to meet you because I've heard so much about you."

"Really? That's nice. I have one lavalier microphone for each room. The portable handhelds won't be charged in time for your meetings. Unfortunately, all three of them were left on overnight, and it will take most of the day to recharge them. I'll show you how the lavalier microphone works."

"I know all about them: we just clip them onto a collar."

"There's a little more to it than that because these are not wireless."

Riley plugged in the microphone. "Your speakers will need to stand near an electrical outlet. I suggest you decide where you would like for them to be and leave them plugged in."

Ava blinked then furrowed her brow. "Don't we just have them pass it around?"

"If you unplug it, it doesn't work. I'm not sure you want people to carry it around looking for an outlet before they speak."

"Excuse me?"

"It's a lot to take in, isn't it? I'll be happy to come to your meetings and explain about how it works, if you like."

"No."

"Let Nora know when you have decided where you want them, and I'll plug them in for you and show you how the volume control works."

Riley scooped up the equipment and hurried to the small dining room. When she reached the kitchen, Nora asked, "How did it go?"

"Just as we expected."

Nora followed Riley into the dining room.

"I think Mrs. Fleet was as close to speechless as she has ever been in her entire life. She's supposed to let you know when she decides where she'd like them plugged in. Is that okay with you?" Riley asked.

"Absolutely."

"I'll leave them in the box; let me know when I can install them." Riley put on her headset.

Riley furrowed her brow. *Ava's on the phone again in the large meeting room.*

"Just hear me out. In spite of all the local lore, I think R. is in the spotlight, which means everyone assumes that she's the one who has saved people and interfered with some of our old associates, but that doesn't mean she is."

"Hadn't thought about it that way; where are you going with this?" Chief asked.

"I had a long conversation with her, and she's not as bright as everyone says."

That's harsh, Ava.

"So who do you think is the brains behind the beauty?"

"Her husband, of course. He's the one we have to silence, not her."

"You know what he does, right?"

"He's a trainee; mistakes are made, and accidents happen during training."

"What do you have in mind?"

"An assignment for Jim. He's capable and dispensable."

Chief chuckled. "You've had a lot of harebrained ideas, and this one tops them all, but it makes sense. Call Jim."

"In all due respect, Chief, I think he needs to hear his assignment from you. He would not agree that this is a decision made at my level."

"I'll call him, and I'll tell him if he needs anything, you are at his disposal and willing to do whatever he needs. Are you okay with that?"

"That's giving him a lot of power; it will go straight to his head and make him insufferable, but yes, I'm okay with that. He'll either accomplish his mission or die when his ego trips him up."

"Or best case, both," Chief added then hung up.

"Do I share this with Orson?" Ava softly asked herself. "No, the fewer that know, the lower the risk to me."

Riley removed her headset, and Toby put his head on her knee.

"What have I done, Toby? Now Ben's their target, and it's all because I think I'm so clever. So what do I do now?"

Toby yipped.

"You're right; Sheriff told me to call him or Deputy Clay, but I'm not sure the sheriff would do anything other than file a report or something, and we don't have time for the official cogs to start moving. I need a friend that I trust like Claire or Mugsy."

Riley's phone buzzed a text. *Claire?*

"My Riley radar just went off the chart. Do I head your way? Or can I rinse out the shampoo suds from my hair first?"

Riley smiled. *This is so tempting.* Riley responded, "Rinse. I owe you a long phone call tonight."

"I'll be waiting."

Riley's phone rang. *I don't recognize the number.*

She didn't answer, then her phone buzzed a text from the same number. "It's Derek. New phone. Call me."

She returned the call.

"I picked up a cheap phone after I turned in my official phone. I watched my supervisor sign her approval for my resignation, so it's official and now I can be unofficial. I came to Atlanta to interview a man named Ike. Have you heard of him?"

"No, I haven't."

"Remember your theory that Jim ordered Shelby's murder? You were right. Ike was there; he turned himself in because he said it was all wrong. Jim told Gus to get a buddy, which turned out to be Ike, to help him kidnap Shelby. Gus slammed Shelby on the head with a baseball bat. Ike said that Shelby was a nice girl, and he didn't know why Gus had to hit her so hard. It broke my heart to hear the details. When Gus and Ike left her alone to get takeout for their supper, Shelby managed to get out of the zip ties on her wrists and legs in spite of the head injury that eventually killed her." Derek's voice cracked. "It was Jim, just like you said. I read Shelby's report; it supports your theory. What can I do to help you? I'm done with airtight cases and cases in general. If I don't go to prison, I'm buying a farm for Hope and me, and we'll raise or rescue whatever Hope wants."

"I need to give Ava time to adjust her plans. You're in Atlanta? Isn't Hope in the hospital there?" Riley asked.

"She is. Do I have enough time to visit her?"

"Absolutely. Ava has her hands full with her meetings starting up, so she won't be adjusting her plans until lunch."

After Derek hung up, Riley said, "I have a friend I can talk to. Derek will be headed this way later, and he'll help me if the sheriff has to go through official channels."

Toby grinned then lay down at Riley's feet and closed his eyes as Riley texted the sheriff.

"I have a little more information. Riley."

She relaxed at the sound of Toby's soft snore then put on her headset and listened as Ava met each of the five couples when they came into the B&B.

"We're in the large meeting room, and our talented chef has provided a lovely assortment of pastries for our continental breakfast, or more accurately, our mid-morning snack." Ava tittered.

Riley stuck out her tongue in a gagging motion as her phone rang.

"Clay's on his way," Sheriff said. "Are you in danger?"

"No, but Ava called Chief. Ava suddenly dropped me as her target because she decided that I was not capable of doing what she had heard from the locals. She told Chief that Ben is the brains behind interfering with criminal activities. Chief will call Jim to give him the assignment to kill Ben. Don't they know who Ben is and where he is? He couldn't be safer, but Ava said that training accidents happen, which scared me."

"I'll turn Clay around and make a few phone calls." The sheriff disconnected.

As the latest guests went to the large meeting room, Ava tapped on the kitchen door, and Nora opened it.

"Nora, I couldn't decide where it would be best to set up the small mics. Would you ask Riley if she would mind installing them where she thinks is best?"

"She's working on another solution for your audience microphones; if she's too involved, I'll send her new helper; I'm a big believer in not disturbing the experts while they do their thing. Shall I answer the door for you, so you can focus on your guests in the meeting room?"

Riley giggled. *Nora's a trip; she's one-upping Ava.*

"That would be wonderful; Orson should be here shortly. He sometimes gets so deep into his meditation that he loses track of time."

Nora opened the door to the small dining room. "I'm sure you heard Ava request your expert opinion on the placement of the microphones. She really irritates me. Do you think she even notices that I'm mocking her?"

"No, but I did."

"Good; go do your razzle-dazzle, but don't be surprised if Ava takes advantage of the fact that the wonderful Riley supports Step Up, which I think is why I invented your imaginary helper on the spot," Nora said.

"Good point." Riley removed her sweatshirt and put on her new Trails End sweatshirt then flipped up the hood.

"That must be what I had in the back of my mind," Nora said. "I can't get over how much you are transformed when your strikingly beautiful red hair is covered."

"Hey, I'm just staff here. We'll see how it works."

Riley went to the large meeting room with the box and stopped in the doorway as she glanced around. One of the younger farmers who stood in the back asked, "Wired microphones?"

Riley nodded. "Backups: one for each meeting room."

"We had those at school; I'll plug this one in. Has it been synched with the amp?"

Riley shook her head.

He pointed to the small switch. "Volume control?"

"Yes, it needs to be synched, and that's the volume control. Let Nora know if there are any complaints."

"Gotcha."

Riley slipped out of the large meeting room. *Ava never even looked up.*

After she plugged in the mic in the smaller room and synced it with the amplifier, Riley returned to the kitchen, and Nora followed her.

"How did it go, Riley?"

"Just like we planned. Your efficient staff did not disturb the meeting at all."

"Perfect. I'll be in the hall or the kitchen if you need me."

"I heard from Derek; he'll be here later, maybe around lunchtime," Riley said.

"That is excellent news, and that gives me an idea. Can you keep an ear out for anyone at the door for a few minutes?"

Riley sat at her console and put on her headset.

"Does anyone have any questions about signing your agreements before I collect them? If you do, go ahead and sign them, and we'll answer your questions when we meet privately," Ava said.

"Can we sign our agreements after lunch?" a man called out, and people laughed.

"I apologize; I missed that," Ava said. "Could you use the microphone, so everyone can hear your question?"

A woman spoke into the microphone. "He asked if we can sign our agreements after lunch. Everyone laughed because that's what all of us were wondering. Do we have to sign to get a free lunch? Could we just pay for our lunch if we want to think about it before we sign?"

Ava chuckled. "Sounds like everyone is hungry; let's take a five minute break, and I'll ask Nora if we have anymore tasty Danishes."

Riley dashed to the kitchen, grabbed the last large tray with pastries on it, and put it on the table in the hallway outside of the kitchen.

"I see Nora has abandoned her post," Ava grumbled as she hurried toward the kitchen. "Oh. She must have taken a quick break herself because here are our pastries."

Ava returned to the meeting room. "Here we are and looks like we have plenty of coffee too."

The grumbling in the room settled down and was replaced by quiet conversations.

Crisis averted. Riley raised her arms in triumph.

Nora came into the small dining room. "I did a quick count of the people in the dining room then called Don. After that, I went on a search and found exactly what I was looking for. I think my husband ordered this sweatshirt for Derek because it's an extra tall.

I'm not sure, but I think he may be six feet, six inches." Nora held up the sweatshirt.

Riley giggled at the length. "It's definitely not yours or mine, is it? I wouldn't have thought that the black lettering and horses would show up on an olive green sweatshirt, but it looks good."

Riley heard the mudroom door creak, but Toby didn't stir.

"Somebody came inside through the mudroom, but Toby didn't alert, so it's somebody we know," Riley said.

"Nora?" Diane called out. "We're here."

Nora hurried to the kitchen. "What do you want to go into the refrigerator?"

"Nothing that I brought in. Don will bring in our two coolers. He'll probably jockey things around a bit to get everything into the refrigerator. He decided on chicken tortilla soup, and I'm making flour tortillas."

"These coolers seem to get heavier every year." Don groaned as he set down the cooler with a thud. "I made a huge pot of chicken tortilla soup, Nora, but I brought only what we needed today. I have a big event next week and this gave me a chance to get ahead a little bit."

While Nora, Don, and Diane discussed the menu, Riley put on her headphone and listened to the five-minute break that had extended to fifteen. *Ava's working the crowd, one at a time.*

"Let's get settled," Ava said in a loud voice.

After the room quieted, she continued, "We'll continue our break until lunch, so everyone can get a few things done this morning before the late afternoon rains start, but you have to be here to eat your free lunch."

Ava paused for the few chuckles. "Leave your contracts here, and I'll keep them, so you don't have to keep track of them. After lunch, we'll have our small group sessions; they won't take long, so everyone should be home this afternoon no later than one thirty or two."

Her audience applauded then filed out of the room.

Riley put down her headset.

"Anything interesting?" Nora asked when she came into the room. "People are leaving."

"Ava called a break for the rest of the morning, and they'll reconvene here for lunch. I see how she really does need Orson to be the obnoxious bull irritating everyone, so she can be the gracious center of sanity."

"Why don't you take a break too?" Nora asked.

"I wouldn't mind spending a little time at the barn. There's not a lot to do, but I'd like to clear my head."

"Take the UTV in case our rain blows in sooner than expected."

"Thanks, I think I will. Are you going with me, Toby?"

Riley headed to the door, and Toby followed her.

Riley glanced at the gray sky as she climbed into the UTV. "Nora may be right about the rain."

When she reached the barn, she rolled her eyes. I thought Sheriff was giving Clay the day off.

Clay met her as she climbed out of the UTV.

"Is everything okay?" he asked.

"Ava gave the group a break until lunch, so I'm taking advantage and getting outside. Where are Dakota and Fire?"

Clay smiled. "They're in the field; I'm not sure, but it looks like they are racing with the rabbits."

Riley went into the barn and checked their food and water but stopped and stared at the floor then peered up at the roof near Fire's stall.

"I noticed the drip marks too," Clay said. "The leak in the roof isn't very big and isn't close to the stalls, but it probably should be fixed fairly soon."

"Derek's going to be here later; I'll mention it to him."

"Derek's coming here? He used to work with horses, but I thought he had another job."

"He's just helping Nora out this weekend. The barn was in pretty bad shape, so he cleaned it and threw away spoiled feed and broken equipment."

"What about you?"

"The horses' hooves needed attention, so I cleaned them and filed their ragged edges on Friday and yesterday."

"I've been thinking," Clay said. "Chief told Ava he would tell Jim that his assignment was to kill Ben, but maybe he didn't, which means that Chief is staying with his original target: you."

"Could be. Ava told him I was here and invited him to come here for lunch."

"Where will you be eating lunch?"

"I told Nora I'd like to come here to check on Dakota and Fire, but Ava or Chief may adjust their plans when they get together. Jim is such a wild card. I don't really know where he is or what he's doing, and Orson's disappeared too."

"Sheriff wanted me here because I could be close, but my cruiser would be out of sight."

"I can't imagine a better place to hang out." Riley smiled as her phone buzzed a text from Nora.

"Sheriff called me. Bring Clay back with you; he's staff now too."

Riley handed her phone to Clay.

"I hope I'm not in charge of cooking unless Sheriff Baker wants me to run everybody off," Clay said as they headed to the UTV.

"We're all in luck. Don and Diane are here."

Toby dashed ahead and waited at the steps to the back door.

"Welcome to our staff, De…I mean, Clay. Here's your uniform." Nora handed Clay a tan sweatshirt.

Clay hung up his long-sleeved flannel shirt with his coat and put on his sweatshirt.

"What are my duties, boss?" he asked.

"Don't call me boss, or I'll fire you," Nora grumbled.

"Can't fire us, boss," Don said. "That's Diane's job."

"Diane, would you fire both of them for me? They're too sassy," Nora asked as she left the kitchen.

"Remind me to fire you two after lunch," Diane said.

Riley shook her head and went into the small dining room as Don and Clay smacked a high five.

After Riley put on her headset, Nora chuckled as she walked down the hall then into the large meeting room.

"I'm just here to pick up the tray and check the coffee," Nora said. "Can I get you anything?"

Riley heard the snap of a laptop as it closed.

"I wouldn't mind some coffee while I catch up on my paperwork, but I don't want to trouble you," Ava said.

"I can bring in the home-size coffee maker that I have and make you a fresh pot. It wouldn't be any trouble at all, and this large pot is almost empty. We'll make fresh coffee for our lunch crowd."

When Nora returned to the kitchen, Diane said, "I'll take the tray. What about the coffee?"

"I'll bring back the large pot to the kitchen. I'm taking my coffee maker to make coffee for Ava. She's camped in the large meeting room with her computer, so she can guard the room, I guess."

"I'll fill the small pot with water and go with you to pick up the large one," Diane said.

"She's been wanting to scrub that large pot all morning," Don added.

Clay came into the small dining room. "Do you have an assignment for me, Riley?"

CHAPTER TWENTY

"It depends; do you want to listen?" Riley pointed to the other console.

"Thanks, I love surveillance, but there's not much call for it around here," Clay said.

After she explained the positions on the dial, he said, "I never had a chance to work with Shelby, but I understand she was amazing." He put on his headset and peered at the console as he listened.

Riley swallowed hard then turned back to her console. *She was amazing.*

The front door slammed, and Orson shouted, "Ava, where are you?"

Ava noisily exhaled. "Please excuse my bellowing son, Nora."

She hurried to the doorway. "Right here, Orson. Do you need some coffee? Nora is making us a fresh pot in here."

"Yeah."

"Isn't that coffee pot heavy? Are you okay with that, Diane?" Nora asked.

"Oh yes, I carry it full all the time, so this is nothing," Diane said as she left the room.

"Your coffee will be done shortly; let me know if you need anything else," Nora said.

While she headed toward the kitchen, Nora whispered, "Wouldn't you love to be a fly on the wall? Oh wait, you are."

Clay snorted.

Riley smiled. *He got Nora's joke. She'll be proud of herself.*

"Close the door and keep your voice down," Ava said.

"That's no good; you wouldn't be able to hear me," Orson muttered.

"Where have you been? I needed you in the meeting this morning."

"Where is everybody? Did they already sign and leave?"

"Nobody signed. I had to give them the morning off for farm work because they balked at signing. When they come back for lunch, they'll sign, but you have to be here."

"Oh, really? Turns out I'm critical after all."

Riley heard the swagger in his voice and rolled her eyes.

"Where have you been?" Ava asked.

"You told me to take care of Jim, so I scoped out a few places for possibilities. Why? Did he call you after all?"

"What do you mean?"

"He finally returned my call, and I told him we had a job. He'll meet me at one o'clock at an abandoned warehouse, but he said he needed to talk to you first."

"I haven't heard from him. What does he want to talk to me about?"

"I don't know and don't much care. Tell me again about how you botched this morning."

"Get out," Ava growled. "Go read or something if you know how."

Orson's cruel laugh sent cold chills down Riley's back; he slammed the door as he left.

"Yeah, well, you're gonna get yours, old woman," Orson mumbled as he headed up the stairs.

Riley exhaled as she leaned back.

"These are not nice people," Clay said. "Are we just going to wait while they kill each other off?"

Riley nodded. "So far, that seems like what's going to happen, doesn't it?"

She turned her attention to the radio when Ava said, "He's such a jerk, but now I can enjoy my morning special cup of coffee in peace."

Ava hummed an offkey tune while she poured her coffee then set it on the table. She sighed. "I deserve a double after this morning."

Riley furrowed her brow at the sound of a splash of liquid. *What's that?*

"Make it a double, kind sir." Ava chuckled.

After another splash, Ava hummed the same tune while she stirred her coffee.

"Ahh. Here's to me." Ava slurped her hot coffee. "Perfect."

She took a big gulp. "The best."

Her breathing slowed, then she gurgled.

At the sound of a loud thud, Riley and Clay ripped off their headsets; Clay snatched up his backpack then passed Riley as they raced to the large meeting room.

Ava was crumpled on the floor under the table. After Clay pulled Ava out from under the table, Riley knelt next to her and put her ear near Ava's mouth.

"She's not breathing; her lips are blue," Riley said.

"Overdose. Call for an ambulance."

Clay opened his backpack then squirted a nasal spray into Ava's nostril while Riley dialed nine-one-one.

"We need an ambulance at the Trails End B&B. We have an unconscious female, not breathing, suspected overdose."

Clay put two fingers on the side of Ava's throat. "Very faint pulse."

"Faint pulse," Riley repeated.

Carter pulled out a second ampule and squirted it into Ava's other nostril.

Ava gasped a breath, and her breathing was shallow and ragged.

Riley pointed to an overturned flask on the floor. "I think she added something to her coffee."

"Don't touch it," Clay said. "Text the sheriff and tell him to come to the B&B. We need oxygen."

Riley texted the sheriff. "Need O2 at B&B."

"Is something wrong?" Nora asked.

"Ava quit breathing, but she's breathing now. I've called for the ambulance, and the sheriff is headed this way."

"I'll keep people away from this end of the hall. Don and Diane can help me."

Riley heard the sound of a siren. "Sheriff's close."

The sheriff burst into the house. "The large meeting room," Nora said.

The sheriff came into the room with a tank of oxygen and a small case. "Do we need to assist her breathing?"

"No, just a nonrebreather for now," Clay said.

Riley attached the tubing of the oxygen mask to the tank port as the sheriff turned on the tank.

Clay placed the mask on Ava's face, and her blue lips slowly turned to a faint pink.

Orson shouted from the other end of the hallway, "Get out of my way. What's going on here?"

"Sorry, sir, but the sheriff has asked that no one go past this point," Don said.

"What are you talking about? You don't have the authority to keep me from going wherever I want. Get outta my way."

"Why don't you have a seat, Orson, and I'll bring you a nice glass of water and an éclair to calm your nerves," Nora said.

"What about one of my cream puffs too?" Diane asked.

"I'll do that," Nora said.

"Your cream puffs? Are you the baker?" Orson asked.

"I sure am. What did you think of them?"

"Lady, they were the best I've ever tasted," Orson said.

"Make that two cream puffs, please, Nora," Diane said.

Riley listened to the wail of another siren on the road. "Ambulance is on the way."

Riley stood back while Clay gave his quick report to the paramedic, then the ambulance whisked Ava away on the stretcher.

While Clay told the sheriff what he and Riley heard and did when they reached Ava, Riley headed toward the kitchen. Don stood in front of the kitchen door. "Are you okay, Riley?"

"Yes, and thanks for keeping Orson from barging in."

"I'll just hang out here until the sheriff releases me."

Riley went into the kitchen where Nora and Diane waited.

"What can we do for you?" Diane asked.

"I think I need a cream puff," Riley said.

"You're supposed to yell at Don first, you know." Diane put a cream puff on a napkin and handed it to Riley.

"I'll do that later; cream puffs take priority. Y'all did a great job of defusing Orson."

"I should be ashamed because I took unfair advantage of his sweet tooth," Nora said. "Can you tell us what happened?"

"I haven't talked to the sheriff yet, so maybe I should wait," Riley said.

"That's understandable, but are you sure you have to?" Nora asked.

"We'll just keep plying you with cream puffs until you crack," Diane said.

Riley giggled. "That won't take long; these cream puffs are wonderful."

"How long do you think it will take for word to get out about Ava?" Diane asked.

Nora's phone rang.

"We should have bet because I would have won." Nora stepped into the small dining room to answer the phone.

"She'll be busy for a while, won't she?" Riley asked. "What are you going to do with all the soup?"

"We'll have lunch, then we'll leave some here with Nora, send you, Clay, and Sheriff home with soup, and have soup ourselves for a day or two."

"I'll collect all the electronic equipment that I can, but I'll need a ladder for the hallway."

"Don can help you," Diane said. "I'll replace him as hall guard."

"Good idea; he's tall."

Diane snorted. "Honey, everybody's tall compared to you."

Riley nodded then picked up a box from the dining room.

When she and Diane left the kitchen, Diane said, "Go with Riley, Don. She wants to collect the electronics but can't reach them all," Diane said. "I'll replace you."

"Let's start in the small meeting room," Riley said, "then work our way back toward the kitchen."

While Riley wrapped up the tabletop microphone, amplifier, and the small remote mic, Don took down two transmitters and gave them to Riley.

They went down the hallway; Don took down the two transmitters there and handed them to Riley.

"There's one at the top of the stairs, but I'll have to wait until Orson isn't around. I think it might be on the railing somewhere," Riley said.

"Give me a second." Don went to the top of the stairs, ran his hand under the railing then joined Riley at the foot of the stairs. "Here it is."

"The last one, except for the large meeting room, is in the kitchen."

Don returned from the kitchen. "Here you go. Why don't we give the large meeting room a try? How many are there?"

"Two."

Don opened the door to the meeting room. "Sheriff, Riley has a question for you."

Sheriff chuckled. "Did Don just throw you under the bus?"

"Definitely. Ask him why."

Don sighed. "I've been out-maneuvered, Sheriff. We're here to take down the transmitters that are in here."

"Right, there's one close to the door, and one midway or a bit closer to the front of the room," Riley said.

Don took them down and gave them to Riley.

"Can we take the amplifier?" she asked.

"You're pushing it," the sheriff said, and Clay smiled.

"Just asking," Riley said.

Riley and Don carried the equipment into the small dining room, then Don replaced Diane as hall guard.

Riley said, "Nora, we collected all the equipment we could. Tell Nick I didn't feel comfortable trying to disconnect the consoles and other equipment."

"Will do; are you leaving?"

"Not until after we eat lunch."

"My ear hurts," Nora said. "Each person that was here must have called ten other people. Did you know Ava was a saint and a crucial part of our local community? No? I didn't either until all the phone calls."

"The sheriff released me," Clay said. "It was nice working with you, Riley."

"I'm glad you were here."

"Is your car at the barn?" Nora asked.

"My cruiser is."

"I'll give you a ride over; I'd like to see how Dakota and Fire are doing."

After the two of them left, Riley's phone rang. "Doc Ned's calling me. Word has definitely gotten around." She sat down before she answered.

"Lizzie wants to know if you're okay."

"Tell Lizzie I'm fine."

"Lizzie wants to know…"

"Oh, for heaven's sake, give me the phone, then you can talk to Riley," Lizzie said. "Ned wanted to talk to you, Riley, but he didn't want to bother you, so he decided he'd use me as his excuse. One of Hope's friends called me; she heard that Hope will come home next week sometime, and she and two other friends want to take a meal to Hope's house for her and Derek. You knew they were a couple, right? She asked me if I'd check with you to see if you were interested."

"That's really nice of them to include me; I'm really honored, but my cooking skills are still a work in process."

"I thought that might be the case, so I'm offering to help you. You and I can decide what you'd like to cook, then we'll cook together. That will give you some practice and Hope and Derek a home-cooked meal."

"That sounds like fun. When would we cook?"

"We won't decide until we hear when Hope is coming home, and what her diet restrictions might be, then we can pick a day that's convenient for both of us. We'll talk later; here's Ned."

"Are you committed to Nora tomorrow? I'm asking because one of my vet techs is stranded at the Denver airport. I guess some heavy snowstorms swept across the Midwest, and many of the airports rescheduled or canceled flights, which always causes a mess and takes several days to sort out."

"I'll check with her. What time would you need me at the office?"

"Whenever you can get there is fine; our appointments start at eight."

"I'll get back to you, is that okay?"

"More than okay, thanks. We could probably limp along, but our Mondays are always busy."

"I'll talk to Nora and get back to you no later than after lunch."

"Thank you; we don't have anything else. Talk to you later."

It will be awesome to be back in my element. I hope Elsie isn't the vet tech that is stranded because she's the only vet tech there I kind of know.

Riley waited in the kitchen while Nora hung up her coat. "Nora, Doc Ned wants to know if you can get by without me tomorrow. He needs me in the office because one of his vet techs is stranded in the Denver airport."

"Those snowstorms really disrupt the air travel, don't they? I'll be fine. My friend who cleans for me will be here tomorrow while I go to the lawyer's office, and I'm sure the new people will want to renew their friendships with Fire and Dakota right away."

"I think you're right."

"I can dust the other bedrooms to get ahead of the cleaning for the week," Nora said. "I hope we can clean the Flint bedrooms tomorrow."

After Nora left, Toby whined. "Okay, I'll go with you for a walk, but it will be short."

Toby pranced to the mudroom.

"We're going outside; I hope it isn't too cold."

"Shouldn't you tell the sheriff?" Diane didn't look up from her bowl while she cut butter into the flour with a pastry cutter.

"He's busy, and I won't be long."

Diane nodded. "I decided against tortillas since we aren't going to have the larger group after all. I'm going to make biscuits instead."

Riley put on her knit cap and her warm coat while Toby nosed the mudroom door.

"Let's go, boy." Riley opened the door and breathed in the cold air through her nose then exhaled noisily through her mouth. "I needed fresh air, Toby, but it's cold out here. I'll take a fast walk down the path a short ways and maybe around the house, then I'm going back in."

Riley passed Don and Diane's van and Nora's truck as she and Toby headed toward the barn; after they turned back, she headed toward the front of the house, and Toby wandered in the other direction.

When she reached the front, she smiled at the wide porch with the rocking chairs that invited visitors to relax. *Nora really does have a knack for hospitality and setting a welcoming atmosphere.* As she turned to go back inside, she glanced at the vehicles in the driveway and frowned. *Sheriff's cruiser, Ava's car, Orson's car, and one extra.*

She stared at the car for a few seconds then shivered and hurried to the back door.

Toby yipped as he raced past her and dashed into the mudroom when she opened the back door.

"You were the one who wanted to go for a walk, Toby," Riley grumbled.

Riley went into the kitchen as Diane set down a bowl of shredded chicken with a little broth on the floor for Toby.

Traitor almost knocked me down for a bowl of chicken. Riley inhaled the soup that was bubbling on the stove. *Not that I blame him.*

Diane turned out her dough onto a floured cutting board. "Don't blame Toby, Riley; he's not the first to fall in love with Don's chicken and broth. How is it out there?"

"It's much colder than I thought."

"That damp cold cuts to the bone, doesn't it? You just missed a guy who showed up; he said he was a friend of Ava's, and she had invited him to join the group for lunch. He sounded terribly disappointed when Don told him the meeting had been canceled, but he was polite and apologized for not checking first. I didn't know Ava had any nice friends, did you?"

"Not at all." *Wonder if that was Chief?*

Toby flopped down at Diane's feet, and Riley glared at him when he grinned, then she went into the small dining room. She glanced at the consoles, headsets, and all the equipment then furrowed her brow. *Didn't Shelby tell me she'd monitor everything else? Wonder if there are any other microphones that I missed?*

Riley put on Shelby's headset and listened to see if she'd hear anything as Shelby's console scanned. *Shelby's console is much fancier than mine.*

She leaned back and closed her eyes until the scan suddenly stopped on a channel. Riley's eyes widened as the men spoke. *I recognize these voices.*

"What are you doing here?" Derek asked.

"I thought it was you when I saw you in town earlier this morning, then when I saw you at the gas station, I thought you might be coming here," Jim said. "Are you working today?"

"I was this morning; I stopped by to make sure the gates were closed; I'm checking in with the owner to let her know I'm finished. What about you? What are you working on?" Derek asked.

Jim snorted. "I could have told you yesterday, but I've been getting conflicting information all day. I tried to get some answers to sort through my options, but now nobody's talking to me. You open for a little freelance job today?"

"What do you have in mind?" Derek asked.

"I need to get a certain guy motivated, so I can close my deal and get out of here. This guy owns an old house on the outskirts of town, and his property is worth ten times what the old broken down house is. I have a buyer ready to put down cold cash, but the guy is dragging his heels about selling; he needs a little help to change his mind. That's not the only property in town with buyers lined up to pay premium prices, but that's the only one that I have all the paperwork in my possession to sell immediately after he signs the deed."

"So far, you're just flapping your jaws; if you don't have any more than that, I've got a few things to do before the weekend's over."

"I don't know much more than the guy needs a little time out to consider his options."

Derek snorted. "That's your specialty, not mine."

"You don't get it. I need the help now, and no one else is around."

"Again, not my problem. Are you working for Chief?" Derek asked.

"How do you know about Chief?" Jim asked.

"I've done some work for him in the past; if you're trying to cross him, count me out."

"What if Chief called you himself?"

"Then it would be a different ballgame, wouldn't it, Jim? I gotta go."

After Derek went inside, Jim growled, "I'll make sure you never work again."

As Jim walked away, he said, "Chief, it's Jim. You're right; she has to be stopped before she warns our owner. Okay, I'll take care of the owner."

A car door slammed, then the car tires spun on the driveway gravel before it sped away. *I wonder if Nick knows where all the bugs are.*

Riley turned off the console. *Was Jim talking about me, and is Ralph the owner?*

When she went into the kitchen, Riley glanced around the kitchen. *No Derek.*

Diane was washing the large coffee pot in Nora's oversized, commercial sink.

"I thought I heard Derek's voice," Riley said.

"He asked for Nora; I told him she was upstairs, but I think he might be talking to Don or the sheriff. You just missed him." Diane's eyes twinkled as she glanced at Riley. "Isn't that unusual for you? I've heard you always get your man."

Riley smiled. "That was a terrible joke, Diane, but it was actually kind of funny, in a way."

She went into the hallway where Don stood guard. "Are you looking for Derek? He's talking to the sheriff."

As Riley headed toward the large meeting room, Don crossed his arms. "Sheriff said nobody was supposed to get past me, Riley."

She glared. "What about Derek?"

"Sheriff came out of the room when Derek asked where he was and motioned for Derek to join him."

Riley headed toward the stairs. "I'm restless; I'll ask Nora if I can help her clean."

"I'd never get that restless." Don chuckled.

Riley saw a pile of sheets in the hall outside the back corner bedroom. When she reached the bedroom, Nora looked up as she put on the bottom bedsheet on the bed.

"I came to see if I could help," Riley said.

Nora straightened her back. "I could use it; I came into this bedroom to dust first, but I realized it's been a while since the bedrooms have had a good cleaning. I've dusted, changed the linens, and swept the floor; next, I need to mop. If you could dust and strip the beds for me in the other two bedrooms, that would be a huge help."

Riley took a soft cloth from Nora's stack of cleaning supplies and went into the next bedroom. She dusted the lamp, lampshade, end table, and blinds on the window then stripped the bed. She shook out the dust cloth on the floor then hurried to the next bedroom. After she finished, she found Nora in the bedroom she had just dusted.

Nora stopped sweeping when she noticed Riley in the doorway. "Finished already? This is going really fast. I have a utility room next to that corner bedroom. Would you take all the linens there? Just leave them on the floor, and I'll load the washer."

"Could I get the first load started for you?"

"Not really; the washer has to be loaded with all sheets I'm comfortable washing at the same time, which is not too many. It's an art." She grinned.

"I'd never want to disrupt an artist's process." Riley smiled.

After Riley went downstairs, Don nodded as she went into the kitchen.

"Is the sheriff still here?" Riley asked.

"No, three GBI agents showed up. Two of them went to the meeting room, so the sheriff left; the third one took Orson to their office to talk."

"I'm surprised Don is still in the hallway."

"He's enjoying himself. He talked about law enforcement for long time, and I caught the bug from his enthusiasm. We've already completed applications but haven't sent them in yet." Diane smiled. "We let things simmer a while before we jump into a decision."

"You'd give up cooking for law enforcement?" Riley asked.

"Don and I will always enjoy preparing meals for family gatherings, but as a career? It's not really us; we do everything together. We didn't really know that's how we were when we were first married because we thought we should be like everyone else; it took a while for us to learn who we were as a couple. We know we're not the norm, but it's definitely right for us."

"Ben and I had the opportunity to go to veterinarian college together when we were first married, but we learned that wasn't what either of us really wanted to do. He has always wanted to be in law enforcement, and I love being a vet tech, especially farm visits."

"Aren't you glad you know that?" Diane reached down and gave Toby another tidbit of chicken that she had on a plate near the sink.

"You didn't see that, right? Lunch will be in about thirty to forty-five minutes; I'll wait until Nora and Don are here before I put the biscuits in the oven. Let me know if you want to eat earlier, and I'll dish up two bowls of soup and put a couple of biscuits in the oven, and you and I can have a girls' hearty lunch."

CHAPTER TWENTY-ONE

While Diane washed the rest of the dishes and talked about the things she and Don had done together since they were married, Riley leaned back and listened until her mind wandered.

Derek's a cop. He would have known that Jim was following him. He wasn't having a casual chat; he was interrogating him. She frowned. *Or am I trying to make excuses for him? I wish I could ask him.*

"Diane, do you know if it's unusual for the land an old house is sitting on to be worth more than the house itself?" Riley asked.

"Actually, it isn't. In fact, most of the old houses around here have a negative value. The costs to bring the electrical and plumbing systems up to code and to have an environmental group decontaminate the house would exceed the price of the house; if you add in the cost for demolition and hauling off the debris…" Diane peered at Riley. "Sorry; I don't see many people because I stay in the kitchen, and I rarely get a chance to talk to anyone, so I go overboard when I have someone around who actually listens."

"Actually, it was really interesting. How do you know so much about houses and land values?"

"I love to research, and I read everything," Diane said. "We frequently have sauces and soup on the stove to simmer all day, but I'm afraid to leave a pot on the stove unattended, so I hang out in the kitchen and read."

Don and Nora came into the kitchen. "A GBI agent put padlocks on Ava's and Orson's bedrooms. I have the upstairs washer going," Nora said.

"The agent in the meeting room did the same thing," Don said.

"I'll pop these biscuits into the oven, then we can eat."

While they ate, Nora asked, "Will you be leaving after lunch, Riley? Nick should be here in an hour or so, but I don't see any reason for you to wait, except I enjoy your company."

"I think I will leave; would you tell Nick that Don and I removed all the transmitters that I knew about. I don't know if there are any more, but he probably would."

"If there are others, Nick could find them," Don said. "I'm sure he'd have an excellent quality multi-frequency wireless bug detector." Don explained the different types of bug detectors for home use and for professional use.

Nora rolled her eyes, but Riley listened intently. *Don researches too.*

When Don finished, Riley said, "You two have to send me your research lists."

Don side-eyed Diane, who laughed. "She's serious, Don."

"We will, if you will, Riley," Don said.

"What a good idea." Diane gave Riley their business card.

When Riley glanced at it then flipped it over, Diane said, "We have an email address that both of us check."

Nora squinted at the card. "It's blank."

"Riley will read it," Diane said.

"Cook's invisible ink?" Riley asked.

Don nodded as Nora rose from the table.

"You people are out of my league; however, I am qualified to clear the table unless anyone cares for more soup," Nora said.

While Nora and Riley cleared, Diane and Don packaged up leftovers then attacked the dishes.

Nora said, "I'll take you to your car in the UTV when you're ready, Riley."

"Ready." Riley grabbed her backpack, then after she and Nora put on their coats, Diane gave Riley a container of soup and a paper sack.

Toby led the way to the barn. When they arrived, Nora parked near Riley's car. "Riley, you're welcome here anytime. I owe you a weekend at a beautiful B&B with no murders or drama. Just give me an hour's notice, so I can chase out the killers before you show up."

When Riley giggled, Nora said, "Oh good; as soon as I said that I realized how inappropriate it was. It was actually funny in my head before it popped out."

"That happens to me all the time." Riley opened the car door for Toby and waved as Nora left.

"Brr. The car's cold, Toby."

After she turned on the engine, she exhaled. "After I turned the key, I thought I should have checked for a bomb before I started the car. I really am more scared than I'd like to admit."

When they arrived at the house, Riley parked, then they rushed inside.

Riley shivered. "That sharp wind took my breath away. We beat everyone here; I thought it would be cold in the house because of the wind, but it isn't at all. Ralph's done a good job of insulating the house, hasn't he?"

Riley put the container of soup into the refrigerator. *According to Jim, I need to warn Ralph. I need to talk to Ben.*

Riley sent Ben a text. "Home."

He replied, "Ten minutes."

When Ben rushed into the house, he grabbed Riley and held onto her. She wrapped her arms around him and tears slipped down her cheeks.

"Are you okay, babe?"

"I am, now that you're home." She sniffed back her tears. "Take off your coat, then sit with me. I need to talk to you."

Ben gazed at her face then kissed her forehead. After he hung up his coat, he joined her on the sofa.

"I know you and Clay tried to save Ava, but I just heard she died in the emergency room," he said.

Riley exhaled then told him about the conversation she overheard between Derek and Jim, and the phone conversation Jim had with Chief as he hurried to his car.

"What do you know about Derek?" Ben asked.

"He's engaged to Hope, and he's an undercover GBI agent."

Ben narrowed his eyes. "Babe, you're not supposed to know the second part. You just answered any questions you might have had about Derek."

Riley exhaled. "That's good news because I thought it sounded like an interrogation."

"You caught that from a short conversation?"

Riley furrowed her brow. "Of course; wouldn't you have?"

"Sometimes I wonder if you're in the wrong field. Moving on to Jim's phone conversation: what's your interpretation?"

"Ralph is the owner of the house that's on the valuable property, so Jim's supposed to take care of Ralph; I'm the one that might warn him, so I have to be stopped, but Jim didn't specify who would stop me or how."

Ben pulled out his phone. "It's turned hot; I need someone at my house."

Ben nodded as he listened. "Perfect."

After he hung up, Ben rose and went to the fireplace. "I'm going to start a fire."

When there was a knock at the door, Riley stayed in front of the fireplace while Ben opened the front door. "Thanks for getting here so quickly; she knows who you are."

"Hi, Riley." Derek followed Ben into the living room. "Are you mad at me?"

"Probably," she said. "What's the plan?"

"Riley, we need you out of the picture," Derek said.

"That's the same thing Jim said to Chief. I actually think that's a terrible idea."

Ben snorted. "Babe, tell Derek what Jim said."

After Riley told him, Derek chuckled. "I kind of agree with you, Riley, so I have an adjustment to my plan. I will take you out of the picture and make sure Chief knows it."

Ben narrowed his eyes. "Where is she going to be?"

"I have a safe house we can use."

"Am I going to stay with Abigail?" Riley asked.

Derek groaned. "That was my idea; now, I'm worried it wasn't as brilliant as I thought. Who knows about you and Abigail?"

"The sheriff does, but I don't see how anyone else could at all."

"Do you know who Chief is?"

"Jim's boss, and he was probably Ava's boss too. I'm pretty sure he's Porter Lewis, the investor that is supposed to be here at two o'clock with Ralph."

"Excuse me." Derek strode to the front door and went outside.

"Is Derek adjusting his plan again?" Riley asked.

"To use your word, babe, probably. How do you put all these pieces together so quickly?"

Riley furrowed her brow as she tried to remember how and when all the pieces came together for her. "I guess I keep dancing. I gave the paper copies of the emails between Ava and Chief to the sheriff after Pamela Suzanne gave them to me. I assumed he would give them to the GBI, did he?"

"You're the one who gave them to the sheriff? Did you say Pamela Suzanne? The Pamela Suzanne we know?"

Riley told Ben about Pamela Suzanne and the packet of papers.

"Who knows about you and Pamela Suzanne?"

"Hope, Doc Ned, and Lizzie know because I was with them at the first Step Up meeting, and Hope because she gave me the knit cap to hide my red hair, but no one except the sheriff knows about the papers."

Derek knocked on the door then strode in. "New plan. Ben, you take Riley to the grocery store; Riley, take your cap that covers your hair, but don't wear it when you go in. Ben, you leave the store then pick up our phony Riley who will be a GBI agent with a red wig. Riley after they leave, put on your cap then leave with Abigail, who already owns a wig that she'll wear."

Toby growled.

"I'm sorry, Toby," Derek said. "You can't go with Riley because everybody knows you."

Toby barked.

"Derek, Toby has a point. When are we going to do all this? Is there a reason you couldn't take Toby to Abigail's in advance?" Ben asked.

"Yes, we need Toby to stick with the phony Riley."

Toby whined.

"Toby doesn't like it, but he agrees, Derek," Riley said. "So, that's a detail. What's the adjustment?"

"I'll take a photo of the dead phony Riley, with Toby next to her. We have a great makeup artist who excels in gruesome."

"What about Ralph?" Riley asked.

"There's another team on that," Derek said.

"Where's Orson?" Riley asked.

"He was questioned and released," Derek said.

Riley wrinkled her nose.

"What is it, babe?" Ben asked.

"It's a fractured plan. Chief, Jim, and Orson are jockeying for the top position because there's a lot of money to be made. There has to be a single plan, or one of them will snatch up the money and disappear when the other one is stopped. I don't think it's likely to be Orson, but both Chief and Jim intend to be on top."

"What would you do, Riley?" Derek asked.

"If you're seriously asking, and not just frustrated, I'll tell you."

Derek rubbed his hand across his face. "I'm asking."

"First, we need Ralph safe. Ben and I should meet with Ralph and Porter Lewis. I'll tell Ralph and Ben about the scheme to sell Ralph's house and its land. I know Porter Lewis will find a way to hear what I'm saying, and I also know he'll tell Jim. Ben makes a call, and a GBI team whisks Ralph away."

"That leaves you, babe," Ben said.

"Yes. Jim's the killer. He ordered the first team to kill Hope, and he intended to kill Shelby then killed Ava. I'm next on his list unless he kills Porter first, which he probably will, then I'm second on his list."

"What about Orson, and will you tell me later how Jim killed Ava?" Derek asked.

"I think Orson knows Jim killed Ava, so he is going after him, but Jim will kill him. Orson's not an experienced killer."

"What do you think, Ben?" Derek asked.

"I think it stinks, but I've never known her to be wrong. Babe, you're setting yourself up as bait, aren't you?"

"No, I'd rather Jim be caught without me involved. Derek, someone needs to find Orson and follow him. I think he'll lead the team right to Jim."

"Do you have anything else?" Derek asked.

"I'd like to know if the team investigating Ava's death found a flask in her purse in addition to the one I saw on the floor."

"Are you going to tell us why?" Derek asked.

"Just proves that Jim killed Ava, and Orson knows it because Jim left the flask on the floor in the meeting room on Saturday. Everyone on her team would have known that Ava liked a little whiskey in her coffee from time to time, which is why she carried a flask in her purse."

"My truck and I have to get out of here, so Ralph and Porter Lewis can look at the house. Ben, call or text me when it's time for the team to swoop in and take Ralph away."

Derek said, "Ben, my career and your reputation are on the line with this. If Riley's wrong, you'll need to go in with me to buy a farm to raise or rescue whatever Hope wants."

"I'm okay with whatever Riley says," Ben said.

"Yeah, I hate that she makes sense too."

After Derek left, Ben said, "You're really something, babe. Would you like some hot tea? I'll start a pot of coffee for our company."

Riley nodded. "That's a hospitality thing, isn't it? Nora's really good at it, and Grandma always had a pot of coffee on in case somebody dropped by."

"Babe, if you and Derek hadn't worked together at the B&B this past week, I don't think he would have listened to you. He was right: he's jeopardizing his job, and he'll probably resign after all this is over."

"Again?" Riley snickered. "He told me twice this week he resigned. I'm not sure he can."

"Really? That's actually good news because he's an outstanding undercover agent."

Ben stood at the bay window to watch the driveway. "Here they are; they came in separate cars."

When they reached the porch, Ben opened the door, and he and Ralph shook hands. Porter held out his hand. "Porter Lewis."

Ben shook his hand. "Ben Carter, and my wife, Riley."

"Nice to meet you, Mrs. Carter."

Riley smiled and nodded.

"Where do you want to start, Mr. Lewis?" Ralph asked.

"Let's go upstairs first."

"You look around and ask any questions you have; I'll do my best to answer them," Ralph said.

Porter and Ralph headed upstairs, and Ben followed them.

"What are your plans to update the second story?" Porter asked after he looked in the first bedroom.

"I updated the bathrooms when I updated the plumbing, and the electrical is updated. Several people have suggested that I don't make the cosmetic changes that a designer recommended for the second floor because of what they called its old world charm; I tend to agree with them."

"It's a different way to see it, isn't it?" Porter said. "I suppose it saves you money."

Aww. Chief doesn't approve.

"Let's look at the downstairs," Porter said.

That was fast.

Porter peeked into the bedrooms from the hall. "Quaint; did you upgrade the kitchen?"

"The kitchen is nice," Ben said.

"I'm sure it is."

Riley followed the three men to the kitchen. When Porter began his examination, Riley asked, "Do you have a minute, Ralph?"

"Sure." He glanced at Porter. "Why don't we sit in the living room?"

"How did everything go at the B&B?" Ralph asked as they sat down.

"That's what I wanted to talk to you about. Someone plans to steal your property. They already have a bidder lined up to pay ten times what you originally planned to ask."

"Ten times? How can they do that?"

"They inflated the value of the property."

"They'll steal my house over my dead body."

"That's actually their plan. They have fraudulent papers all ready to go. You die, and they collect money from the buyer."

Ben stood in the doorway. "I heard that. We need to put you under protection, Ralph, until we get to the bottom of this."

Ben pulled out his phone and sent a text. "I've asked my supervisor to send a team here immediately."

"Immediately?" Ralph asked. "Is it that bad?"

Riley nodded. "Yes, that bad."

Porter came out of the kitchen. "Thanks for giving me the opportunity to examine the property more closely. We'll be in touch, Ralph."

He hurried to the door and left.

After he was on the road, a silver car drove up, and two uniformed GBI agents stepped out; Ben met them on the porch, then they went inside the house.

"Mr. Wagner, we'd like for you to come with us for your own protection. Your wife is waiting at a secure location for you."

"Are you sure about this, Ben?"

"Positive. GBI has been investigating this for a while, but Riley's news is a huge breakthrough."

"Will you come along too, Ben? I'd feel more comfortable," Ralph asked.

"Up to you, Agent Carter," the lead agent said.

Ben glanced at Riley, and she nodded. *That's perfect.*

"I'll call you, babe, if I need a ride."

"Toby and I would love it."

Ben sent her a text. "I let Derek know you're alone. He's going to pick me up at the safe house, then we'll be there as fast as we can. Twenty minutes tops."

Riley chuckled. "Toby, I think we're about to see a race between the good guys and a bad guy."

Riley's phone rang. I don't recognize the number.

When she answered, Porter said, "Ralph gave me your number, Mrs. Carter. I'm sorry, but I don't have your husband's phone number, and I have a technical question for him."

Good one, Chief.

"I'm sorry, but he's not here right now; maybe I can help you. What's your question?"

"I'll call back later. Sorry for the interruption." Porter hung up.

"Porter just checked to be sure I was alone, Toby. Do you think Jim was with him?"

Toby exhaled.

Riley nodded. "And so, we wait."

When a car came down the driveway and parked, Riley said, "I don't recognize the car, but there are two people in it."

Toby whined then went to the kitchen and nosed the back door.

"Good idea, Toby."

My coat's too heavy; I couldn't move it out of the way fast enough if I need to draw.

Riley put on a sweatshirt that zipped up the front and held it together with one hand as she stepped out. Jim stepped out of the driver's seat.

Still has his wingtip shoes.

Jim roughly pulled out Diane from the passenger's seat and pushed her as he stayed behind her. Diane's hands were bound in front of her.

Diane gazed at Riley then glanced down at her hands then returned her gaze to Riley then glanced down at her hands again. When she glanced up at Riley, Riley's nod was almost imperceptible. Diane raised an eyebrow then blinked three times, and Riley nodded again with the same slight movement.

"The cook's here to help me out, Riley." Jim pulled out his gun from his waistband. "Drop your gun. I know you have one. Drop it, or the cook's dead."

Riley focused on Diane's hands as Diane pointed to the ground with one finger, two fingers, three fingers. On the third finger, Diane flung herself to her right and hit the ground. Jim stared at her then pointed his gun at her; Toby's growl distracted Jim's attention, and Riley pulled the trigger. Jim's gun fell near his hand when he dropped; Diane kicked it away from him.

Diane flinched at the abrupt sound of a siren as a car sped down the driveway.

"Who's that?" Diane asked.

"The cavalry," Riley said.

Derek and Ben jumped out of the car and rushed to Riley and Diane.

"Can we go inside?" Riley asked. "We're freezing."

Ben put his arms around both of them and walked them into the house.

After Ben helped the two of them sit near the fire and removed the duct tape that Jim had used to bind her wrists together, Diane said, "I'm really embarrassed; he jumped me when I took out the trash. I know it was a rookie mistake, and it won't happen again. Can you let Don know I'm okay?"

"He called us," Ben said. "He'll be here in a few minutes because he knew where your abductor would take you; he just didn't see who it was. I want to hear details, but we'll wait for Derek. Two hot teas?"

Diane smiled, and Riley nodded.

Derek opened the front door, and Toby came inside. After Don and more GBI agents showed up, Derek came inside.

"Is it okay if I take my wife home?" Don asked.

Derek nodded. "An agent will be by later to talk to you, Diane."

After they left, Derek said, "You were right about Orson, Riley. After we received a report of a shot fired earlier today, we found Orson dead in the hotel parking lot in Macon where he was staying."

"Jim didn't waste any time, did he?" Ben shook his head.

Derek continued, "Jim shot Porter at a public park then went straight to the B&B and kidnapped Diane. He was moving much faster than we expected. I'll say one thing for him: he was smart enough to bring a shield when he confronted you."

Riley told them how Diane signaled her then threw herself to the ground, so Riley could shoot.

"He pointed his gun at Diane with his finger on the trigger, and Toby growled. When Jim glanced at Toby, I shot him."

After Derek left, Ben put another log on the fire and sat with Riley as he stroked her cheek.

"Aren't you proud of me for not going solo?" Riley asked.

"You're pushing it, gunslinger, but I loved you first," Ben kissed her cheek.

"Yeah, honey, but I love you more."

Ben tossed a quilt onto the floor in front of the fireplace. "Prove it."

"Every chance I get, Doubting Cowboy."

Later, as they lay together wrapped in the quilt, Ben drank his beer while Riley sipped on her wine.

Ben said, "Derek wants to hire you."

"I don't think I'm the right type to be in law enforcement," Riley said. "You know, follows orders and stuff."

"You got that right, babe."

ACKNOWLEDGEMENTS

Huge thanks to my husband for his patience, support, talented technical expertise, and willingness to listen to me while I talk about the problems of the people who exist in my readers' minds.

Thanks to my editor for her dedication to commas, semicolons, colons, and other punctuation magic that eludes me.

Thank you for reading. *You keep reading; I'll keep writing!*

What to read next?

Visit BARRETT BOOK SHOP

Browse and Shop for your next Judith A. Barrett book!

www.BarrettBookShop.com

Subscribe: to the newsletter!

Look for the Subscribe button on www.judithabarrett.com

ABOUT THE AUTHOR

Judith A. Barrett is an award-winning author of mystery, crime, and survival science fiction novels with action, adventure, and a touch of supernatural to spark the reader's imagination. Her unusual main characters are brilliant, talented, and down-to-earth folks who solve difficult problems and stop killers. Her novels are based in small towns and rural areas in south Georgia and north Florida with sojourns to other southern US states.

Judith lives in rural Georgia on a small farm with her husband and two dogs. When she's not busy writing, Judith is still busy working on the farm, hiking with her husband and dogs, or watching the beautiful sunsets from her porch.

You keep reading; I'll keep writing!

Website www.judithabarrett.com

Barrett Book Shop www.BarrettBookShop.com

Subscribe to the eNewsletter via her website

Let's keep in touch!

Made in the USA
Coppell, TX
27 April 2023